SCRIPTED FOR LOVE AND POISON

A SOL AND LUKE MYSTERY ROMANCE

PATRICIA PUENTES

ALSO BY PATRICIA PUENTES

Sol and Luke Mystery Romance Series

Book 1: Cluelessly Unscripted

Confidential Hearts Series

Love, Lines, and Alibis

Cover design by Ashley Santoro

Editing by Brenna Bailey-Davies at Bookmarten Editorial

ISBN 979-8-9913992-4-1 (paperback) | ISBN 979-8-9913992-5-8 (ebook)

To Xavi, you're total book boyfriend material.

January 2024

"This is *not* happening," Sol said for the tenth time. But even if she was set on denying the facts, they all pointed to one awful, hideous, horrible conclusion: Her checked bag had been lost. It had been carefully packed by her expert self to contain all the essential clothes, cosmetics, shoes, bags, and sundry accessories she'd need for her four-day stay in Los Angeles—and then some in-case-of-emergency or last-minute-invitation-to-a-lavish-party extra stuff. Yet, despite the perfection of its contents and how much Sol Novo really required them *all*, it was nowhere to be seen.

She and Luke had been at carousel number three of LAX's international terminal for more than forty minutes. The latest of the London passengers had picked up their checked luggage, yet Sol's hadn't been among the delivered suitcases.

"Andiamo al banco bagagli, Sol. I'm starting to see bags from a flight from Roma on the carousel," Luke told her, but she wasn't listening. She hadn't even cared that her London-born-and-raised lover had talked to her in Italian—even if that always made her melt.

But she would not go to the baggage counter. She knew what happened there: People were always given the same terrible news—their bags were now forever lost.

"This isn't happening," she repeated yet again.

She had been stranded by volcanoes. She'd sleep-walked through terminals, waiting for much-delayed connections. She'd napped in uncomfortable airport seats. She'd been inside long-haul airplanes with malfunctioning lavatories and no running water. She'd even had to head back home—on more than one occasion—after spending the whole day at the airport, only for her flight to go from eternally delayed to canceled. But Sol counted herself fortunate because never, in her many decades as a seasoned traveler, had her bags been lost. Not even momentarily misplaced.

Luke was dragging his carry-on bag with one hand and had taken Sol's hand with the other. He was guiding her to their airline counter at the arrivals area of LAX. Once there, he addressed the sole attendant filling the post.

"Hello. My partner's bag hasn't turned up at the carousel, and we were wondering if—"

"It has to be somewhere!" Sol said, taking both hands to her heated cheeks.

"Ma'am, calm down. Do you have the receipt for the checked bag?" the airline attendant said.

Sol handed over the receipt, sore from having been called *ma'am*. How old did the airline attendant think she was?

After what felt like an eternity—but was probably only a couple of minutes spent inputting the number of the receipt in a computer—the attendant said laconically, "We've found it."

"You have it!" Sol felt something akin to ecstasy. She was *that* attached to her things. "I thought I was going to have to buy a whole new wardrobe!"

"You may still have to do it," the attendant continued in their curt style.

"What do you mean?" Sol asked.

"I told you we found it, not that the bag was here." The attendant shrugged, not looking up from the computer screen.

Sol arched her eyebrows in confusion. "That sounds ominous."

And it did, but not as ominous as what happened next.

Her editor was calling her. It had to be urgent, because Julie McQueen never had the habit of making a phone call. Not to Sol. Infinite email chains were more her style. But Sol needed to take that phone call because Julie was the one editor who threw well-paid freelance work her way on a regular basis.

Sol left Luke dealing with the airline attendant so that they knew where to deliver her suitcase once it made its way back from its undisclosed location. It wasn't like her to let someone else handle a lost-luggage situation, but over the past few months together, she'd learned to trust Luke. He'd proven himself constant and dependable. So Sol was sure he'd do everything to get her things back and instill all the required urgency into the airline people dealing with her belongings.

"Julie, hi. Is everything okay?"

"Are you in Los Angeles already?" her editor answered promptly. She was a competent woman who Sol enjoyed immensely as a professional colleague. She was a stanch believer in the less-is-more motto, never over-edited, and still had a decent contributor budget. She wasn't a great conversationalist, but Sol could overlook that.

"Just landed, trying to sort out a luggage thing."

"They lost your bag," Julie stated. Not asked, but stated.

Sol paced nervously a few meters away from Luke, her eyes pinned on him while he dealt with her problem. "They did. I'm a bit panicked, to be honest."

"Don't be, that'll hardly serve any purpose. You'll still have nothing to wear and be panicked on top of it. And, believe me, *no one* wants to see a panicked woman over forty," Julie argued. Her editor sounded sadly somewhat reasonable. "But I don't have time for chitchat."

"Right," said Sol. When did Julie ever have the time, or the inclination, for chitchat?

"I assume you've read my email."

"I'm afraid you've assumed wrongly. As I was saying, I just landed and haven't even had time to clear customs or get out of the airport yet." If she hadn't been working with Julie for a few months and had learnt to understand the woman's way of communicating, she'd be panicking about her editor's tone. But unlike most of the editors Sol had worked with throughout her career, Julie was all bark—that was a common editor trait—but no bite—an uncommon one.

"There was no Wi-Fi on the plane?" Julie asked.

"Gods, Julie, have you had your full caffeine intake today?"

"Sorry, hon, but a dear friend may have died, and I think I'm obviously more touched than I expected."

"I'm so sorry," said Sol, now feeling bad for her jab at the editor. "What happened?"

"Well, that's why I asked you if you'd read my email. I'd

put it perfectly there. Now you'll get the not-so-polished spoken version. Simon Smith has gone missing."

Sol's brows knit together. She wasn't following whatever Julie was trying to tell her. "Missing as in . . . ?"

"Missing as in kaput, hon. It looks like foul play to me. I've been telling him for years he needed to lay off on the vitriol. And he's been getting hate mail for ages. But this!" Julie continued, without making much sense to Sol. She didn't even know who Simon Smith was.

"Can we recap a little bit? You said someone died?"

"Yes! Probably . . ." said Julie. "Simon, obviously. Do you even know who I'm talking about?"

"I feel I may be overplaying it, but do you realize I just landed from an eleven-hour flight and my luggage is lost! And no, sorry, I didn't read your email. The name sounds familiar, but I can't place it right now." Sol continued pacing up and down, eyeing Luke as he was still chatting with the airline attendant. She could feel a headache coming and was massaging her temples.

"Simon Smith, *The Showbiz Reporter*'s main film critic and one of the most divisive people in our business."

"Divisive because?"

"The last time he actually liked a movie was probably 1999," said Julie.

"I mean, it was such a great year but . . ."

"There's life after *Fight Club*, *American Beauty*, and *Eyes Wide Shut* . . ."

"Don't forget about *The Matrix*," Sol contributed, stopping her pacing.

"Yeah, Simon didn't like *The Matrix*, actually."

"Seriously? What's wrong with him?"

"See, that's why I'm so worried about him!" Julie said. "Everybody hates him. Even his editor at *The Showbiz*

Reporter, Jason Zit. I just called him, and he's not worried. And he hasn't heard from Simon for two days! He sounded relieved to be rid of him. He's had it out for Simon for years!"

"Okay, Julie, I can see you're clearly upset. What can I do for you?"

"Well, I need you to find Simon, of course! But I'm afraid it's too late and he's going to be six feet under, buried in the California desert somewhere. And that's a dreadful way to die!"

2

Sol didn't immediately return to Luke's side after hanging up Julie's call. She breathed deeply first. She was feeling all the stress from the last days catching up to her.

She knew she should have booked the flight to LA to leave a couple of days earlier so she'd have been able to get some rest before the frenzy of activities that awaited her in the Californian city, but things had been hectic—someone would argue even a bit crazy—the past few weeks. Nothing had gone back to the normal bliss she and Luke had enjoyed pre-Christmas. But how could it? The holidays had been dreadful—an absolute, utter disaster. And now she'd lost her bag and was supposed to find a missing reporter!

Just thinking about the days before the LA trip both infuriated her and made her heart sink. Her past experience dealing with the acute stress-inducing holiday season should have prepared her for this recent one. Yet, there she was: forty-three, two husbands and a couple of significant lovers down, and she still hadn't been able to confront the latest end of the year in the smartest, most rational way. And rationally is how you should always do Christmas.

How Sol should have proceeded was having a serious talk with Luke and *telling him* how things would go their first Christmas as a couple: She would fly back to her hometown, as she always did, and would spend the festivities in Barcelona with her family and friends. He would remain in London and do whatever he normally did during that time of the year.

Even if Sol had been living in London for almost four years, all her knowledge about British traditions for the holiday season came from watching *Love Actually,* so she assumed Luke's family would be serenaded by neighboring carolers, would buy not-necessarily-exciting-or-needed presents, and would eat panettone—Luke's family was Italian, after all.

And the thing was, Sol had sat Luke down and had tried to tackle the Christmas issue—only not in the clearest way. Because Luke had interpreted her words in the opposite way they were meant and had assumed she wanted them to spend that time together.

In his defense, they had been spending almost all the previous time together—except for work and socializing with friends, and the four summer days she'd spent with her parents in Greece, agonizing through monuments and ruins under the scorching sun. Of course, the source of the misunderstanding with Luke could also have been that Sol was having a hard time disentangling herself from him for any extended period of time, so she hadn't made herself clear on purpose. Even if she knew better.

Even if the two-person detective agency Luke ran with his friend and professional partner, Divya Bakshi, meant that he sometimes wasn't available on evenings or weekends because he was on surveillance duty, he still spent most nights at Sol's quaint Georgian cottage on Roupell Street. And on those occasions when he couldn't make it to London's South Bank for whatever reason, Sol usually trekked to his cozy (read really *really* tiny) studio flat by Finsbury Park.

Sol had to admit that she hadn't been expecting things would be so comfortable—and easy—with Luke when they'd started seeing each other in a committed capacity the previous spring after they'd met in a less-than-ideal situation.

Theirs hadn't been a meet-cute. She'd been the prime suspect in a theft investigation. He'd been in charge of investigating her. She wasn't his type. He was ten years younger than she was. She didn't want a relationship. He shouldn't have seduced a person of interest. And yet somehow, they had ended in bed together and been unable to sleep apart even for one night since then.

Only they should have slept apart. During the whole of the Christmas season. Instead of that, and against her better judgment, Sol had brought Luke to spend the first part of the season in Barcelona. The Novo clan hadn't exactly taken to him. Not only did they consider Luke too young and unsuitable for their daughter, Sol's two past divorces prevented her parents from warming up easily to anyone anymore. Not that they had ever been too warm to begin with. Plus, her mother was adamant in her belief that Sol should never have left her first husband and was still sore about it.

To make things worse and even more uncomfortable, Sol's apartment in Barcelona had been unavailable, as there had been problems with the heating system that weren't repaired on time. Sol and Luke were forced to stay with Sol's parents as a result. There's nothing like spending a couple of days in your old room with your partner to make you want to go back home for a little bit of peace—and intimacy.

After the mainly glacial silences and charged stares of the Novos, Sol and Luke hadn't gone back to London as initially planned but to Reggio Calabria. New Year's Eve was spent with the Contadinos, and the family had decided to all fly to their grandmother's home in Southern Italy. That had been even more disastrous. Not because Luke's parents or his two older sisters, or his aunts and uncles and many many *many* cousins, hadn't liked Sol, but because they'd been so nice and *warm* with her. And yet, she hadn't enjoyed the experience.

It wasn't them, though, it was *her*. They were all perfectly nice people. She would have liked any of them if she'd met them under different circumstances. But the reality was that her two divorces had left her scarred, and—as a result—she had a pathological mistrust of in-laws. She couldn't avoid thinking that, if things came to an end between her and Luke, they would all turn on her—the same way it had happened in the past.

It also didn't help that the old Contadino house was picturesque and lovely but not necessarily equipped to host so many people at the same time. Luke and Sol had slept on a bumpy sofa bed, sharing the room with at least two of Luke's cousins.

She would have preferred to be home, just her and Luke. Or Luke could have been celebrating with his family, but she'd have still preferred to be home, by herself—not having to share a bathroom with at least twenty other people. The only silver lining to the whole holidays-with-the-in-laws affair was that there had, indeed, been panettone. Plus, she'd discovered zippuli con alici, fried anchovy-stuffed dough in the shape of balls, and pitta 'mpigliata, a typical Calabrian Christmas pastry filled with nuts, honey, and spices.

But nothing had been the same between Luke and her since the dreaded Christmas together. Their conversations felt short and rushed. It was as if they were eternally tired and almost hadn't enjoyed any quality time together. And she *knew* Luke was thinking and feeling the same.

And now there they were, in Los Angeles. He hated being away from London. She had no clothes. And she was supposed to help Julie find a cranky journalist.

3

uke wasn't happy. But his discomfort came from reasons completely unrelated to what Sol had been musing about. And he certainly didn't mind having to take care of her missing luggage for her. If anything, he loved the occasions in which she let him take charge of the situation. They were rare.

But he couldn't deny the fact that they were now in a foreign country, and he hated traveling. He'd tried—he'd *really* tried doing it right. For her. Luke Contadino had gone as far as rewatching *Up in the Air*, taking notes about everything George Clooney's character had to say on the subject of packing. Especially considering that Sol had been obtusely vague in her directions: "Oh, bring whatever you feel you'll need there. And don't forget the suit!"

As if that had made anything any clearer. He hadn't forgotten the suit, though.

They'd met for their LA-bound flight directly at Heathrow Airport. It had been deemed easier that way, with each of them coming from their respective homes and packing on opposite sides of the Thames. Luke had been so proud about his compact carry-on bag—until he'd seen her lugging the most ginormous of rolling suitcases and carrying an equally big carry-on weekender.

"We are still coming back in four days, right?" Luke had asked her, suddenly afraid. Accepting to go to Los Angeles with her had been anxiety-inducing enough—there was no way of overstating how much he hated to be far from London. He'd just hoped Sol hadn't had a change of heart and wanted to spend a whole month there or something. By the looks of her baggage, she was carrying stuff for at least that many weeks.

"Of course. Just so that we can attend the thing, see some friends, and fly back. Why?" she'd asked him, confused.

He'd simply looked at his luggage and then appreciated the size of hers with his eyes.

"Am I judging you because of that ridiculously small roller you're bringing?" she'd said, but her tone did sound judgy, and Luke had started doubting his packing method. Perhaps it should have been less minimalism, more anything goes. "I never travel light. My toiletry bag alone doesn't fit into a carry-on. Are you sure you have everything you'll need?" she'd inquired, just short of accusing.

The irony of it all wasn't lost on Luke: Sol's stuff was now missing, and his own carry-on was safely tucked next to him. Not that he had any intention of telling her that.

Especially considering that things hadn't necessarily improved for them during the flight after the luggage discordance. He liked to think that he'd come to know his romantic partner quite well. He suspected that Sol would have bought first-class tickets if he hadn't insisted on paying for his own. She'd tried persuading him against it. But he'd told her that the only way he was going to join her on that trip and accompany her as her plus-one for a work commitment she had in Los Angeles, was if he paid for his own plane ticket.

In the end, she'd acquiesced, but Luke suspected she would have preferred to be traveling solo and in first class instead of with him and in the *plebeian narrowness* (her words) of a premium economy seat. Compared to Luke's limited past flying experience, the seats they had occupied in an exit two-seat row—Sol had been by the window, him by the aisle—were ample, comfortable, and almost luxurious. But she'd complained and grumbled when they first boarded the plane.

She didn't look uncomfortable for long, though, as she soon fell asleep, decked with all the complements of a frequent flier. Luke had been a bit taken aback by Sol's frequent-flier persona, in fact. He felt almost tempted to say that Sol was the worst travel companion ever. He'd assumed the trip would be an opportunity to spend more time together. The two of them had been quite busy. Long gone were the ten days by the beach they'd both spent on a Mediterranean island that summer with nothing to do but to eat, sleep, read, sunbathe, and shag—not necessarily in that order. He'd thought the quick escape to Los Angeles would mean another opportunity to enjoy each other's company.

But from the moment they boarded the plane, Sol had acted with the absolute independence and detachment of someone used to traveling often and exclusively alone. She'd put on her noise-canceling headphones and isolated herself from the rest of the plane, even from him. He had been going to propose to watch a rom-com together on the infotainment system, but she hadn't given him that option. She didn't even bother taking her headphones off during mealtime. They'd barely made it in the air, and she'd already been placidly sleeping. How could that have been even possible? They were such different travelers.

She was so used to flying that not even a rapid succession of turbulence had spooked her or even awakened her. She'd just barely turned on her seat and muttered something under her breath. She ended up invading Luke's space. He didn't mind that. He liked having her close.

But Luke feared she was finally going to realize he was too young and unsophisticated for her. Could she be wondering about the adequacy of their match?

Then he saw Sol coming in his direction after hanging up the phone call that had taken her away from the suitcase crisis. Even after the longest, most tiresome of flights, she looked refreshed and bloody gorgeous. Her chestnut hair, cut just above the shoulders, was tousled in the sexiest way. She wore leggings and a boxy crop T-shirt that showed off her slender figure in all the right ways. And she was smiling at him. He filed away his worries and started walking toward her, a smile also tugging at his lips.

...

"I think I got us a job."

"Us?" Luke asked Sol, visibly surprised. "A job? We don't need a job."

"Speak for yourself," Sol answered.

They were finally inside the Uber that would take them to the Fairmont Hotel in Century City. Sol was still missing a big suitcase full of such basic things like extra sunglasses, block heel sandals, and a party clutch, but she'd decided to stop complaining about it for one full minute. Luke had assured her that she'd get her stuff back soon enough. So she was sharing some pressing news with him.

"That was my editor calling me at the airport," started Sol.

"Julie McQueen?"

"You remembered her first *and* last name?" Her heart skipped a beat. Not only was he sexy and smart in confusingly equal measure, he'd just dealt with airport employees on her behalf and remembered her editor's *full* name. He had the uncommon quality of paying attention. Finding someone who cared *and* listened was exceptionally rare. And if one was fortunate enough to find such a person, they normally never looked like an Italian model with perfect, tousled dark waves and even more perfect pillowy lips. And yet, he was seated next to her, looking at her intently—and still waiting for an answer.

"Julie, yes," Sol finally said. Her neck was a bit sore from the nap on the plane, and she was trying to massage it. "She's worried because one of her friends, who sounds awful, has gone missing. She actually thinks he's dead, but I tried talking her down about that—"

"Missing?" Luke took his left hand to her neck and started kneading her muscles with a perfect, alleviating pressure.

"He won't return any of Julie's texts, calls, or emails," Sol said, her eyes now closing. She enjoyed the expert touch of Luke's hands on her neck.

"Sol, you know I like Julie," Luke said, not stopping his work on her tight muscles. His voice sounded deliciously coarse. "She's kept you employed while you try to get your novel published, and I realize that she's one of the only editors who doesn't cause you an allergic reaction. But could this friend be on a trip and away from his devices? Or maybe he just doesn't want to speak to Julie."

"Is that what you tell all your potential clients?" She opened one of her eyes and narrowed it on Luke.

His voice dropped, rough and deep, making every word land heavier. "No, that's the version for the person whose neck I like caressing."

"So not all your clients get such outstanding service," she said, both her eyes open now and a note of sexy flirtation in her tone.

"Definitely not," Luke said, leaning in, voice playful. "But tell me more about this job you've gotten us."

"Julie is in London, of course. So she asked me to go to her friend's place and check on him since she can't do it herself. He lives here in LA."

"What if we don't find him at home because he's on a trip—or went to the supermarket."

"We'll leave a note," Sol said matter-of-factly.

"A note?"

"Yes, asking him to give us a call because Julie is worried. And tomorrow we'll have another chance to find him, because he's supposed to be at the same awards ceremony we're attending."

"Remind me again, how many people are attending this thing tomorrow?"

"Upward of fifteen hundred," she said sheepishly.

"Should be easy enough," Luke said, not even pretending to mask the sarcasm. "I'm afraid to ask, but are we getting paid for this job?"

"We're doing it as a favor to Julie."

"Are we?" he said, his hands still at her neck, his eyes pinned on hers, a wolfish smile on his lips.

Perhaps things between the two of them weren't as strained, after all, and the only thing they'd needed was to get out of London. There was nothing like traveling to remind her of everything she loved.

4

There was nothing like traveling to remind Luke of everything he abhorred because he was away from London.

He knew he could be perceived as narrow-minded, even limited, but gods did he miss his hometown. Everything was objectively better there. For one, they were in the right time zone. But here he was, eight hours behind his natural biorhythm. His body just wanted to slumber, yet the sun was shining with an unnatural intensity for January.

What was this place? Sol had assured him their hotel was in a perfectly centric location, yet you'd never have said it just by looking at it. The Fairmont Century Plaza was a slab of glass and concrete towered by two skyscrapers. There was no hustle and bustle of pedestrians on the street as one would assume from any *central* location. Luke was still unsure whether the hotel was accessible on foot since it was surrounded by a two-lane driveway.

After checking in and having a quick shower, Sol had forbidden him from sleeping. She'd argued something about the need to adapt to the time change and mitigate jet lag. It was easy for her to say since she'd taken a seven- or eight-hour nap on the plane. But he hadn't slept a wink. He'd never been good at sleeping in public spaces. Passing out and drooling in front of strangers wasn't exactly his brand.

Of course, there had been no drooling coming from her while she slept on the plane. The woman had some faults—lack of patience being the worst—but he had yet to catch her in a bad moment. Not even fresh out of bed and hungover did she look disheveled.

But Luke was tired and sore from the long flight, and he was afraid he didn't look exactly refreshed after the shower. As if lack of sleep wasn't bad enough, Sol had taken him on an *emergency* shopping trip in the mall next to their hotel. Maybe that was what Sol meant by centric? The fact that the hotel was flanked by a labyrinth of seamlessly endless small high-end stores and at least three department stores.

After three bags full of garments that would get any normal person dressed for a month and a falsely advertised *quick* visit to a beauty shop, they had left all the merchandise in their room. Luke had given the California king-sized bed an appreciative, lusty look, but he hadn't been permitted to act on his desires.

He was so sleepy that he had stopped by the first random place in search of a much-needed (and craved for) English breakfast tea. Sol had said something about going someplace different, but it was a simple tea. It shouldn't be that hard. Apparently, it was, and it *really* hit him then that he no longer was in the UK. He was served hot water in a paper cup. The barista had added a splash of milk on top of it and then they'd opened a wooden box by the register with tea bags so that Luke chose his preferred one and dunked it himself in the now extra-lukewarm milky water.

That thing was never going to be the right strength, color—or flavor.

After the tea calamity, he and Sol sat in traffic inside an Uber, trying to reach Simon Smith's home across town. For some reason unbeknownst to Luke, public transportation hadn't been an option to make their way there, even though he'd been assured the critic's home was also in a *centric* location. He was starting to believe the word meant a completely different thing across the Atlantic Ocean.

"This couldn't get more LA authentic," Sol said enthusiastically.

Was she really trying to make the fact that they were stuck in the worst kind of rush-hour traffic sound like the perfect touristic experience?

In her defense, he hadn't been exactly transparent with her about his lack of knowledge of the Californian city. Sol was under the impression that Luke had been to Los Angeles and had visited all the landmarks during a work assignment several years before. And while that had been technically true, the reality was that he'd been too busy and tired to get to know the place or enjoy it.

It had been a full week of endless driving and fast-food consumption, trailing their client's ex-husband, who'd just moved to Los Angeles from London. The client had wanted Luke's agency to find something about his ex, anything that would render him ineligible to get their children's custody. Or some story similar to that one—Luke didn't remember all the particulars. The case had happened almost ten years before, when he'd just started working in his first agency as a contractor. He was so junior—and young, merely twenty-three and out of uni—that he'd been employed mostly as the driver and errand person of the senior detective.

Driving in that city had been an absolute bore that occupied most of his days there. Congestion and bad traffic were such common occurrences that he couldn't remember going more than 10 mph, on the motorway or the streets. He still could savor the elation he'd felt when the case had been deemed over and he was able to return to London. When his flight from Los Angeles to London had touched ground at Heathrow, he'd almost been one of those enthusiastic clapping passengers on planes. He suspected that trip, and Los Angeles, had instigated his longtime dislike of travel.

But he was with Sol now. If there was someone who could bring the charm up in Los Angeles for Luke, it was her.

"Remind me again, where does this mate we're looking for live?" he asked, taking Sol's hand, which had been resting on the car's seat, and lacing his fingers with hers.

"North of Montana in Santa Monica, quite close to my old place actually," she said.

"Really? Should we go and visit your old neighborhood after checking on the critic?"

Sol had shared a few details about the decade that she'd spent in Los Angeles after leaving Barcelona in her twenties, but she'd never been forthright about her California era. Luke was curious about the years she'd lived there before her move to London and before meeting him.

"Not sure there's anything interesting to see there," she told him, hoping Luke wouldn't insist.

Sol's second and least favorite ex-husband still lived in the house they'd both shared in Santa Monica, and the last thing she wanted was to accidentally run into him while strolling through the old neighborhood. "But we can go to the beach after this. I think we're here," she said, checking her cell phone and making sure their driver had reached their destination.

They thanked their driver and got out of the car in front of a new-construction, courtyard-style apartment building. Sol was trying to figure out how to get access to the building if Simon was indeed not there—or not answering the door—when she saw the police cars and uniformed officers crowding the sidewalk by the building's entrance.

"Is everything okay?" she asked one of the closest officers, who looked to be in charge and was in plain clothes.

"Afternoon, ma'am, everything is hunky dory," the officer said. He was around her height and looked to be in his forties. Sol just wanted people to stop calling her *ma'am*. "How can I help you?"

"We're here to see a friend of a friend and were wondering if we could get inside the building," Sol started, and she realized she had no clue where Luke had gone. He'd gotten out of the car with her, but he was nowhere in sight now.

"Afraid the building is off-limits right now unless you're a neighbor. Do you happen to live here?" The officer had an extremely musical Southern Californian accent.

"No, I don't."

"Then I can't let you in, ma'am," the officer said with the most fastidious smile.

"But see, my friend really wants me to check on her friend who lives here. I've come all the way from London."

"You flew from London for a house visit?"

"What? Of course not. But since we were already in Los Angeles—"

"Then I'm sure you'll be able to come back at a less inconvenient time," the officer went on with his best smile.

Sol was going to protest despite the futility of it, but she saw Luke coming her way.

"Want to go to the beach now, cara?" he asked her, and she would have tried to persuade him to stay and help her convince the officer to let them in the building, but she recognized the hint of mischief in Luke's eyes.

...

"Are you going to tell me what you were doing when you disappeared?" Sol asked as she and Luke made their way to the Santa Monica beach from Simon Smith's building.

"Curious, are we?" Luke asked her, smirking.

"Please, you hardly need to be a sophisticated detective such as yourself to know I'm dying with curiosity," Sol said as they strolled side by side.

"Sophisticated, huh?"

"You know you are. But can we cut to the chase? What were you doing?"

The hint of a smile tugged at one side of Luke's lips. "While you were chatting with Officer Hunky Dory, I went around the building and pretended to be a neighbor looking for a lost kitten. And I managed to find some sympathetic tattlers."

"Really? You? Looking for a lost kitten? I can hardly see how anyone could resist it."

He couldn't suppress the smirk. Even if he wasn't vain, she could still describe him as occasionally cocky, and she knew he liked it when she acknowledged that he was pretty much irresistible. It was hardly a secret that he was. He basically embodied the beauty canon. He was tall, strong jawed, lean, muscular, and fetching.

They had stopped walking, waiting for a traffic light on

Montana Avenue to turn green, and Sol returned Luke's flirty smile. For a moment it was as if everything else had ceased to exist or stopped having any relevance. It was just the two of them, together and hungry for each other. He'd made her forget about everything else going on in her life: the chance of running into a much-despised ex-husband, the novel she'd finished writing that still hadn't landed a literary agent, the journalistic career that continued dwindling by the day, the lost suitcase, and the missing critic she couldn't care less about, even if she probably should.

The vicious honk of a car waiting to make a left turn at the traffic light jolted Sol and sent her straight back to reality.

"You were telling me you just pretended to have lost a cat to get some intel," Sol prompted Luke.

"I talked with a couple of neighbors and a copper who were gossiping about Simon Smith. The door to his apartment was fully open this afternoon, apparently. His flat had been completely ransacked, but he was nowhere to be found. They still haven't been able to locate him, and no one seems to have seen him. And there were big blood stains all over the place."

"Blood?" asked Sol, horrified. The mention of someone else's blood made her feel queasy.

"Why did Julie suspect he'd be dead?" asked Luke, suddenly more interested in that story than ever.

"Because he hadn't liked a movie since 1999," answered Sol. When she saw Luke's face, she realized that, once again and like when they first met, she'd have to be a bit clearer while giving him background about her professional environment. "Because he's ruined more than one movie—and their filmmakers' and actors' careers in the process—with his penchant for vitriol."

"Still think it's a big jump to go from 'I can't reach my friend' to 'I think he's dead.'" Luke was thinking out loud.

"She's always had a flair for the dramatic. I don't think she actually believed Simon was dead."

"It doesn't look good for this Simon bloke, but we don't know he's dead," Luke said.

"You just told me there was blood at his place, and he was nowhere to be found!"

"Precisely, no body. But I still think you should call Julie. I can see how this thing is going to leak soon. I'm sure I won't be the only one to lure my way into the confidence of a couple of friendly elderly neighbors and a junior police officer."

"Don't underestimate your charm abilities," Sol said, and she was ready to forget about that whole unfortunate, bloody business until the following day. It was too late to call Julie in London, so she decided to savor the magic-hour lighting while watching the sunset with Luke on the beach.

Sunsets on the Pacific had a bewitching quality to them, and Sol wanted to simply enjoy the moment with him. But as they took their shoes off and made their way to the ocean through the expanse of the Santa Monica beach, Sol's cell phone started buzzing. It was Julie McQueen.

"You found Simon?" Julie blurted the moment Sol picked up her phone.

"Julie, isn't it like one in the morning there? What are you still doing up?"

"Waiting for your call, hon," Julie deadpanned.

"I thought you'd be sleeping. I was going to call you tomorrow."

"Well, I'm obviously not sleeping. You found Simon?"

Sol and Luke were in front of the ocean, and the sun was almost completely hidden under the horizon line. Tones of pink and indigo painted the sky. The bustling Santa Monica Pier was to their right, buzzing with laughs and movement in the distance. Sol looked for her lover's eyes at that moment, not knowing what to tell her editor and friend. She wasn't necessarily good at delivering empathetic messages.

"Let me put you on speakerphone with Luke, who's also here. He'll give you the professional take," Sol said and put the phone between her and Luke with a pleading expression in her eyes.

Luke acquiesced with his gaze and took the lead in the delivery of bad news. He was more used to that sort of thing.

"Hello Julie, Luke here. I'm afraid we have a bit of bad news right now, but please don't worry yet."

"Simon is dead, isn't he? How can he not after that awful review he wrote," said Julie.

"Julie, right now the only thing we've been able to confirm is that he's missing from his flat and that the place has been vandalized. But we don't know whether he's dead or not, nor do the police," Luke explained. "Why are you so sure he's dead? Did he tell you someone had threatened him?"

"And what were you saying about an awful review he wrote?" added Sol.

"You're going to laugh at me and think I'm a silly old woman," said Julie.

"I can guarantee we won't do that." Luke's jaw tightened, and Sol knew he meant it.

"We chatted on the phone the other night. He told me about this review he'd written about that movie *Haughty Horizons*. He'd completely panned it. *Haughty Horizons* was supposed to be a December surprise during awards season, and Simon managed to squander all possibility of nominations with his review."

Sol couldn't suppress the feeling that Julie was being overly dramatic once again. "I mean, I'm sure the director of the movie is not too happy with Simon, but surely you don't suspect him. Was it Victor Lago who directed it?"

"I'm not saying he did anything, but someone did. *Haughty Horizons* cost $250 million, and it doesn't look like it's going to recoup any of that. And they'll get nominated for nothing."

"Two hundred and fifty million?" Sol's eyebrows shot up. "For a non-IP, non-star-driven, very serious movie?"

"Don't forget it's written and directed by a white, straight man," Julie deadpanned.

"Ah, I guess that'll do," Sol decided. "But let me go back to what you were saying while I got sidetracked by that budget. You don't mean someone at the studio did something?" Sol tried to follow Julie's thread.

"I don't know! But Simon told me he had gotten some threatening messages."

"What kind of threatening messages?" Luke was quick to ask.

"Mostly of the colorful variety and posted to his social media accounts," Julie explained. "But he told me some of them were a bit more extreme than the regular disgruntled fan who is disappointed their favorite auteur got criticized. I told Simon he should report them, but nobody ever listens to me . . . And then that night, I had this dream where Simon died. He was beaten in his flat and bled to death."

"You dreamed it?" asked Sol, blinking in incredulity. After all, she hadn't been the one to promise Julie they would not judge her. "Since when do you believe in dream premonitions, Julie?"

"I don't, hon, but it was such a graphic dream. And then the following day, I was worried and tried contacting Simon, and I haven't been able to talk to him since, and now you tell me he's missing from his flat!"

Luke hesitated, then spoke with measured calm. "Could it be a coincidence?"

"Coincidence or no, Simon is still missing and not answering my calls, and someone threatened him," Julie reasoned. "Sol, I know your boyfriend is very busy, but could you convince him to keep looking into this? I'm worried about Simon."

Sol took a steady breath. "He's not my boyfriend, he's my romantic partner." She hated when people didn't use the proper qualifiers for her relationship with Luke.

"Same difference. Who cares? You two don't even live together. Can he look into this for me?" Julie dismissed her.

"*He* is actually here," Luke said, keeping his voice relaxed. "Julie, I'm not sure I can take on this investigation as this is a Los Angeles affair and I am, very much, based in London. But tomorrow Sol and I are going to that awards ceremony organized by the critics organization she's a member of. Sol tells me Simon is also a member, and what I can promise you is that while we're there, we'll keep an eye out for him. We'll try to figure out if someone else has seen him or knows anything."

"Please find out what happened to him, but you two should be careful," said Julie.

That sounded ominous.

6

"These heels are eight inches high, so you need to promise to be by my side all night. I need you as my extremely handsome walking accessory. I would literally fall to my face otherwise," Sol told Luke, gripping his arm and walking much slower than her usual brisk pace.

They'd landed in Los Angeles less than twenty-four hours before. She'd incessantly grumbled because her suitcase still hadn't been recovered. Yet she'd managed to find a party dress in which she looked even sexier than in the one she'd originally packed. She kept complaining that the black slip dress she was presently wearing was too simple and a bit too sheer. Luke didn't agree with the first part and had absolutely no problems with the second.

He'd put on the suit she'd selected for him in London and was now escorting her to the entrance of the hangar in the Santa Monica Airport to attend the awards ceremony they'd come to Los Angeles for. He was still surprised that such a lavish and glamorous party was taking place in such an odd location. One that seemed hardly equipped for the throngs of celebrities descending on the red carpet.

He was taken aback by security that could be described at best as lax and at worst as neglectful. The all-clad-in-black team at the entrance had barely checked the two printed invitations Sol had produced out of her clutch, and Luke had the feeling anyone dressed in the right way and who had the right attitude would easily slip through unnoticed. Things didn't get much better once they were inside the venue.

Of course, as a Londoner, he was somewhat used to the odd occurrence of bumping into Peter Dinklage after having breakfast in a popular spot in Notting Hill, seeing Felicity Jones making her way out of a West End theater, or even chatting to Emma Thompson at his regular yoga studio. What Luke wasn't prepared for was the sheer number of so-called celebrities currently together under the same roof in a too-densely-populated room where actors and popular filmmakers were prey to many journalists wanting a word, a picture, or even a hug.

"I think I just stepped on Kiefer Sutherland's foot by accident," Luke whispered in Sol's ear, abashed.

"I know, it's crazy. This is way too packed," Sol told him, her eyes scanning the room avidly.

"I tried apologizing, but he left with the same stealthiness he'd used to end up under my foot."

"Don't worry," she said, absentmindedly.

"Are you looking for Simon?" Luke suddenly also felt compelled to check the room for the missing critic, following her gaze.

"Who?" Sol asked. "Oh, Simon. No, I was looking for Greta Gerwig, actually. She's nominated for *Barbie*, and I'm dying to see her."

"But you remember we promised Julie we'd look for Simon, right?" Luke asked her, amused.

"*You* promised her. I merely facilitated the conversation." She glanced up at him, the corner of her mouth lifting coyly.

He was about to tell her how gorgeous she looked and kiss her, but they were unfortunately interrupted by a petite, middle-aged woman making rapid progress toward them and talking in a shrill tone.

"Sol Novo! You didn't tell me you were coming!" the woman screamed while still more than two meters away, and that got Sol's attention.

"Claudia! I didn't know you'd be here!" Sol said in a similar tone. For the second day in a row, Luke was surprised by an aspect of his partner's personality he'd still not learned about. Her English had become louder. Her statements suddenly sounded like questions, and her accent had turned to pure California Uptalk. It was as if she was a different Sol, one he hadn't been exposed to before. But unlike her frequent-flier persona, Luke was somewhat charmed by this California Girl Sol. "But of course you came," Sol added.

"I come every year. Don't you?" the woman named Claudia said, hugging Sol and eyeing Luke with an appreciative stare.

"This is the first year I've come since I left LA, actually," Sol explained. "It's so far from London ..."

"Nonsense! But you need to introduce me to this eye candy of a man by your side," Claudia said.

"This is my partner, Luke. He's a private investigator," said Sol. "Luke, this is Claudia Hopkins. She was my editor and manager at *Performance Weekly*, where she still works as an executive editor."

"Nice meeting you," said Luke, going to shake Claudia's hand. But she dismissed him, clapping him on the shoulder with the tip of her encrusted clutch instead.

"Oh my god! That accent!" said Claudia in an even louder tone. "Why didn't you tell me you were coming and that you had a hot British boyfriend!"

"Not my boyfriend," said Sol. "Luke's my romantic partner."

"Tomato, tomahto. No wonder you don't want to leave London, though!" Claudia continued, and Luke was starting to get annoyed by her brazen personality and the fact that he could sense Sol's discomfort. "And you said he's a private investigator . . . That sounds naughty."

"Luke co-owns an agency in London with quite the success rate in high-profile entertainment cases, actually," Sol said.

"He does, huh?" said Claudia. "It's a pity you're so attached to London, because the right position just opened up, and I would offer it to you on the spot."

"Now I'm intrigued," said Sol, and Luke could see her thinking behind a veil of perfect composure and nonchalance.

"Travis is *finally* retiring," said Claudia. "And we're looking for an experienced TV reviewer with a personal point of view to replace him. And, of course, I thought of you immediately!"

"Thanks. That's so . . ." Sol was apparently too flustered to find the right words. "Will you send me the job posting so that I can take a look? It sounds so—interesting."

"Sending it right this moment." Claudia took her over-sized iPhone and a pair of equally big and bold reading glasses out of her minuscule clutch, and she started typing.

"There, I sent it. But the position is going to be based in Los Angeles—New York perhaps, for the right candidate—and I'm not sure you want to lose sight of this cutie."

Sol fake laughed uncomfortably, and Luke imitated her, but he could sense her body going stiff.

"Listen, we need to go grab a drink, as I can't do these things sober, but I'm so glad we bumped into you," Sol said, her California drawl fully on. "And thanks for thinking about me!"

"Nonsense! You'd be doing us a favor. But you can't leave yet, because I haven't told you all the gossip!"

"What gossip?" Luke could see Sol was reaching the end of her limited patience with Claudia, even if the editor was seemingly offering her a job.

"Simon. Smith. Has. Gone. Missing," said Claudia, getting closer to them and exaggeratingly enunciating each word. "Rumor has it that he pissed someone off again with one of his incenciary reviews and finally got what he'd been asking for for years."

"You can't mean to say someone made him disappear because he dissed their movie?" asked Luke, full of curiosity.

"Look at you, sexy and sneaky!" said Claudia, bumping Luke's shoulder again with her clutch and looking at him with eyes that could almost be described as appreciative. "But you seriously should read what he wrote about *Haughty Horizons*. I would have *killed him* if he said that about a movie I'd written and directed after spending ten years developing it like Victor Lago has."

"Wow, yes," Sol said. "I'd forgotten he'd been developing it for forever."

"But enough about Simon. Where did you two meet?"

Claudia suddenly changed subjects just when things were starting to get interesting.

"London, of course. But we're going to go get that drink now. I loved seeing you," Sol said, putting an abrupt end to the conversation. She grabbed Luke's arm and steered him away from the editor in the direction of the bar.

"Why are we moving away from the woman who could have given us more information about Simon Smith *and* was offering you a job?" Luke murmured into Sol's ear, guiding her through the sea of people, an arm around her waist.

"Because I can't stand the woman!" Sol brushed his neck with her nose as she spoke.

"She was offering you a job." He tried navigating around the incoming celebrities and their considerable entourages surrounding them in all directions.

"And I'll take a look at it, but she's literally one of the reasons why I hate her profession so much, so forgive me if I tell you that if she is going to be my boss again, the offer doesn't sound too enticing," Sol said. "And that was *before* she said I'd have to move back here."

Luke had always been supportive when it came to Sol's career, but he had to admit he also hadn't liked the idea of a job that would take her away from London. Even if the position, to him, had sounded perfectly fine, and he didn't want to be the reason she wouldn't contemplate it.

"She seemed to have some information on Simon." Luke continued whispering in Sol's ear while they were still moving toward the bar.

"We're in a room full of journalists. It's going to be easy to find someone else who babbles. News travels fast in this sector, and the best thing is, you don't even have to pry people for information. Everyone is probably already hammered and loves gossiping. The food is not only not good, and I wouldn't recommend having any of it, but there's really not that much to begin with. But everybody knows there's plenty of free booze," Sol said. "Plus, the woman was annoying me even more than usual. She was getting handsy with you."

Luke couldn't repress his smug smile.

7

"**This isn't happening!**" Sol protested when they reached their table inside the big hangar where the ceremony would take place.

Luke narrowed his eyes at her, silently questioning. "Sol, you keep saying that, and then things still happen."

"She's sitting with us," Sol said, referring to Claudia Hopkins's name on a seating card placed next to her own on top of table number 13. "I've never been seated in a better position in all my years attending these things. I can literally almost touch the stage from here. There's even some talent sitting at the table with us. And she has to also be sitting here! The one time I'm lucky with the seating lottery in an awards ceremony, but of course it can't be all good luck!"

"Maybe it's going to be a good thing, and she can tell you more about that position she mentioned," Luke said, and Sol wanted to strangle him. Why was he so fucking reasonable? Yes, she'd always been attracted to the part of him that respected and supported her career, but was he actually suggesting she should leave London? He was literally the most attached-to-London person she'd ever met. A job offer in LA had to sound preposterous to him. She wasn't still sure how he'd said yes to accompany her here when it meant leaving his dear hometown for four full days—more, counting the many hours spent in the air. Yet all of a sudden, he wanted her to contemplate a job *away* from London? Could he be getting tired of her and that was why he was pushing that idea so much?

She'd decided she couldn't wait to find out the answers to those pressing questions until later that day, when they'd finally be done with the circus of the awards ceremony and alone. She was going to try to take him to a more private place to talk about everything—the Christmas debacle included. But although having that conversation was all Sol needed, they were interrupted once again.

"Look who's here!" Claudia's high-pitched voice reverberated behind Sol, and she decided the person she most wanted to strangle was her former editor and not the man standing next to her, looking dashing.

"It looks like we're seated together, yes," Sol said, trying to sound cordial and unannoyed but not sure she'd achieved it.

"You need to tell me what you have been doing in London," Claudia said to Sol. "Other than picking up sexy men, of course."

Sol didn't know how to tell Claudia that it wasn't okay to objectify Luke in that way, even if he looked more like the character of a soapy TV show than a real person sometimes. She could testify to the fact that he was, indeed, an actual human whose feelings could be hurt.

"He's quite smart, too, you know?" Sol said. She didn't want to confront Claudia too overtly. The ceremony would drag for more than three hours, and she didn't want to be seething and angry, seated next to a person with whom she'd just had an argument, during all that time. But she also didn't like the way Claudia had spoken about her lover.

"Is he now? So, how's life been treating you across the pond?"

"I've been writing a book and freelancing for *Red Carpet*. I normally work with Julie McQueen. Is it possible she told me you folks know each other?" Sol asked Claudia, attempting civility and hoping Claudia would take the hint.

"Yes, yes, dullest woman in the business." Claudia waved a hand, brushing Sol off. Sol begged to differ. She would take Julie over Claudia as an editor any day, but she wasn't allowed to protest, because Claudia continued voicing all her thoughts. "But look at you, acting all grown-up and writing a book!"

Sol decided not to say anything. She was forty-three. She would have objectively said she'd started acting like a grown-up at least a decade before. That's what homeowner-ship did to people, right? It crashed their youth. Plus, that book of hers was not only unpublished, ever since she'd written its closing paragraph, she'd felt a sort of dread at the idea of no longer being able to spend time in that world.

"You know who else was writing a book, right?" Claudia said, taking Sol out of her reverie. "Simon Smith."

"Really?" Sol said, and she could sense Luke's body tensing next to her, paying closer attention.

"It was supposed to be a tell-all, first-person account about his experience as a movie critic. I'm told he shopped it all over town, and no one was buying it." A hint of a satisfied smirk played on Claudia's lips.

"I mean, I can relate to that," Sol said. "Agents haven't exactly been jumping at the opportunity of representing me, either."

But she couldn't ask Claudia any more details about

Simon's thwarted literary endeavors, as the other guests occupying their table arrived then, and she was surprised to recognize none other than filmmaker Victor Lago among them.

...

In hindsight, Sol should have realized that Victor Lago was going to be one of the guests at their table. He'd had an ongoing romantic relationship with showrunner Abbie Domingo for more than a decade, and Abbie's name was on one of the seating cards on the table next to another one that read *Abbie Domingo's Guest*. The second season of Abbie's show, *Slowing Down*, had been nominated in several categories and was one of the favorite drama contenders of the night. It was clear that Lago had wanted to show support to his partner, even if his own movie, *Haughty Horizons*, had been a darling a mere few weeks before but hadn't amassed any recognition after Simon Smith's review.

"Hello, everyone, I'm Abbie," the gracious showrunner said while getting to the table. The fifty-something-year-old had a small frame but a presence that filled the room, dressed in a stunning eggplant sleeveless gown. "So glad to be here tonight. So honored to be nominated. I'm a bit nervous, though."

Abbie laughed anxiously while shaking Claudia's, Luke's, and Sol's hands.

"Nervous?" a curmudgeonly Victor Lago said, falling ungraciously over a chair, not acknowledging the rest of the people at table 13. Next to Abbie, the filmmaker looked pale, tired, and even slightly disheveled with his short gray hair sticking up and his tuxedo hanging awkwardly on him. "This is a joke of an awards show!"

Abbie's laugh suddenly turned from nervous to embarrassed.

Things started to feel extra uncomfortable at table 13 when a couple of journalists joined the group: Jason Zit, who was Simon Smith's editor at *The Showbiz Reporter* and had overseen the publication of his review of *Haughty Horizons*, and critic Travis Wise from *Performance Weekly*.

"This is getting more and more interesting by the minute," Sol shared with Luke in an almost inaudible tone. She proceeded to introduce herself and Luke to the newcomers. "And I don't know if you remember me," Sol said when she addressed Jason Zit and Travis Wise.

"Of course, Sol, how are you doing?" Travis said in his usual affable style. He was a Black sixty-something-year-old who had a few more white hairs than the last time Sol had seen him.

"I don't remember you, actually," Jason said, abruptly.

"She worked for me for a while," intervened Claudia, as all of them had worked together at *Performance Weekly* a few years before, while Sol still lived in Los Angeles.

"Oh, you worked at *Performance Weekly*. I also worked at *Performance Weekly*," said Jason. "I'm an executive editor at *The Showbiz Reporter* now."

"We were there together for a couple of years at *Performance Weekly*. Travis and I worked together for longer, though," said Sol.

"Really? I still can't remember you," Jason said.

Sol blinked. She didn't know what to make of that. The fifty-something-year-old man with wispy hair and yellowing teeth had worked on the same floor as her, a mere couple of desks down from her, four years before. She had to admit that a pandemic had happened after that, and she, too, had seemed to forget some things, but still.

"Oh, please don't hold it against him," a tall and slender redhead woman of around fifty told Sol. "He won't admit to it, but he's completely face blind. His main fault is not even trying to hide it."

"Okay, I guess," Sol said, confused.

"I'm Emily, Jason's wife. If it's any consolation, I do remember you from a couple of holiday parties organized by *Performance Weekly*," the redhead continued, and that made Sol feel bad because she couldn't remember her. And she knew she wasn't face blind herself. "But you were there with someone different." Emily pointed to Luke, who was standing next to Sol.

"I probably attended those with my husband," Sol said and immediately realized the blunder. What was she thinking? Being in Los Angeles and surrounded by former colleagues had brought back vividly a period of her life that was now over. She felt Luke by her side, looking at her with confused eyes. "My *ex*-husband," she corrected herself.

"Ah," said Emily.

"Yes," added Sol awkwardly.

"I personally think she totally traded up with the new beau," Claudia felt inexplicably compelled to say.

8

They had reached that unavoidable point in awards ceremonies in which Sol was officially tired. They were two and a half hours in, and most of the main awards had yet to be announced, but she was bored, hungry (Sol had deemed the provided food not desirable), and would much rather have stayed in and watched the whole thing from bed, in her pajamas. The bought-in-a-hurry shoes were killing her even while seated, and the dress she was wearing couldn't be described as comfy athleisure.

Even the continuous comings and goings of famous, beautiful people inside the venue was starting to get old. She no longer cared if Jennifer Aniston was wearing a stunning black bustier with matching pants. Or if Jonathan Bailey was himself stunning.

To make things worse, *Slowing Down* had been on a winning streak, taking award after award. Sol wouldn't normally have had a problem with that. In fact, she'd voted for the show to win in several categories. The problem was that every time *Slowing Down* won something, one of the handheld video cameras covering the floor went to table 13 for a reaction shot from Abbie Domingo. And Sol had grown weary of having cameras pointed in her general direction. She felt compelled to look good and not make a face every single time. She didn't want to look bad on network TV—or worse, become an internet meme—but looking good was simply exhausting.

"You're getting tired," Luke leaned in and whispered. He'd learned to read her so well.

"I wish we'd stayed at the hotel, ordered room service, and watched from bed, to be honest," Sol told him in a hushed voice that would not be overheard by their neighbors. "Or we could have skipped the whole watching and still stayed in bed."

They looked at each other, and she could feel the longing in Luke's hungry eyes. Between the disastrous holiday break, work, the franticness before their trip to Los Angeles, and jet lag, they hadn't had sex often those past few weeks, and that was uncommon for them—and unacceptable.

Sol had almost interpreted this sudden lack of sex as an ominous sign that the last sentence in her story with Luke could have been already written, like the last sentence of her book. But his mischievous eyes told her a completely different thing.

"Let's get out of here," she said.

"Are you sure about that?"

"Absolutely. We've done the fancy, glamorous party already. No need to stay till the end. The longer we wait, the harder it's going to be to get a ride back to the hotel. And I have a sudden urge to get to the hotel."

"I'm also feeling the urge, but I thought this was important for your work," Luke said, and she needed him to stop sounding so reasonable.

"I've already said hi to everyone I like, like Travis, and even a few people I don't like, like Jason and Claudia. The real reason I wanted to come wasn't to attend this but because I wanted to show you the city where I lived for so long. And I still haven't been able to do it. I'm sure you'll end up loving Los Angeles."

Luke gave her a skeptical arch of his eyebrow.

"Plus, Simon Smith is clearly not here, or Claudia would have found out about it. Nothing escapes her. And we haven't been able to get a word out of Victor Lago all night, even though judging by all he's drunk, he should be quite talkative."

"No, but I've caught him checking you out at least a couple of times," said Luke, his eyes flicking to their table neighbor.

"I don't think he's been checking me out more than any other woman who isn't his partner," said Sol. She'd also noticed Victor's eyes on her and a few other people. "But in any case, we haven't neglected our promise to Julie."

"What about Greta Gerwig?" Luke asked. "We still haven't spotted her."

"I want to believe she would tell me to go ahead and leave with my sexy partner."

"Let's go then," he practically growled. They were already standing up to leave, taking advantage of one of the many commercial breaks during the ceremony, when they heard a shrieking yell, audible even in the crowd.

They remained frozen for what felt like a few minutes but was only one or two seconds. Sol experienced all the symptoms of a burst of adrenaline: heart pounding, blood pumping, a cold sensation that traveled through her body, and sweat. And then she saw Luke going in the direction of the scream. She was going to complain, because he was leaving her behind and she'd been very specific about her need for his support to be able to move, when she realized the terrifying source of the scream had been Emily. Luke was not abandoning Sol but simply going around the table to assist. The whole room was in a frenzy around them, and everyone seemed to be on the move, either trying to figure out what had happened or running away from the source of that scream. There was complete chaos.

Sol saw Luke talking to Emily, who was pointing to a passed-out Travis. His head had landed on top of his plate on the table.

"What happened to him?" Luke asked.

"He was nibbling on some of the food on his plate, and suddenly his head collapsed on top of the table," Emily said. Her hands were shaking, and she kept clutching the pearl choker at her collarbone, making the pale skin around it red with the friction.

Luke took Travis's vitals and was quick to lift the critic's head from the plate. He untied the bow tie around his neck and undid the first two buttons of Travis's shirt.

A paramedic team that had been standing by for emergencies at the entrance of the hangar arrived at the table. They put an oxygen mask on Travis as they worked quickly to stabilize him. Before the commercial break was over, the critic had already been taken away on a stretcher. It wasn't only that his life could be at risk—the show must go on.

Luke had a short conversation with the paramedics, relating what happened, then he made his way back to the seat next to Sol.

"Did Travis's face look extremely red and blotchy to you just now?" Luke asked Sol in their usual whisper.

"Perhaps, why?"

"And is it me, or is there a faint bitter almond smell in the air?"

"Now that you say it, yes," Sol admitted, paying more attention to the aromas that surrounded her. "Why?"

"Because I'm not sure that was a heart attack or a stroke. I think Travis may have been poisoned."

Sol's eyes widened in shock and surprise. "I told you not to eat anything!"

9

"That was Claudia," Sol told him, her voice still hoarse from the sleepiness.

Daylight had only just begun to creep in, but he'd been awake for at least an hour. He hated jet lag so much. They'd made it to their hotel extremely late the previous night, as the circumstances surrounding TV critic Travis Wise and his emergency trip to the ER had been thoroughly discussed by several ceremony attendees. Everyone had wanted to talk to Sol and Luke as they'd had a first-row view of the events. They'd tried to leave the venue for at least an hour, being intercepted every single time by another journalist or critic who wanted to ask them about Travis's near-encounter with death. Luke had resented all of them. Journalists had to be the most unabashedly nosy professional group he'd ever met. By the time he and Sol had finally managed to arrive at their hotel room, they'd simply crashed, exhausted from the lack of sleep and the adrenaline-fueled events of the evening.

But despite the extreme tiredness, he'd still woken up unseasonably early that morning. He had just started to finally fall asleep again when Sol's phone, which was normally silenced, started ringing, waking both of them up.

It was Claudia, Sol's former editor.

Sol took the call, and when she was done, she said, "You were right. Travis was poisoned." She stood by the room's windows, the morning light filtering through the cream-colored curtains. She was wearing black, cheeky knickers and a white, see-through T-shirt knotted at her waist that she'd borrowed from him. He would have fixated more thoroughly on the sexyness of her state of undress if it wasn't for the message she was delivering. "They found traces of cyanide in his blood. He was lucky, apparently, to have ingested a very small amount of food during the ceremony, or he could have been dead."

"Someone tried to kill him? Is he doing okay?" Luke managed to ask, still in a semi-dazed state but pushing himself to sit up in bed.

Sol clutched her phone in one hand, playing nervously with the hair at her nape with the other. "Claudia just talked to Travis, and he's doing fine. I'll try calling him later. I've always liked him. Everyone likes him. He's the nicest guy in the business. I don't really think anyone would want to kill him."

"You always think everyone is innocent. But it looks like someone did try to kill him. What about one of the creators of the TV shows he reviewed? There was a screenwriter sitting at our table, right?"

"Travis isn't like that. Even if he doesn't like something, his reviews are always polite, considerate. I learned a lot from him," Sol said. She was visibly distressed. "And I think I read his review of *Slowing Down*—that's the show from the showrunner at our table, Abbie Domingo. Travis liked it."

"True. It was the chap who didn't remember you, the

one who had worked with Simon Smith on the review dissing *Haughty Horizons*." Luke tried remembering everyone who was at the table with them yesterday. "And they think the cyanide was at the food from the ceremony?"

"That's what I gathered. We'd been inside the damn hangar for almost three hours by then. Anything he may have eaten before that was poisoned would have acted much quicker. Claudia said they think he was only saved because he barely ate anything from his plate. Travis has a severe nut allergy and only nibbled a bit of the hummus and grapes, afraid they might have been in contact with some nuts."

"So his allergy to nuts could have saved his life?"

"I mean, when you put it like that . . ." Sol climbed onto the bed to sit crossed-legged next to him. "Claudia talked to her bosses at *Performance Weekly*, and they are thinking about investigating this."

"I think it should be investigated," Luke admitted.

"Since you were there last night, and I mentioned you're a private investigator with experience in the industry, they were wondering if you'd be willing to take the case," Sol said. Did she sound tentative?

"I think we are," Luke said, even if the idea of having to stay in Los Angeles for longer than necessary made his skin crawl.

"We are?" Sol asked in disbelief. She seemed to have realized he hadn't exactly been wowed by this whole California experience.

"Not *we* as in you and me, cara. But *we* as in Divya and me, as soon as I talk to her and *if* she agrees," he clarified. The last thing he needed was for Sol to get enmeshed in this case. It was true that they'd met and fallen for each other because she'd ended up entangled in a previous case he was investigating. But, on that particular occasion, poisoned critics hadn't been a feature. "In the last twenty-four hours, one critic has gone missing under mysterious and apparently violent circumstances. And another one got poisoned and almost died. It's as if there's someone out there trying to get rid of critics, and I have a vested interest in the well-being of the profession, particularly when it comes to one of its members."

Sol's eyes widened. "What? You're doing this because you think I could be next?"

"I'm doing this because there's clearly something to investigate, and as you've put it, the Bakshi & Contadino Agency specializes in Hollywood matters. That, and I want to make sure you won't be next. So, who's the client exactly? And are we getting paid this time?"

"You know you sounded exactly like Cybill Shepherd in *Moonlighting*, right?"

He gave her his sexiest, most rakish of smiles and kissed her. The case could wait for a bit. There was something more important that they needed first. But Sol's phone started ringing once again. Claudia wanted to know if he'd take the case.

He couldn't avoid thinking about how much he wasn't enjoying the whole Los Angeles experience. Was it so much to ask for a decent sleep and uninterrupted time alone with one's romantic partner?

10

"So how is LA treating you?" Divya asked him.

"Do you want the truth?" Luke was currently strolling along Abbot Kinney Boulevard, following Sol's advice, while she had lunch with her friend Lola. Sol had provided Luke with at least three different recommendations in case he wanted to grab a bite alongside the popular street on Venice Beach. He was weighing his options while walking. He missed walking so much.

"You know I always want the truth," Divya teased him, and he had to admit that hearing Divya's Mancunian accent made him feel more homesick, even if he was a staunch Londoner.

"I can't say I'm taking to it much. I just don't get it," he finally said.

"What don't you get, exactly?"

"This place. The traffic is horrendous. If you want to walk, you need to drive first to a walking-friendly area. Everyone looks like they're out of a TV show . . ."

"And that last is a problem because . . . ?"

"I guess you're right, and that last thing is not necessarily a problem. But I swear I've not seen a single crooked tooth since we've landed."

"Again, what are you complaining about?"

"I've forgotten that you had a sweet spot for Americans," Luke said, as Divya had been dating a Texan TV staffer called Moon whom Divya had met during the same case that brought Luke and Sol together.

"Should I remind you Sol has an American passport on top of her Spanish one?"

"No need," he said, defeated. "But I'm a bit homesick, and the Americans have threatened to give us a job."

"What, seriously? What job?"

Luke relayed the events of the previous night and how the publication Travis Wise worked for had expressed their interest in hiring private investigators. He also explained the facts surrounding the disappearance of Simon Smith and how he thought both occurrences were somewhat connected. It was too much of a coincidence, and at the Bakshi & Contadino Agency, they didn't believe in those.

"I hope you've said yes," said Divya when Luke finished talking.

"I was waiting to talk to you first, and to be clear, we're only getting officially hired and paid to investigate the poisoning of Travis."

"Yes, yes, let's take it," Divya said.

"Argh," Luke growled. "Really?"

"Luke, we've got nowt on the books right now. That's why I said it was a good time for you to head off for a couple of days and spend some time with Sol in LA. Honestly, this couldn't've come at a better time. We needed clients, and somehow, you've gone and found them."

"But I found them in bloody Los Angeles!" Even he

could hear how ridiculous he sounded. The truth was that the Bakshi & Contadino Agency needed cash urgently. He'd been worried before traveling to Los Angeles because of that. He'd almost told Sol that he couldn't join her in the end because of how short on money he was, but he'd feared she would see it as one more reason why they weren't a good fit.

"I'm sure you can survive wearing board shorts and drinking kale juices for a few more days," Divya teased.

"You're joking, but you don't even realize. I haven't been able to read a restaurant menu where all the dishes didn't feature either kale or avocado—if not both. You ask a waiter to suggest something to order, and they always invariably say the brussels sprouts or the asparagus!" And yes, he'd almost told his romantic partner he wouldn't accompany her there not only because he was broke but because he was a consummate reluctant traveler.

"Still not understanding why you're complaining."

"Alright, aren't you going to join me in the ingestion of kale and avocado?"

"Are the clients willing to pay for my flight there?"

"Shit, probably not."

"Then I'll have to help you from here. And, if you need some help there, you can ask Sol," Divya said.

Luke's jaw was tight as he spoke. "I'm not getting Sol involved this time."

"The way you told me the whole story, Sol is already quite involved," Divya said. He knew that, but hearing it out loud didn't help. "The last time she was involved in a case wasn't that bad. You got a detective agency and a relationship out of it."

"There's a missing critic whose apartment is bloody. And another one who only made it alive out of an awards ceremony because he has a nut allergy. This isn't like the last time Sol was involved."

Divya's tone sharpened as she spoke. "Careful she doesn't hear you. Last time, her reputation and career were at stake. Not sure she sees it as nothing."

"And I'm not saying it was nothing! You always take her side, even when she's not here." He ran a hand through his hair in frustration.

"Don't get jealous, will you?" Divya teased him.

"I'm not jealous. I'm just saying that I have the feeling this case may be dangerous, and I don't want her near danger." Saying it out loud helped him realize how much he didn't want Sol getting involved in the new investigation.

"Absolutely, but so far you just have a gut feeling that this may be dangerous and you know those—"

"Don't solve cases," Luke finished.

"Què t'ha passat?" Lola asked Sol in Catalan, visibly concerned about what had happened to her friend.

"It's not that bad, is it?" Sol replied, also in Catalan, to her screenwriter friend who lived in Los Angeles. They'd met when Sol lived in California, and they bonded over their common Barcelona homesickness. They'd remained close since then. Even after Sol's move. She'd perfected the art of long-distance friendships.

Lola looked at the normally stylish Sol and shrugged. They were meeting on Third Street in West Hollywood, in front of the salad and healthy-foods staple Joan's on Third.

"The airline lost my suitcase, and I've had to improvise. They still haven't delivered my clothes!"

"Oh no!" Lola said, understanding dawning on her face.

"I did some emergency shopping for underwear,

toiletries, a damn party dress, and the most uncomfortable shoes in the history of heels . . . but somehow I managed to forget about jeans, sweaters, and most basics. Hence the—" Sol gestured to her look.

She wore a pink Bimba y Lola cap to protect her face from the sun, which had been miraculously packed in her carry-on, black leggings that she'd remembered to buy because she had attended a Pilates class that morning before heading there, and a giant navy sweatshirt that she'd borrowed from Luke. It was stamped with the word *ITALIA* in big letters, and apparently it had been a souvenir gift from his sister Gaia, who was four years his senior and had gotten it at the 2016 Rio Olympics.

"Okay, I understand your luggage got lost, and you had to make do with your partner's hoodie, but did he go missing with the rest of your wardrobe?" Lola asked Sol as they both made their way inside the restaurant and lined up at one of the deli counters to order their lunch.

"What do you mean?"

Lola lifted an eyebrow, clearly annoyed. "Where's Luke? You've been telling me all about him for months, and I thought I was going to meet him."

"Ets una xafardera," said Sol, dismissing her friend.

"I'm dying with curiosity, yes."

"I promise I'll introduce you before we leave, but I wanted to see you alone," said Sol.

"Why?"

"Because I want to talk about him, obviously."

Lola uncrossed her arms, suddenly understanding. "Ah."

"I was actually going to propose—"

"Not another marriage!" Lola interrupted.

"Of course, not another marriage," said Sol, her tone just

shy of annoyed. "I'm never getting married again! You know that. But I was going to propose to Luke to move in together with me. We've been practically living together since the summer, and it would save him some money. His place is all the way up, almost in the outer limits of North London, and not very convenient for me."

"So you want him to move in with you?" Lola said.

"Yes, of course. My place is much bigger than his. Ridiculously small by any Californian standard but apparently quite big for a London cottage."

"Perhaps phrase it differently when you bring up the subject with him," Lola said, choosing her words cautiously. "Don't just assume he's going to see your place as the most desirable one."

"But it is!"

Lola breathed deeply, as if bracing herself to find the patience to deal with Sol. "Didn't you tell me he's a North Londoner through and through? Perhaps he doesn't fancy living south of the Thames."

"Okay, okay. Point taken. That's why I wanted to talk about this with someone with the capacity for empathy, because I know I tend to be clueless sometimes. But the thing is, I'm no longer sure if moving in together is a good idea," admitted Sol. She didn't add anything else as it was finally their turn to order food, and she hadn't even had time to check the menu.

She copied Lola in her choice of the quiche of the day and a side of greens.

"What happened? Why don't you want to propose anymore?" Lola asked Sol as they both sat at one of the outdoor tables, waiting for their food to be brought out.

"Nothing, really. I mean, these past few days haven't been perfect. But a relationship cannot be perfect all the time, I *know* that. But then we came here, and it brought me memories of so many things, of everything that can go wrong."

"Los Angeles is reminding you of your ex-husband David, and now you don't know if you want to commit to another relationship because you're afraid it'll be the same as that last one," Lola said.

"That, basically." Sol hadn't realized the extent of her doubts until she heard her friend's words. "And I want you to know the only reason I don't have a professional therapist analyzing every single aspect of my disastrous life is because I have you doing an amazing job for free."

Lola gave her the judgy eye. "You don't have a disastrous life. Quite the contrary, I'd say. I've seen pictures of Luke, remember?"

"He is awfully handsome," Sol admitted.

"He also seems to know how to make you happy, which is something David certainly forgot how to manage by the end of your marriage."

"And the middle of it. So you still think I should propose?"

Lola shrugged, as if contemplating the options. "Think about it. There's no rush."

"It's not like I haven't made any commitments already with him. I got a fucking IUD inserted," Sol said.

"Those can be painful!"

"But what if he doesn't want the new commitment that moving in together implies? I'm no longer sure we want the same things . . ."

"Then he'll probably let you know," argued Lola, and it sounded reasonable. "Why don't you see how things go, and tell him something by the end of this trip. Traveling with someone is a great opportunity to learn new things about them."

"I think Luke is hating this trip," Sol said.

Lola arched her eyebrows in an almost offended stare. "He doesn't like LA?"

"I don't think he does," Sol realized. "In his defense, I haven't made a proper effort to show him the city. And we both know Los Angeles can be hard to know for a European. He's one of those people who likes walking everywhere, so..."

"He'll get nowhere that way."

"Plus, the awards ceremony yesterday wasn't necessarily a fun activity with Travis getting poisoned."

"Poor Travis. I like him. When my last TV show opened, his was the nicer review. He really understood what we were going for. Which can't be said about the rest of your profession," Lola dissed, pointing in Sol's direction.

"Ouch." Sol feigned offense with a hand over her sternum.

"Which is why I don't understand why they're firing him."

"What?"

"Haven't you heard?" Lola said. "*Performance Weekly* fired him. This is his last week at the job."

"You mean there were layoffs, and they let him go?" said Sol. "He'd been there forever, so he was probably making more than most of the other staff."

"No, no. The way the story has been told to me, he wasn't laid off but fired," Lola said, happy to share some gossip with Sol.

"But Claudia told me he was *retiring!*"

"Who's Claudia again?"

"My former editor at *Performance Weekly* and Travis's boss," explained Sol.

"So another journalist?"

"Yes."

"Sol, guapa, you're my favorite journalist. But you're aware your sector has a way of saying things that aren't completely accurate when it suits a narrative, right?"

"What do you mean?"

"That perhaps Claudia told you Travis was retiring because she didn't want to tell you why they'd fired him."

"I think I should call Claudia and ask her."

"Not so fast!" objected Lola. "When is it again that I'm meeting Luke?"

11

"Where are you?" Sol asked Luke when he picked up the phone.

"Trying to decide whether I should eat at Gjelina or a place called The Butcher's Daughter that seems like the perfect spot for unemployed screenwriters and their puppies." Luke was famished, yet he couldn't seem to make a decision.

"When in doubt, Gjelina is always the answer," Sol said.

"But I just told you there were cute dogs at the other place."

"And how come you still haven't eaten?" she asked. Did she sound upset?

"I wasn't feeling hungry, and now all of a sudden I'm absolutely famished," Luke explained.

"How many times do I need to explain how jet lag works?" It looked like he'd managed to make her lose her not-so-ample-to-begin-with patience—again. "If you want to be out of this travel-fatigue loop, you need to start doing things when they're supposed to happen here, not in London time!"

He let out a slow breath. "Sorry to disappoint."

"It's not that, I'm also tired. We haven't been able to have a moment just to be with each other. Now there's this new case getting in the way. And I know you hate being here."

"I don't hate being here, it's just that I don't fancy it much," Luke admitted. "I do fancy you, though, a lot. And I know this was an important work trip. And all of a sudden it became a work trip for me, too, which isn't ideal, but Divya tells me we need to take this case because we're basically skint. Not that I needed to be reminded about it. The state of my bank account speaks for itself."

"And you're hating the idea of having to spend even more days in Los Angeles and away from London," Sol said.

"Yes, but mainly I hate the idea of being away from you. Especially considering we haven't exactly been spending proper time together lately and most certainly none since we arrived in Los Angeles."

"Don't worry about that, you won't be away from me," she said, a playfulness in her tone.

"What do you mean? We were supposed to fly back to London tomorrow. I'll have to reschedule my flight to work on this case," he said, and he really couldn't believe he'd be the one to stay.

"I'm also postponing the return. Julie called me. Since we're here, she wants me to cover a last-minute junket for *Red Carpet*. It's actually an interview with Victor Lago. Apparently they're doing a second round of press for *Haughty Horizons*."

"Doesn't *Red Carpet* already have a correspondent here?"

"Do you want to get rid of me or what?"

"Of course I don't want to get rid of you! I'm just making sure no more journalists have gone missing," he protested.

"No one else has gone missing! *Red Carpet*'s regular

correspondent has to cover something else happening at the same time. It's a very common occurrence. Julie wanted their regular correspondent to try to do both but now decided to take advantage of me being here, and she's put me to work," Sol explained. "She still wants us to find Simon."

"Of course she does, and again, there's no *us* when it comes to the case," Luke said, and he sounded as commanding as possible. "I don't want you getting involved."

"Okay, okay. I promise to stay away from *your* case," she finally conceded.

"Good, but I'm very relieved I won't be alone in this awful maze of motorways and retail parks that calls itself a city."

"Oh my god! You're such a snob!"

"And I'm looking forward to seeing you often in a strict non-case capacity," Luke said.

"You mean if we finally find the time to actually have a nice fuck?"

"We haven't been shagging as often as before, right?" he said, and he was happy she'd also realized it, and it wasn't that she'd been actively avoiding him because she was thinking of splitting up or any of the other theories that assailed him sometimes.

"We most definitely haven't, and I haven't as much as seen you naked—let alone touched you—since we've landed in LA."

"And you're wondering why I'm not taking to this place ..."

"You're not liking it because I haven't shown it to you. Once I discover Los Angeles for you, you're going to fall in love with the city."

"Allow me to remain skeptical about that. But I'll be happy to see the city with you," he admitted.

"Okay, here's what's going to happen. You're going to head to Gjelina, where hopefully they'll give you a table right away, because who has lunch at 2:30?"

"Unemployed screenwriters with their puppies?" he tried aggravating her, but he could hear her contained laugh while she kept talking and pretended to ignore his comment.

"You're going to order the pomodoro pizza with burrata and one of the salads. I trust you'll be able to make an informed decision. The traffic is bad-ish," Sol said. He liked it when she got bossy.

"Obviously," he said, but Sol ignored his quip, again.

"But I should be there in about forty minutes. We can order some dessert and then go to the beach."

"Again?"

"Could you be a bit less obtuse? The other day we went to the beach in Santa Monica. This is Venice. I promise you'll like it."

"But just so that we're clear, you're not implying we're going to swim or anything, right?" he said, still not understanding her beach obsession in January.

"Of course not! The water is freezing!" Sol exclaimed. "We're going to stroll and people watch."

"It's going to be one of our passeggiate."

"Precisely. But we're not going to stay to watch the sunset this time. Because I want to get to the hotel early and see you naked."

"I may be finally starting to like the idea of staying in this city," he said, his tone laced with mischief.

It had been a glorious afternoon. Almost perfect. It played like the montage sequence in a movie: the sexy couple walking, their arms wrapped around each other. Taking every chance to touch, look at each other, smile.

Sol liked the idea of making new memories in a city that had been among her favorites for so long but that she'd been forced to keep out of her mind after the divorce. It was as if everything that she associated with Los Angeles—the sun, the ocean, the laid-back vibes, and the surfer energy—had become indistinguishable from her marriage with David.

She had avoided thinking about Los Angeles just to keep David out of her mind. But she was starting to have new experiences there, and some of them were now synonymous with a new Sol. And with her relationship with Luke.

After a stroll by the Ocean Front Walk, where Sol would have said that Luke was starting to show some signs of fondness for the place, they'd grabbed an Uber and made their way back to the hotel. They were now finally in front of their room at the Fairmont. She would have been able to open the door if Luke hadn't been distracting her from the moment they got inside the elevator. He hadn't relented even when they got out.

"You need to stop kissing my neck for two seconds," she begged him.

"Really?" he whispered, pressing his chest and hips against her back, biting one of her earlobes, and making her shudder.

"I'm so—" she tried.

"Turned on?" he helped her, running his tongue slowly down her neck.

She arched her back against him, acquiescing. "That I can't get the door to open."

She'd tried the room's key card four or five times, always getting a red light in the process. She was starting to feel extremely frustrated.

"Try my card," he told her, still tickling her nape. "But you'll need to find it first."

"Really?" she said, but she couldn't avoid smiling.

She turned, facing Luke, her back against the room's door, his body pressed against hers. He continued torturing Sol with the most devilish neck play while she started going through the contents of his back pockets.

"Not there." He bit her earlobe again, and she needed to find that damn key and open that door, or she'd combust in the hallway.

After feeling the perfect roundness of Luke's ass, she got her right hand in one of his front pockets but decided he wasn't going to be the only one to play the game of keeping the other aroused.

"That's definitely *not* it," he said, his voice shaky and even sexier than usual as she stretched the fabric of his pocket and slowly palmed his length. "Okay, let me help you," he finally said, taking his card from the other pocket and trying to open the door himself. But that also didn't work.

"Argh!" Sol cried when she saw the red light on the door's lock. She was officially frustrated.

12

Sol was inside one of the suites of the Beverly Hilton Hotel, waiting for her interview with Victor Lago to start. Describing her as irritated would be putting it mildly.

For one, she was supposed to interview the director for a movie she had yet to watch. The commission from Julie had been so last minute that she hadn't had time to see *Haughty Horizons* before her chat with Lago. And everyone in her profession knew there was nothing that upsets filmmakers and creatives more than lack of knowledge when it comes to their work.

Granted, the movie had been released a few weeks before, and she should have *technically* already watched it. In theory she should watch *everything*, but there were way too many films and TV shows and not enough time. Not even for a professional critic.

The reality was that she'd read a few of the online reactions generated after Simon Smith's initial review and decided she didn't want to watch a bad movie—especially one that dealt with existential dread, a haunted ranch, and the machinations of a local political boss. She'd read the plot of *Haughty Horizons* and thought, *Bleak drama that takes itself too seriously. No, thank you.* Of course, she now realized that had probably been a prejudiced mistake. Reviewing was such an subjective business that Simon's initial criticism could have negatively influenced consecutive reviews of *Haughty Horizons.* And maybe the movie deserved better. It probably did, since the studio was giving it a new promotional push. That could only be seen as their belief in the film's potential. Yet she still hadn't watched it.

But Sol wasn't only unhappy because she felt ill prepared for an interview. She was also extremely sleepy, tired, and still quite frustrated. If the heat level of the makeout session with Luke in the hallway of the Fairmont Hotel the previous evening was any indication, she should have probably been still dazed from all the good-mood hormones and fantastic sex. But she wasn't.

After both their key cards had failed to open their door at the Fairmont, Luke and Sol had gone to the hotel's reception. There they'd been informed not only that they would not be able to extend their stay as initially planned, they were, in fact, no longer guests. Sol had made an inexplicable mistake while booking their hotel. In her defense, it had been while listening to her mother enumerate all the reasons why she didn't think Luke was a good match for her —and she'd selected the wrong end date.

After spending a cramped Christmas at the Novos' and then the Contadinos', and after a busy start to the new year, what Sol and Luke needed was some quality time and the comfort of a solid bed. Instead they were told that the hotel was completely full, and they would sadly have to leave. Not only that, Los Angeles was buzzing with several awards ceremonies and events. So much so that they hadn't been able to find another suitable hotel room. The few available were either expensive suites going for several thousand dollars a night or out-of-the-way motel rooms that didn't inspire much confidence.

After hours of hotel perusing from the lobby of the Fairmont, Sol had called Lola. The silver lining had been that her friend had finally met Luke in person. The not-so-ideal situation was that she and Luke had slept on an inflatable mattress in Lola's living room in her family's Craftsman Bungalow in Los Feliz.

"Sorry I'm late." A low-pitched voice took Sol out from her inner musings as Victor Lago entered the room. "I needed to make a phone call."

"No problem," she said, her professional smile and demeanor fully at play, even if she did feel more tired than usual. "I don't know if you remember me from the ceremony this Sunday?"

"Yes, of course. Unlike your professional colleague, I'm extremely good with faces." Victor Lago sat in front of Sol. But even though his words were polite and kind, there was something about his cheeky demeanor that didn't make him very trustworthy.

"It was a night difficult to forget by any measure," Sol said, and she wasn't exactly sure what had made her do it. She was normally all business in those kinds of settings, but Julie only wanted one quote or two from the director, and Sol had been promised fifteen minutes, so she inferred she could do some small talk before asking Lago about *Haughty Horizons*.

"I'm glad that there were medical professionals close by. Was it a heart attack?" Lago asked, still sounding a tad fickle. He produced a hip flask from the interior pocket of his tweed jacket and took a swig.

"What happened to Travis, you mean? It wasn't a heart attack. They believe he was poisoned," Sol explained, unfazed by the mid-morning drink. It wasn't exactly the first time she'd encountered that during an interview.

"Poisoned? By who?" Lago said, surprised. Even his accent sounded different. It had been a perfectly modulated and somehow artificial Mid-Atlantic English until that point, but it turned to a broad and expressive New Yorker after hearing Travis had been poisoned.

"No idea about that," Sol said, realizing she should probably not have shared that piece of information. She made a mental note *not* to tell Luke about her babbling too much. "Did you know Travis? Before Sunday, I mean."

"I'm sure we've seen each other at press functions over the years, you know how it goes. The same faces keep popping up, but I can't say I knew him personally." Lago's Mid-Atlantic English was back at play. And was it weird that he'd just described himself as someone who was *extremely good with faces* and now seemed to have only a vague recollection of Travis's features?

"Yes, every time I come to Los Angeles I keep seeing the same journalists everywhere," Sol said. She suddenly realized she wasn't sure how she'd introduce the questions Julie wanted her to ask. "My editor at *Red Carpet* was very excited when the opportunity of talking to you arose. She feels that perhaps we didn't cover *Haughty Horizons* properly before."

"If so, I'm afraid that you weren't the only ones," Lago said. Again, his words and manners were polite, but they still didn't ring as sincere to Sol.

"Do you feel the movie hasn't been treated fairly?" she pressed.

"I don't think I'm the most objective person to make such a statement, but yes, I don't think the movie was judged in a fair manner." Lago sipped again and then offered the flask to Sol.

"Why?" Sol shook her head to the offer of booze, and then she tried to soften her words. "If you don't mind me asking."

"Of course I don't," Lago said, yet it sounded like he did mind. "Despite my requests for a wide promotion, the studio insisted on showing the movie initially only to an extremely small number of select critics. I wanted to reach as many movie reviewers as possible and do word-of-mouth screenings, but I was told that would be a mistake. So we took the studio's approach, and the initial reviews were middling. Of course, only a very small batch of critics had seen the movie, a very homogeneous group."

"You mean that the critics that had access to the movie were mainly middle-aged, white, straight, cisgender men," Sol deciphered Lago's code.

"Without getting into specifics, the studio felt a certain demographic would respond better to the movie," Lago continued. Sol thought about her own response to *Haughty Horizons* and the lack of appeal the movie had to her.

"Did you read those reviews?"

"I never read reviews," Lago said, and Sol didn't know how she knew it, but he was lying.

"So you don't know if there was anyone in particular who hadn't understood what you tried with *Haughty Horizons*?" she surprised herself by asking. Was she baiting Lago to get him to talk about Simon Smith?

"You'd have to ask our publicity team. I know they keep clippings of everything that gets published." Once again Lago was all professionalism. And Sol couldn't avoid thinking that if they were having this conversation in a bar, instead of the setting of an interview, and without her phone recording the director's every word, those words would be a bit different and more revealing. Especially considering Lago was probably already tipsy.

"So they didn't tell you anything about critic Simon Smith's views on the movie?" She would normally never risk antagonizing an interviewee in such a way, but Julie probably wouldn't mind. After all, Sol was inquiring after her editor's friend.

"I'm afraid I have no clue who you're talking about," said Lago in an icy tone that Sol recognized only too well as a warning. The director's patience was wearing off.

"How has the studio persuaded you to do this again?" she asked. "I know doing press is tiresome and draining."

"No, no. I love doing press."

Sol almost chuckled. No one loved talking to journalists for hours on end and repeating the same answers over and over again. "But how are things different this time for *Haughty Horizons*?"

"Well, for starters I'm talking to you," Lago said with his best smile. "I love talking to women about my films."

"To women?" Sol frowned, unsure what exactly Lago was implying.

"You're much more gentle and understanding," the director said, with the confidence of someone who thought he'd just paid a compliment. "By the way, where has your editor at *Red Carpet* been hiding you? I don't think I've seen you around before, and it's most definitely a pity."

There was nothing Sol liked less than a man pretending to be something he wasn't. And Victor Lago, regardless of what he may think about himself, clearly wasn't aligned with feminist values.

13

While Sol was having a not necessarily comfortable conversation with filmmaker Victor Lago, Luke was making his way to the offices and central kitchens of the catering company that had provided the food at the event on Sunday evening, where critic Travis Wise had ended up poisoned. Before Luke left Sol's friends' house that morning, Alex—Lola's precocious thirteen-year-old kid—had warned Luke that the catering company was in an extremely inconvenient part of town.

Luke, once again, didn't know what to make of that information. So far, he'd had to take a car there like everywhere else, the traffic had been atrocious like every other time since landing in California, and absolutely nothing in the landscape of that urban sprawl reminded him of an actual city.

He still wasn't sure whether he hated Los Angeles solely because of its complete lack of convenience and traditional urban planning, or because the trip had started morphing into a nightmare from hell.

Luke was now not only still jet-lagged and tired, but also extremely irritated. He missed Sol. Even though they'd spent more time together than usual over the past few days, it hadn't been quality time. He was starting to really resent the lack of verbal—and sexual—communication with her. He just hoped they'd be able to fix that before their return to London—mainly because there was no date in sight for said travel back.

Throughout his late twenties and early thirties, he had a recurring nightmare in which he waited in a nondescript airport terminal and was denied boarding a London-bound flight every single time he tried leaving. He felt he was now living through that scenario. Only here there was no chance of waking up and finding himself comfortably abed in his London studio flat.

"Can I help you?" An attractive woman in her thirties, dressed in a pristinely white chef's jacket, took Luke out of his thoughts when he entered the offices of the catering company.

"I'm looking for Chef Gill García," Luke said.

"Then you're in luck, because you found her," the woman told him with a smile.

"I'm Luke Contadino," he said, extending his hand and not knowing if the famously germophobic Americans still practiced that manner of formal greeting post-pandemic. There was a reason Luke didn't like working outside of London—not mastering the behavioral code of the place made his job harder. "I called earlier. I'm investigating the incident at the awards ceremony."

"Ah, the *alleged* poisoning," Gill said, taking his extended hand in a firm, warm handshake and giving him an appraising look he was almost tempted to interpret as seductive.

"The alleged poisoning," Luke conceded.

"The police have called me about it," Gill said. "But they definitely didn't sound as sexy as you."

Alright, perhaps working outside of London had some advantages. He had found exactly zero people there more willing to talk to him just because of how he sounded.

"I can talk to you now, if you follow me to the kitchen and promise to give me your honest opinion." Gill quirked an eyebrow. "I'm testing a new spinach and artichoke appetizer and need fresh taste buds."

"Sounds promising," he said and followed Chef Gill García to the interior of an industrial kitchen, where at least half a dozen other cooks were already hard at work.

"Were you working at the venue on the night of the awards, or is your job done beforehand?" Luke asked Gill as she served three small glasses of fragrant, chilled, creamy green soup from three different containers on top of the kitchen counter.

"We did a lot of work before, but I was there that night," Gill said. "Try this one first," she added, pointing at the slightly paler of the three glasses.

"And you oversaw each one of the dishes being served?" Luke realized he had somehow agreed to try the food cooked by a person of interest *and* potential poisoner. That would have never happened to him in London. He'd be fully awake and alert if they were in his hometown. He wouldn't have slept on a half-deflated mattress in the middle of a too-bright living room if they were in London. What was he thinking when he'd taken this job?

Right, he was broke.

"Relax, I'll also have a taste of that," Chef Gill said, as if reading his mind, ladling some of the same soup into a small glass for herself. "And no, obviously I didn't oversee all sixteen hundred plates being served. I had a team of ten cooks and an army of waiters working there with me that night." She sipped delicately from the glass.

Any of them could have tampered with the food.

"Creamy," he offered after tasting the subtle notes of artichoke but no spinach in the soup.

Chef García made a note in a big notebook, and Luke couldn't avoid thinking *he* should be the one taking notes. And yet he'd completely forgotten about packing the most basic tools in his profession. In his defense, not in his wildest dreams had he imagined he'd have a case to solve and notes to take in Los Angeles.

"What about this one?" the chef asked about the greener of the soups. She also tasted it.

"Too much celery," Luke offered after just one sip. "But it could be just me. Not a fan of celery."

"Such a pity. You were showing so much potential," Gill said with a slow, knowing grin.

"And there's something else there, but I can't place it," he said, taking another sip and not minding the celery this second time around.

Gill gave him a teasing glance. "Secret ingredient, but I'd be willing to reveal it if you ask nicely."

Luke ignored Gill's insinuating gesture. "Any chance you know who in your team plated and served the food for Travis Wise?"

"Is that the dude who got *allegedly* poisoned? Nobody tells me anything around here," Gill said, and Luke couldn't help but feel the chef was extremely relaxed, considering she was being interviewed by a private detective and her reputation could be on the line. What chef wants to be associated with food intoxication?

"It is." He confirmed Travis's identity, which had been all

over the news, as the event had been packed with journalists. So Chef García's not knowing about it rang a bit improbable.

"You wouldn't happen to know where he was sitting, right?" Gill said as she unlocked her cell phone and started looking for something.

"I do because I was also there. Table 13."

"You were, huh? Fancy party you were attending." Gill continued searching her phone, her tone laced with flirtatiousness.

"I was there with my partner. She's a member," Luke felt compelled to say. He had flirted his way out of many interviews before in the name of making progress and getting information but didn't feel like that would be the right approach with this particular subject. For one, the chef was too willing to charm him, and he didn't buy it.

"You are too hot to be off-limits. Tell me you're not exclusive," Gill continued, and even if Luke felt flattered, he couldn't fully believe the overtness of the chef. Could she be concealing something from him, opting for such a distracting technique?

"Very much exclusive," he said, the smile not quite reaching his eyes as he tried deciphering the woman in front of him and deciding whether she was hiding something and why.

"Try the third one while I find this," Gill said, and Luke took a shot at the third glass of soup, the tastier by far and also bearing notes of something he couldn't quite place. "It looks like I took care of table 13 personally and Travis Wise's food in particular. As he reported a nut allergy."

"You're sure?" Luke said.

"It says so in the schedule for the day. And I always oversee personally all the food allergies," Gill said. Luke felt grateful she was finally answering questions and not trying to divert.

"And you don't recall lacing Travis Wise's food with a few drops of cyanide?" Luke asked, his most seductive smile now at play.

"I don't." Gill returned his gesture. Did he believe her?

"Who else could have touched the food that night?" Luke asked.

"From my team, you mean? Because anyone could have tampered with that food once it was placed on table 13. It looks like Travis didn't start eating until two hours into the ceremony, and we served it before it started. So there was plenty of opportunity for others to touch the food."

"I'm aware," said Luke, and he was. "But how do you know Travis didn't start eating until late in the ceremony?"

"Every adept whodunit fan out there knows cyanide poisoning symptoms occur within minutes of ingestion," Gill said, smiling, and Luke preferred not to pry. "But you can talk to Vinny."

"Vinny?" Luke finished the last of the soup from the third glass. "And this is definitely the winner for me."

"I noticed you didn't finish the other two," Gill said. "Vinny Green. He was the waiter in charge of serving table 13. I'll give you his contact details as he isn't working today."

"That would be great, thanks so much," Luke said. "But why am I feeling suddenly light-headed?"

14

"Where are you?" Sol said when he finally picked up the phone.

"Literally no idea."

"You don't know where you are?" Had she managed to lose her perfectly considerate and gorgeous Italian British lover in the immensity of Los Angeles? If so, Sol would never forgive herself. There was no chance she'd ever be able to replace him or forget him. And did that make her feel uneasy? Certainly it made her feel less independent and self-sufficient than a few months before.

"Not really." Did he sound cagey? "But thank gods for technology. I'm requesting an Uber now to go back to Lola's place. We're meeting back there, right?"

"I thought we could do something different," said Sol.

"I think Lola said her husband was going to cook something special for us tonight."

"You need to stop sounding so reasonable." Sol's voice thinned with irritation. "I was hoping we'd spend some time together. Alone."

"You found us a place?" She relished the enthusiasm and insinuation in his tone.

"I didn't," Sol admitted, defeated. "Unless you don't mind a shared room in an Airbnb by the airport."

"I think I'd rather stay at Lola's for another night if that's the only option and they don't mind us cramping their living room. But we can't just disappear. The husband is cooking. Should I get a bottle of wine or two?"

Sol let out an exasperated sigh. "The husband is always cooking! I can't believe we're arguing because you're hungry and think a dinner is a better option than spending some time with me."

"What are you talking about? I just want to be courteous to your very nice friends, who've taken us over and given us a roof," he said, and he really needed to stop sounding so sensible, or she was going to flip. "I'm not even hungry. I just interviewed the chef who cooked at the awards ceremony, and she fed me a bunch of stuff."

"You took food from someone who may have poisoned someone else?"

"I mean, when you put it like that. I wasn't the only one eating. She was also trying all the stuff."

"Such a relief!" Sol didn't even try to mask her discontent.

"I guess this is *not* the moment to offer you full disclosure and tell you the chef may have been chatting me up for most of the interview."

"Seriously?" Sol said, the bite in her remark perfectly audible.

"Would it have been better if I didn't tell you about it? She didn't mention that some of the food had hard liquor in it, and I'm a bit pissed right now. Hence the oversharing."

"Most definitely better if you hadn't said a single thing," she said, feigning absolute indifference when all she wanted to ask was whether he'd flirted back. Was he only telling her that because he wanted to make her jealous? He'd most definitely achieved it. "Listen, I need to let you go. Claudia is calling me back. And I've been trying to talk to her all day," Sol said instead of coming clean.

"Right, see you at your friends'?"

"Sure." She hung up, fuming.

"Claudia, thanks for calling me back," Sol said when she picked up her former editor's call. She tried breathing deeply. She needed to relax. The conversation with Luke had spiked her heart rate and angered her to inexplicable levels.

"I only have a couple of minutes before I get into a dreadful planning meeting," the editor said. "I need awards season to be over!"

"Don't we all?" Sol commiserated. "Listen, I checked your job offer. It sounds interesting."

"So you said the other day," Claudia said, her tone just shy of icy. "Yet somehow I had the impression you couldn't be less *interested*."

"It's not that," Sol said, and for once she'd have liked to not always be so transparent and direct. "You caught me by surprise."

"You didn't want the beau to know you may be leaving him and moving to Los Angeles for the right opportunity, eh?"

Sol remembered how much she disliked her former boss. Claudia always assumed she knew what everyone was thinking and feeling, and she was an absolute busybody.

"It's not that," Sol cut in. That wasn't the reason she hadn't cared about the position, and she wasn't talking about Luke right then. Not when she was furious with him, and not with Claudia. "It's just that I've heard some rumors."

"You're a veteran journalist and a smart, old woman and you're listening to *rumors*," Claudia said. Why was everyone so adamant in reminding her that she was no longer young?

"Precisely because I'm a veteran journalist and a smart, *old* woman, I listen to rumors. It doesn't mean I always believe them, but I consider what small fraction of truth they may hold. Is it true that you fired Travis?" Sol finally let out the true reason for that call.

"Ah, those rumors," Claudia said, displeased, but she didn't offer anything else. Sol was tempted to do the nice thing and fill in the silence, but she knew well not to do it. She wasn't giving Claudia an easy way out of an uncomfortable conversation. "We had to let him go."

"You told me he was retiring."

"He's sixty-nine!" Claudia said, and Sol couldn't help thinking the editor was being a cretin and a bit of an ageist, especially considering she couldn't be far behind Travis agewise. "He should have retired years ago. We offered him a very nice buyout during the second-to-last round of layoffs, and he wouldn't take it."

"But he's such a great writer and has a devoted following," reasoned Sol.

"Which is why we didn't lay him off when we could," said Claudia. "But he makes a lot of money, which we cannot keep paying."

"I see, you're looking for a *cheaper* replacement."

"Cheaper, perhaps, but the position still comes with an eighty-thousand-dollar salary, full benefits, the comfort of a staff position where you don't have to hustle for assignments every single day, and the prestige of *Performance Weekly*."

Both Sol and Claudia knew well that even if the magazine wanted the experience and responsibility Travis had for far less money, something like what Claudia was offering was rare and coveted for a mid-level critic like Sol, who still had decades of career ahead of her and not many prospects at present.

"As I said, it's a very interesting position *and an attractive one*," Sol admitted. "If you're still serious about the offer . . ."

"I am," Claudia said. "Mainly because the last thing I want is to interview several candidates only to find out I can't stand the ones whose writing I actually like and vice versa. I know you're a good writer and relatively easy to be around."

"When should I give you an answer?" Did she feel a pang of guilt because she was having that conversation?

"A couple of days ago, when I offered you the job the first time," Claudia deadpanned. "But the end of the week will do. I'll start interviewing candidates on Monday if I haven't heard from you."

"Sounds good," Sol said, and she let the editor go back to her busy afternoon.

She'd prefaced the conversation with Claudia using the job offer as an excuse to talk to her and ask her about Travis. She wanted to know why she'd lied and whether Claudia could have been involved in any way with Travis's poisoning.

But Sol had been sidetracked when she'd truly realized what was being offered. Should she not even contemplate the position? She was well aware how rare a television critic opening was. Was she being smart by avoiding working with Claudia a second time? It had been an absolute nightmare the first time around. She hated the editor's bossy, snarky style. And was she simply closing herself to that opportunity because the idea of running into her ex from time to time if she moved back to Los Angeles terrified her? Was the Californian city off-limits for good because David still lived there? Had she been that scarred by her marriage to him?

And, of course, there was also the difficult-to-ignore man in her life right now. But was Luke an important enough reason to stay in London?

15

The following morning, Luke was standing on the open-air walkway of a run-down, two-story apartment building in yet another part of town deemed unhip by Alex. Luke was aware he should probably stop taking the opinion of a thirteen-year-old so seriously but couldn't avoid doing it. He liked Alex. The introverted, scrawny kid reminded Luke of a version of himself at his age. Minus the skateboard and the tie-dye Crocs. And Alex seemed to genuinely like Luke, as well. It was nice to be surrounded by nice people, especially when he was so far from home and his romantic partner still hadn't forgiven him for being drunk and saying the wrong thing the day before.

It was as if Sol was freezing him out. And the lack of personal space wasn't helping. Luke's plans for the day were interviewing Vinny Green, trying to finally talk to Travis Wise, and finding a hotel room for him and Sol. They needed to move out of Lola's living room and start communicating again.

He put thoughts of Sol aside for a moment as he

knocked on Vinny Green's apartment door. The sooner the case was over, the sooner they could go back to London and resume their perfectly heated relationship. After a second knock, a blond woman in her late twenties holding a few stapled pages opened the door.

"Can I help you?" she said, not taking her eyes off the pages in front of her, which looked like a script. Was it possible that everyone was an actor in this town? At least every waiter and waitress he'd encountered so far looked like an aspiring one.

"I'm looking for Vinny Green," Luke said.

"Who?"

"Vinny Green, he's a waiter at Star System Catering." Luke had a bad feeling.

"You got the wrong address. There's no Vinny Green here. And no clue who that is. I also temp for Star System Catering sometimes, though," the wannabe actress explained.

"I see," Luke said. "And by any chance were you working a couple of nights ago?"

"For the critics awards ceremony? I had to skip that one. I'd booked a role in a toothpaste commercial," she said, flaunting the most perfect of white smiles. It was so fluorescently white, it almost blinded Luke.

The story checked. Luke thanked the actress for her time and made his descent to the street, but before requesting another car and wondering if he should think about renting a vehicle full-time, he called the number Chef Gill García had given him for Vinny Green and got exactly what he was expecting: a no-longer working number.

"The plot thickens," he said out loud while he dialed Divya's number and waited for his Uber to arrive.

I will not fall asleep, Sol kept reciting to herself, but it was difficult to follow her own precise instruction. She was at an almost-deserted showing of *Haughty Horizons* at The Grove. A full hour of the movie had already gone by, and she still couldn't tell what the movie was about or why had it ever been greenlit.

She was utterly bored. And tired, so tired. She loved Lola, but as inflatable mattresses went, her friend's was the most uncomfortable one Sol had ever slept on. And that was counting the whole of her twenties and even a few of her thirties.

But Sol feared it hadn't been the discomfort of the mattress that had caused her to sleep extremely poorly the night before, but Luke's humming presence lying next to her. Silent. He was so close. Yet the farthest apart from her she'd ever felt him. Even when they'd just met and had just started knowing each other, he hadn't felt so out of reach. He hadn't stopped flirting with her back then. But now, for all she knew, he was flirting with someone else. Why else would he have told her about the chef hitting on him?

She needed to stop obsessing about him and pay attention to the damn movie. She was supposed to write about the damn movie! But she knew there was no way she'd get even minimally interested in the story of *Haughty Horizons*, and she resisted the idea of thinking about Luke, plus those seats were definitely more comfortable than Lola's mattress. So she finally allowed herself to give in and sleep. She just hoped she wouldn't snore much.

She was woken up by a movie usher, the ending credits of the movie rolling on the screen and not another moviegoer in sight.

"I'm so sorry!" Sol told the usher when she realized she had, indeed, fallen deeply asleep.

"Oh don't worry, ma'am, it's this movie. I feel the director has stumbled on the cure for insomnia," the usher said, and Sol couldn't avoid laughing out loud, even if she had yet again been called *ma'am.*

Her cell phone buzzed the minute she disabled airplane mode, and she left the screening room, thanking the usher one last time. It was Luke calling, and she felt the only way the two of them were communicating lately was telephonically. She hated that.

"Luca," she answered, using the affectionate version of his name she had for him, momentarily forgetting she was supposed to be mad.

"Ciao, cara, sorry to bother you," he said, and she felt they had perhaps reached some kind of tacit truce.

"You never bother me," she said. It was so much easier to not be mad at him. She didn't want to be mad at him. Why was she mad at him? Some miscommunication nonsense.

"How was the movie?" he asked, because of course he'd remembered she'd mentioned she was going to watch *Haughty Horizons* when they'd all had breakfast together that morning like a big happy modern family. Lola's husband had made whole wheat pancakes with blueberries and Shinko pears, and everyone had shared their plans for the day. Not only that, Luke had listened. Not that the same could be said of her. She had no clue what everyone else was doing at the moment.

"The movie was dreadfully boring," she admitted.

"I'm sorry," he said, and he did sound as if the idea of her being dreadfully bored was appalling. As if that wasn't already enticing enough, her mind decided that was the perfect moment to remind her how he looked completely naked, and Sol concluded she was a fool and had been acting like one for the last few days. There was absolutely no reason why she should be mad at such a man.

"Don't be sorry, I had the most restorative of naps," she said.

"That mattress is also killing you, huh?"

"Most uncomfortable thing I've ever slept on."

"I know," he said, a conspiratorial tone in his voice. The half-deflated mattress suddenly sounded much more appealing. It was the most tortuous sleeping device, but she'd shared it with him. "Listen, I have a bit of an odd request."

"Uh-huh," she said while she headed to the nearby Barnes & Noble. She sure could treat herself to some book buying now that she no longer was fuming against her partner.

"I know the answer is probably no, since everyone you seem to know is somehow associated with the showbusiness industry," Luke continued.

"Except for you," she said, a smile reaching her lips.

"Except for me," he said, and she could hear him smiling as well. "But would you happen to have any contacts in law enforcement here? If I were in London, I'd have reached out to my and Divya's contacts at the Met already. We both feel a conversation with the LAPD would probably help right now but don't know where to start."

"The investigation is stalled?" she asked.

"Very much so." He sighed. "I have a missing witness, a chef who won't pick up the phone, and Travis still doesn't feel strong enough to talk to me or anyone else, apparently. I was just texting him, and he told me he needs a few more days. But I really want to wrap this up and head back home as soon as possible."

"I see."

"Sorry again. I know I said I wouldn't get you involved."

"I may know someone," she said, even if she regretted it the moment she uttered those words. But she wanted to help Luke. "Can't promise anything, but he's an assistant district attorney for the city."

"That's exactly what I need! I'm trying to get the official police file and whatever they may have on Travis's and Simon's cases."

Sol hesitated for a beat, then said, "Sending you his info right now. Tell him I gave you the contact."

"Grazie, cara. I'll call you later. See you at Lola's?" Luke asked.

"Sure," Sol said before hanging up. Should she have told Luke how she knew someone in law enforcement? He was so caught up in the case and fixated on going home that he hadn't even thought about asking.

16

"How was the movie, Sol?" Lola's husband asked thoughtfully while serving steamed miso salmon, brown rice, and broccoli sautéed to perfection.

"Hideous," she pronounced. "How was your day, Geoff?" she asked in turn, realizing she couldn't remember what Lola's husband did, even if she'd known him for almost a decade. She was the worst friend ever. In her defense, she'd asked him in the past at least three or four times and never managed to understand what he did.

"Not much better than yours. This crazy weather is making things difficult to forecast. There have been mudslides in Big Sur, and we've had to swap the older models because all the priors keep changing."

"Right," Sol said, and she could see Lola's amused face across the table from her. She was sure her friend knew she hadn't understood a single word. But she wasn't going to translate Geoff's lingo for her.

"How's the investigation going, Luke?" Lola asked.

"I may have finally made some progress," Luke said,

proceeding to devour Geoff's culinary achievement. "This is delicious, by the way."

"Thanks, it was nothing. I'll send you *The New York Times* recipes if you like," Lola's husband said, slightly abashed, and Sol smirked. There was nothing Geoff liked more than people praising his food. She should remember to do it more often. "But please, tell us more about the case. We're very curious."

"Well, without giving too much information away—because this is, of course, sensitive and mostly confidential," Luke started.

"Of course," Sol, Geoff, Lola, and even Alex said in unison, leaning forward on the table, unable to conceal their overall curiosity.

"And I need to thank Sol for the progress, because she has a friend who put me in contact with the officer at the LAPD in charge of both Simon Smith's disappearance and Travis Wise's poisoning."

"They also think they're linked?" asked Sol, wanting to deflect attention from herself and her so-called friend.

"I think so. Will know for sure tomorrow. I'm meeting with an officer Tom Owens."

"Sol, I didn't know you had friends with contacts at the LAPD," Lola said distractedly while she focused on her food and didn't catch Sol's pleading gaze in her direction. "Could you also introduce me? I'm working on this new police drama, and it would be great for research if I could— What?" Lola *finally* caught Sol glaring at her.

"Nothing." Sol tried acting normal.

"You need to introduce David to Lola, Sol," Luke said.

"David?" Lola almost shrieked. Why her friend was still talking was something that Sol couldn't understand. Weren't Sol's flaring eyes a clear enough message to shut the fuck up? Geoff was acting like the perfect husband-of-a-friend that he was and had remained silent the moment he saw Sol's distress and realized the identity of her supposed friend. Was it too much to ask the same from Lola?

"Mom, seriously? It's, like, Sol's ex!" Alex decided to participate then after having remained silent for most of the dinner.

Luke froze, the realization dawning on his face. "Ex, as in your ex-husband?"

"Um, it's, like, her *second* ex-husband!" Alex specified.

Sol had always liked Alex. He was smarter and more polite than most of the kids his age, and he was Lola's son, but right then Sol decided she hated *all* adolescents, Alex included.

"We're going to finish eating in the kitchen and give you some space to talk about this," Geoff said, standing, grabbing his plate, and indicating Alex to do the same.

"Please don't leave," Sol said. "We've already invaded your living room, and now you want to also decamp the dining room."

Lola crossed her arms and lounged back in her chair, making herself comfortable. "I'm not going anywhere. I want to hear this."

"Seriously?" Geoff pleaded with his wife.

"I was the one here when this one finally decided to leave David and needed a place to stay and a shoulder to cry on," Lola said.

"And I'm immensely thankful and will never forget," Sol told her friend.

"I don't need you to stay thankful. That's what friends are for!" Lola didn't raise her voice, but her words left no room for argument. "What I need is you to remember your resolution *never* to have anything to do with David again. And now you go and put your partner in touch with him!"

"Luke needed a contact for his case! So that he can return to London!"

"But you didn't tell him who David was," Lola argued.

"What do you mean so that *I* can return to London?" Luke said. "Aren't you also coming?"

"Geoff, this was a lovely dinner, as usual. If you'll excuse me, I need to go for a walk—*alone*," Sol said, standing from the table, then leaving her friends' place.

She wasn't sure exactly where she was supposed to be heading. It was dark and cold, and she hadn't exactly grabbed a jacket, her wallet, or even her phone. But she just started walking alongside the jacaranda tree–lined residential street. And pretended she wasn't about to break.

...

"Please get inside the car, you are shivering." She heard Luke's worried voice from a nearby car, which had pulled over at the curve and stopped next to her.

She didn't know how long she'd been wandering around the neighborhood. But she'd had time to cry her agitation out, analyze everything that had happened, and even make a few resolutions. She was feeling energized and better. But it had started drizzling halfway through her restorative walk, and she was soaked and freezing.

She turned in the direction of the voice and went to the car, getting into the front passenger side. The moment she was inside, she saw Luke's face. She'd never seen him wearing such preoccupied features. They didn't suit him. She didn't like being the one who'd contributed to his discomfort—or his diminished prettiness.

He took out his midnight-blue bomber jacket and wrapped it around Sol's shoulders. His hands made circular movements around Sol's arms and back to warm her up.

"Lola let me borrow her car," Luke explained, as she was still not talking. "The moment you left, we started arguing about the best course of action."

"Arguing?"

"Geoff thought you deserved privacy and being left alone and in peace like you had requested. Lola and I wouldn't hear of it," Luke explained while he kept heating her skin through his jacket. "By the time Lola and I decided it was me who had to go look for you, you were nowhere in sight. I've been driving around Los Feliz for twenty minutes."

"I'm so sorry."

"Don't be," Luke said. "I'm the one who's sorry. I know these past few days haven't been great."

"We should have stayed in London," Sol said.

Luke leaned forward and shot her a half smile. "Believe it or not, I think coming here was a good idea."

"Has all this driving on the *wrong* side of the road permanently traumatized you or something?" Sol snapped. "What are you talking about? I thought you hated it!"

"Don't get me wrong, I do thoroughly *hate* it. And there's plenty of reason for it. We've had two cases thrown at us while we were supposed to enjoy some much-deserved downtime. Your luggage was lost. and you've been forced to wear my clothes."

"I like your clothes, they smell of you," Sol said, getting closer to him.

"You have one editor asking you to write about a movie you don't care to even watch." Luke hesitated, then pressed on, his voice clipped. "And one former editor offering you a job you feel you should take."

"But that I know very much that I *don't* want to take," she said.

That was one of the conclusions she'd reached during her walk. There had been several reasons that had driven her away from Los Angeles, and not all of them were her ex-husband David. She was *not* returning to the city. Not now. Not to work with Claudia. And not alone.

Luke's tone shifted, softer now. "You were thrown out of the four-star hotel we were staying at, haven't had a good night's sleep since landing in California, and have had no sex for days."

"And I'm incredibly pissy and cranky because of that," Sol admitted. "I also miss you in an almost painful way but haven't been able to find the way to tell you."

"You miss me? I thought you were cross with me."

"You see, I haven't been able to communicate. But that's not even everything," she said. She was finally ready to voice what had been keeping her wrapped up for days. She raised her gaze, holding Luke's chestnut eyes inside the dark vehicle.

"The next time we go to Barcelona, I'll introduce you to Miquel."

Luke blew out a sharp breath through his nose, jaw tight. "Your first ex-husband."

"Yes. He's a bit obnoxious but a very nice person, and we've been friends for decades. I think you'll like him."

"I reserve the right not to do it. I'm not a jealous person but only to a point," Luke said, and Sol knew he was trying to keep the conversation cordial. He wasn't a fan of the exes.

"But I never had the intention of introducing you to David," Sol continued. "Divorce is never easy, but I had already done it once with Miquel, and I naïvely thought that it could be the same with David. Hard, yes, but we could get through it in a civilized manner and remain friends. But the breakup with David wasn't exactly amicable. The divorce was an absolute legal nightmare. He did everything possible to make the situation unbearable. His family got mixed in the negotiations. Whatever good memories I may still have had from the first years we spent together were shattered after months of accusations and bickering. And when the conversation about what money belonged to whom started, things got very ugly."

"You never told me about it."

"I don't like talking about it. It's a period of my life that I don't like recalling. I don't know what I'd have done if it wasn't for Lola and her family. But they took me in, cheered me up, and fed me."

His mouth curved in a quiet smile. "I like them."

"I like them too. Even if Lola is nosy as hell, Alex has the ability of only speaking at the most inconvenient moments, and, to this day, I don't know what the hell Geoff does for a living."

Luke snickered. "He's an actuarial scientist for an insurance company."

"A what?" Sol asked, perplexed. "Never mind, not important. What I was trying to tell you is that coming to Los Angeles has brought up memories about my past relationship and hasn't helped with my present one."

"Why did you introduce me to David? You said you never had intention of doing it," Luke asked.

"You needed the contact for the case."

"If I'd known everything, I'd never have contacted him. You may introduce me to Miquel, and *perhaps* I'll find him agreeable."

"You'll love him, believe me. He has that effect on people."

"You're not really helping. I don't know how I feel about a guy who was married to you and makes everyone around him fall in love with him," he said, his jaw clenched again.

"Don't worry about Miquel, I have lifelong immunity to all his charms," Sol explained. "You, on the other hand . . ."

"Let's stop talking about your ex's charms, or I'll stop not being jealous," Luke said. "What I was trying to say is that, after what you've told me, there's no way I'm ever going to tolerate David."

"You shouldn't," Sol confirmed.

"I know this is a bloody pain, cara," Luke said, caressing Sol's cheek. "There are still two extremely inconvenient cases to solve, no sign of your suitcase anywhere, and the prospect of another night spent on a very uncomfortable mattress."

Sol shuddered at the mention of the torturous sleeping device.

"There's something else."

Luke's eyebrows shot up, and he seemed to be bracing himself for another bit of bad news.

"Julie sent me an email. I just saw it before dinner. She wants me to stay in Los Angeles for a few more days. There's another thing she wants me to take care of," Sol explained. She realized Julie's request hadn't helped her mood. And the worst part was, Sol hadn't been exactly truthful in her description to Luke of what Julie had asked her.

"So we still have no clear return date to London." It was Luke who was shuddering now. "But we both want to go back to London, right?"

"Believe me, I absolutely want to get back to London. I have an appointment with my colorist that I absolutely can*not* miss," she said, and he let out a soft laugh. The kind reserved just for her.

"I know we're not exactly thriving right now. But are we at least *fine*?"

"Definitely fine," Sol admitted as he knit his fingers through her wet hair strands. "And I suspect that we could even be upgraded to a perfect match with a flourishing relationship once again if we finally had sex."

"This may sound a bit far-fetched or desperate . . ." Luke said.

"But . . ." Sol continued.

"I've seen people eating in their cars, napping in their cars, even shaving or putting on makeup in their cars in this city. I can only assume a car is a perfectly acceptable place to indulge in a steamy exchange with another human, right?" Luke said, his hungry eyes fixed on Sol. "If we make sure to return it in pristine condition to Lola afterward."

"Right," Sol answered, not even thinking about what she was doing. After the lousy few days she'd had, after having to revisit a failed relationship she'd vowed to keep buried, after the exhaustion that lonely walk in tears had caused, the only thing she wanted was to feel alive. And she always felt young, beautiful, sexy, happy—and very much alive—when he held her close. When his body enveloped her. Plus, they were currently parked in a dark enough spot of a non-transited dormant street, no?

She let Luke's jacket slip off her shoulders and drew near him in a swift motion. She crouched so as not to hurt her head with the car's roof and found herself seated on top of him, straddling him. She took his T-shirt with one hand and pulled him toward her, meeting his mouth with hers in an urgent, nearly desperate kiss.

"I need you," she told him in between breaths as she inched closer to his body.

Her right hand found his skin, getting underneath his T-shirt and exploring the taut warmth of his chest. She ached to trace every inch of his torso with reverence. But that hand was needed elsewhere.

She took her mouth away from his for a ragged moment, smiling wickedly when she recognized the same need she was feeling in those beautiful, warm eyes. She bit his lower lip and groaned in pleasure as he kissed her not-so-delicately behind her earlobe and licked the column of her neck.

She ground herself on his lap, feeling his hardness against her clit through the fabric of his jeans and her leggings, resenting the barrier in between their bodies. She stood slightly on her knees, her right hand now finding his erection, stroking it. She could feel each one of Luke's husky pants against her hand. She found the waistline of his jeans and started undoing his button first, then the zipper. He swiped her closer to him in a frantic movement, grabbing her ass and bringing their bodies flush, her throbbing breasts grazing his chest.

She smiled as she felt his cock in her hand. Naked. Rock-hard. Demanding.

He returned the smile, high on the heat of the situation, fighting with the extremely high waist of her leggings for a touch of her body.

The real world came crashing down then. Again. As the neighbor in front of whose house they'd parked came out on their front porch, a lantern and its bright-white light pointed in their direction.

"Who's there?" they heard the neighbor called, a dog barking in the background.

In a quick move, Sol untangled her hands from Luke's body, left his lap, and sat on the passenger seat.

"Go, go, go," she ordered him. "Drive!"

"Seat belt!" he said as he fastened his own and got the car to move.

"This is a decent residential street!" the neighbor yelled as they were leaving.

They drove for a couple of blocks in silence.

"You have literally no idea how much I hate this city right now," Luke finally said, a bite of frustration in his tone.

"Oh believe me, it's starting to rub on me too," she admitted. "And I'm not the one with the zipper down."

They both exploded in a tension-releasing laugh.

17

Sol had plenty of reasons to be anxious and irritated. Yet she found herself calm and almost cheerful. She allowed herself to go over everything that had taken place in the last hour one more time as her Uber made its slow approach to her destination that morning. She had more than a hunch that her present satisfaction had a lot to do with what had just happened.

She'd been showering in Lola's guest bathroom, which retained all the charm and discomfort of an original 1920s design. It featured bright-green tiled walls and a separate bathtub from the narrow shower alcove. Sol was shampooing her hair in the shower cubicle when she found herself not alone in the minimal space. Luke was also there. Naked.

He'd taken his index finger to his voluptuous lips, as if asking her to remain silent.

"Everyone just left," he'd told her in an almost whisper. "But let's keep it quiet. I don't want more neighbors complaining."

"And why exactly should the neighbors complain?" she'd asked him insolently, a smile tugging at her lips.

"I thought you could do with a bit of relaxation." He helped her rinse the shampoo from her hair in what had to be the sexiest gesture she'd ever seen. And she'd watched Robert Redford taking care of Meryl Streep's hair in *Out of Africa*.

Of course, in that movie there had been no steamy shower scene, which was exactly what Sol had anticipated would happen next. And, for the first time in days, she hadn't been disappointed. Not completely, at least.

"When I thought about this little escapade, I massively overestimated the size of this space," Luke told her in a growly tone while he kissed her neck. He made a slow descent along her collarbone, finding one of her breasts and biting mercilessly at her nipple. "I'm going to have to improvise."

He used his lips on her mouth, her earlobe, her nape. But it was his teeth on her nipples. Had there been any room for it, she knew he'd have knelt between her legs and used his tongue. But he had to do with his fingers at her clit. He proved just as competent, relentlessly tugging, throbbing, stroking her core, sliding first one, then two fingers inside her.

"Love your improvisation skills," she told him in a breathy moan.

"You sure?" His voice was pure insinuation. Rough and sexy in a way he sounded only when they were together and alone.

He had somehow gotten even closer to her, pressing her against the wall, his body against hers, his lips on hers, his fingers inside her. The warm water streamed over their skin, making everything feel hotter.

What was it about shower sex that turned on something in her body, blocking all her insecurities and just making her want to *feel*. She arched her back against the tiled shower wall and moaned—audibly.

It was his satisfied snicker against her breast, his mouth still there, his hand at her center, that pushed her to the edge. She panted with pleasure as the release shook her whole body. He silenced her repeated moans with his lips, kissing her as the two of them shared in the fleeting moment.

"My turn to play," she'd told him, still breathless, when she came out of the dizzying orgasm.

A sly smile curled at his lips. "Would love to let you *play*," he drawled, his tone thick with implication. "But you're going to be very late for Julie's thing."

"Fuck!" she'd groaned in frustration, getting a towel and leaving the shower and Luke's body. She hadn't even allowed herself a last look in his direction. She knew she'd probably decided to stay with him and, indeed, play. And was she regretting not having done it now?

That image of Luke's naked loneliness inside a green-tiled shower was the reason Sol felt only halfway satisfied as her car dropped her off at the Hancock Park address. Not only had she left her partner naked and dissatisfied inside the shower, she'd lied about the nature of her appointment.

...

Twenty minutes later, Sol was comfortably seated on the ginormous modular sofa she could have sworn she recognized from a Roche Bobois catalog, where it retailed for more than twenty thousand dollars. She was also brightly aware the living room where the not-cheap-sofa resided pertained to a six-bedroom, six-bathroom Colonial Revival mansion-like home that Redfin had told her was estimated to cost only shy of seven million dollars. Did editors really make that much more money than writers? Because, if so, Sol had clearly opted for the wrong profession.

Unless, of course, the house hadn't been procured with Jason Zit's money but his wife's, Emily's. What was it again that she did for a living? Something incredibly lucrative that still permitted her to be home on a Wednesday at 10:30 a.m., offering perfectly brewed tea and pastries to Sol. Then again, Jason was also there. He'd grumbled about his working-from-home status and having to leave a meeting early even if Sol had been exactly on time, thanks to Luke's foresight—and his resignation.

"I love your home," Sol told Emily and Jason in what was probably the most genuine exchange she'd had with them. "It's so tastefully decorated."

"Oh, thank you. Nobody ever seems to notice," quipped Emily, visibly pleased by Sol's compliment.

"Really?" Sol said incredulously. She allowed her gaze to wander over the perfectly fluffed pillows, artfully designed bouquets of fresh flowers displayed in elegant vases, and the discerningly curated art hanging from the walls. "Is that an actual Banksy?" Sol couldn't help asking about a print depicting model Kate Moss, imitating the style and colors of Andy Warhol's infamous Marilyn Monroe portraits.

"It probably is. Emily likes expensive stuff," Jason Zit said exasperatedly. "So, to what do we owe the pleasure of your visit? I was a bit surprised when you contacted me yesterday."

"Julie asked me to talk to you," Sol explained.

"Julie?" Jason asked.

"Julie McQueen, she's an executive editor at *Red Carpet* and one of Simon Smith's longtime friends," Sol said.

"Ah, the obnoxious Brit who won't leave me alone because she thinks I have something to do with Simon ducking out," Jason seemed to recall.

"She's very worried about Simon."

"Is he still ghosting her?" Jason said, and Sol thought he sounded unnecessarily cruel.

"*Honey*, please. The man has gone missing." Emily seemed to echo Sol's thoughts.

"Has he really?" Jason sounded genuinely surprised.

"The police can't seem to locate him," Sol offered.

"Have they checked the bars?" Jason continued, chuckling at his own attempt at humor and apparently finding himself hilarious. "I'm sure he's just drinking his sorrows away with cheap chardonnay somewhere between the office and his home."

"Was that something that he did often?" Sol asked, resisting the urge to get her notebook and take notes. She needed this to look like a friendly chat, not an interrogation.

"Let's just say that he liked to drink," Jason said.

"Oh please!" Emily protested. "Many journalists like to drink. He was hardly an exception, *honey*."

"So you also knew him?" Sol asked Emily.

"I know all of Jason's colleagues. That's how I met you as well, remember?"

Sol smiled demurely, because she still couldn't remember Emily. And she felt a bit bad about it. Emily was a very nice woman, and Sol was well aware that she herself could hardly be described as such.

"And did he look distraught, more reserved, different these past few weeks?" Sol continued.

Jason leaned back on the sofa, pausing for effect. "He looked his usual curmudgeonly self."

"Not really. Don't you remember?" Emily intervened again, and Sol was starting to feel both aggravated by her but happy that she was there to jog Jason's obtuse memory and keep him on a short leash. "He was even more grouchy than usual. I think it's because he was having a hard time finding a publisher for his book." She said those last words in a lower, compassionate tone.

"Could that be reason enough for him to do something silly?" said Sol hesitantly. She wasn't equipped to deal with that kind of questioning. She should have told Luke what Julie had asked her to do, but he'd been so adamant about her not getting involved in the case . . .

"Something silly? Do you even hear how you sound?" Jason barked. "It's as if you were playing detective! No, he wasn't so distressed that he couldn't sell his book that he would have killed himself. If that's what you were insinuating!"

"He'd poured body and soul into that book," Emily said.

"To the detriment of his journalist work!" Jason threw up his hands, scowling.

"Do you mean that his reviews were getting worse?" Sol said.

"His reviews had always been bad!" Jason's voice was rising. "But they were simply atrocious lately. Look at what he did with *Haughty Horizons*, which is a perfectly masterful film by a visionary *auteur*. He eviscerated it!"

Sol tried maintaining a calm tone, even if she realized Jason was getting agitated. "So you didn't share his views on the movie?"

"Of course I didn't! I've been complaining to our editor

in chief for years about Simon. But does anybody listen to me?"

Did Emily roll her eyes at her husband's last remark?

"The awards ceremony the other night was absolute agony," Jason whined, no longer shouting. "To be seated at the same table with Victor Lago. I wanted to tell him I didn't share Simon's views on his masterpiece of a film. He pretended he didn't care, but he was flabbergasted. But then that unfortunate incident with Travis happened, and I could never explain myself to Victor."

Sol would have sworn that Jason was annoyed at Travis for getting himself poisoned and thus robbing Jason of his chance of fanboying with the filmmaker.

"That must have been hard, editing someone whose views in movies were so different from yours, I mean," Sol said tentatively. She kept a close eye on both spouses. "And then having to interact in real life with the people who made those movies."

"That's literally my job as an editor."

"So you didn't resent Simon?" Sol prodded.

"What are you trying to say? Do you think I had anything to do with Simon's disappearing act because I don't like how he writes? Are you demented?" The editor was shouting again.

"There's no need of calling Sol names, *honey,*" Emily said, and once again Sol noticed the woman was using the term of endearment when she was clearly exasperated with her husband. She did seem to be able to calm him, though. "Julie asked her to come talk to you because she's worried about Simon, and Sol did just that," Emily continued in the type of high-pitched and exaggerated tone one would use with a bratty child. "I'm sorry we weren't able to be of more help," she told Sol with her grown-up voice, cutting the conversation short.

"No problem," Sol said. "And thanks so much for the tea."

"Oh, I love having guests," Emily said. "Let me see you to the door."

The two women left Jason brooding at the couch and walked toward the house's grand entrance.

"I didn't want to say anything in front of Jason," Emily told Sol in a whisper by the front door of her home. "But Simon sent me his manuscript."

"He did?" Sol said, not sure what Emily was implying.

"I never told Jason, because I don't think Simon shared it with him as well. They were never very *friendly*," Emily continued. "But I suppose I could share the book with you, see if there's something there that could help you find him."

"Would you? That would be great!"

"Sure, it's in my office somewhere. Hold on a second," Emily said.

The woman disappeared behind a door, and Sol waited patiently at the entryway, hoping Jason wouldn't make his way there. The last thing she wanted was to see the rude editor again.

While she was waiting, Sol saw a recently delivered box from Cacao Vieille with the name Jason Zit as the recipient. She just hoped the gourmet chocolates would make the sour editor a bit less grouchy. Emily came back a mere two minutes later, holding a thick stack of copy paper in one hand.

"That must be at least five hundred pages long!" Sol's eyes widened.

"Six hundred and eighty-seven, to be more precise."

"Have you, by any chance, read it?" Sol asked.

"I did start but never found the time to finish it. I told Simon I was looking forward to the Meshflixx miniseries adaptation of it," Emily said cheerfully.

"But it's not fiction, right? I heard he wrote a first-person account of his experience in Hollywood."

"I only read a few pages, but I think you'll recognize a few people in it," Emily told her, a note of insinuation in her tone.

Sol thanked Emily one last time and exited the Hancock Park home, ready to roam the neighborhood. If she didn't recall it incorrectly, there was a perfectly charming Café Gratitude on Larchmont Boulevard, where she could start doing some reading while sipping on some goddess green tea and nibbling on some vegan superfood or other.

She also needed to think about what exactly she was going to tell Luke. She'd realized she'd lied to him so blatantly because she didn't appreciate being told what to do—or not to do. But she didn't like lying to him. And there was no way she could hide that mammoth of a book from him for long. He was not going to be happy.

18

To say that he wasn't happy was an understatement. He was fuming. Not only had he been stood up by officer Tom Owens that morning, he was starting to get breathless. Running after a potential witness at full speed for more than ten minutes would do that to you. Even if, like Luke, you ran often. But there was the stay-in-shape type of running and the this-potential-witness-is-looking-more-suspicious-by-the-minute type of running. And this was most definitely the *second* kind.

After several repeated calls to Chef Gill García that had yielded no fruit that morning, Luke had called the main line at Star System Catering. There, a friendly receptionist had informed him that Chef García wasn't avoiding his calls. She was simply enjoying a much-deserved break, taking a three-day, completely off-the-grid backpacking trip somewhere called Lost Coast. Luke had rolled his eyes when he'd heard that. How could people be and sound so stereotypically Californian? And who would find the prospect of sleeping on the ground and being exposed to the elements even for three days alluring? He was currently doing the whole sleeping-on-the-floor thing with a roof over his head and still hating it.

As for the elusive Vinny Green, Luke had somehow managed not only to get a telephone number for the waiter who'd allegedly served Travis Wise's food at the awards ceremony, but an actual home address from Star System Catering's helpful receptionist. Luke was starting to realize his London accent may have some advantages with the locals. They all seemed charmed by him the moment he opened his mouth.

After getting Vinny Green's information, he'd replied to Alex, who'd wanted to make sure he was all right after the *beef* with Sol the previous night. Luke had assured him that all was good and then had asked the Angeleno teenager about the appropriateness of the new address he had for Vinny Green. Somewhere called Long Beach. After being informed his new destination was, once again, far and extremely inconvenient, if somehow charming because of its proximity to the ocean, Luke had resignedly taken an Uber bound for Long Beach. He wasn't big on California beaches—or California anything else, for that matter.

He'd been barely out of the car for two minutes and had knocked on a door on the first floor of a run-down, two-story apartment building similar to the one he'd visited the day before. After five minutes waiting at the door, he'd been convinced the whole trip there had been in vain when a dirty-blond, long-haired man in his early-to-mid-twenties holding a joint on his lips had opened the door. He wore a neoprene wetsuit unzipped and peeled down to his waist, exposing his bare chest, and he had only flip-flops on his feet. He was almost like a much shorter version of Chris Hemsworth in *Thor* (and in surfer mode), and Luke couldn't help but wonder if *everyone* in that town really looked like a movie star. The man had taken a look at Luke, pushed him aside, and started running. And Luke, of course, had followed.

Leave it to a suspect who was probably high, and wearing flip-flops, to make Luke sweat! Was the detective really tired of jogging through alleys and swerving trash bins in the otherwise calm and quiet beach town? He was. Not only that, the surfer chap was getting farther away from Luke every passing minute. Could he be in better shape than Luke?

"He's probably ten years younger than me," Luke muttered under his breath, still chasing the suspect. He realized he was starting to sound like Sol. He'd never understood her obsession with age when she looked as great as she did. But he was beginning to share in his partner's insecurities. He'd make sure to let her know that he understood her a little bit better the next time they were alone, if that ever occurred. Surfer chap was getting farther ahead and, with him, Luke's chances of finding out who could have poisoned Travis Wise's food—and getting on a plane back to London.

Surfer chap turned around as if to see how far he'd managed to get from Luke. He laughed at Luke's breathlessness, the joint still hanging from his mouth. But he hadn't seen a second surfer chap skating through the alley, his wetsuit unzipped and open at the chest, carrying a giant board on his right side.

Luke watched it happen almost frame by frame. The skater hadn't been able to avoid the collision with the runaway surfer chap, who hadn't noticed him approaching.

They both ended up on the ground, accompanied by a big thud of the surfboard hitting the pavement and the skateboard rolling aimlessly on the street. Luke accelerated in their direction.

"Are you alright?" he asked the wetsuit-wearing men, scanning them both to make sure they were unharmed. "Got you," he told the surfer chap he'd been pursuing, grabbing his right arm to help him stand up—and to make sure he wouldn't flee again.

"Dude, karma really is a bitch!" The short Chris Hemsworth laughed and showed the most perfect of white smiles.

...

Ten minutes after that, Luke and the surfer chap, who'd turned out to be Vinny Green, were sharing a concha de cacao and a pastelito de guava at the sidewalk patio of Gusto Bread. Would Luke have preferred to be savoring an English breakfast tea with those pastries instead of a yerba mate? Obviously. But he was doing his best at pretending to be cosmopolitan and open-minded.

"So Chef García told you I was looking for you?" Luke asked Vinny as he took out his sunglasses from the interior pocket of his jacket, put them on, and let himself enjoy the warmth of the sun on his skin. Wasn't it supposed to be winter here as well? The idea of an alfresco snack in January in London would absolutely be out of the question. But he was *not* enjoying the LA experience at all, nonetheless.

"Yeah, man. She called to warn me that some hunky British dude—looks like an Italian model or something—is convinced I poisoned that critic guy at the party the other night."

"What? I never said such a thing!" objected Luke,

though he couldn't help but feel pleased with how he'd been described.

"Gill said she tried to, like, run interference or whatever."

Luke knew the chef's supposed interest in him had been dubious. Turns out she was playing him. "She gave me a fake address and fake telephone number."

"But she said you'd probably bust me and try to pin it on me," Vinny continued.

"That's why you ran away?"

"Nah, dude, if I come clean, I'm not gonna get in trouble, right?"

"Did you put cyanide in Travis Wise's food?" Luke asked Vinny.

"Cyanide? Whoa, that sounds nasty! I don't mess with chemicals, man. I'm all about the natural stuff. I only bathe in water, coconut oil, and lavender infusions."

"Of course you do," Luke said.

"That thing does wonders for your skin, man. You're totally welcome to join me next time I bathe. I'm all about saving water, so I usually only do it once a week, but hey, I'd totally make an exception for you." Vinny winked at Luke.

"Thanks for the offer," Luke said, blushing. Was his accent so irresistible, really? Why did everyone in this city keep flirting with him? Even if sometimes it was fake flirting. "So you didn't poison Travis Wise, then?"

"Nah, man, not with that cyanide stuff," Vinny said.

Luke's eyebrows drew together. "What do you mean?"

"That's why I bailed when I saw you, man. During the awards, Gill told me there was a nut allergy at table 13, and she gave me the plate for the dude with the allergy. But I got distracted and totally spaced out."

"Distracted?"

"I was carrying two plates—one regular, one no nuts. But as I was heading out of the kitchen, this chick offered me a vape, and you know, it's kinda rude to say no, right?"

"You mean you stopped for a smoke?"

"Yeah, man. Life's short, and it's the little moments that count."

Luke had to admit there was a lot of wisdom in Vinny's words. "So what happened to the plates?"

"I left them—somewhere."

"Unattended?"

"I mean, there were lots of people around—waiters, partygoers, celebs. It's not like the plates were alone, dude," Vinny said, and he laughed at his own attempt at a joke. "But I think I ended up serving that Travis Wise dude the regular food instead of the no-nuts grub, man."

"Whose food did you serve Travis?" Luke said, straightening his back on the chair and feeling like he was finally making some progress.

"Dunno, the one for the guy who was sitting next to him, I think."

Luke went back to the night at the awards, picturing everyone seated around table 13. He knew exactly who'd been by Travis Wise's side. But had the poisoned food been intended for that person?

Luke's phone buzzed then, and he saw Sol's name on the screen.

"Mind if I take this? It's my partner," Luke told Vinny. He wouldn't normally take a personal call while talking to a witness, but he knew Sol would be texting first if it wasn't important.

"Nah, man, gotta keep the main squeeze happy," Vinny said with a wide smile. Luke wasn't sure how Sol would take it if she knew she'd been referred to as his *main squeeze.*

"Ciao, cara," Luke answered the phone the way he liked doing with her.

"I think I got into trouble." Sol's voice sounded anguished.

"What happened?"

"There's been a death, and apparently I'm the last person to see the victim alive. The police want to talk to me," Sol explained.

"Are you alright?" Luke stood from his chair and gathered all his stuff, making an apologetic gesture to Vinny. He needed to find her. "And who's dead?" he asked, even if he had a slight premonition.

"I'm perfectly fine. But Jason Zit, apparently, not so much."

19

A little bit more than an hour later, Luke got out of a car in front of the police station in Beverly Hills. Sol was already there. The moment he laid eyes on her, he almost forgot he was mad at her for hiding information from him. She was dressed in her LA-staple combination of leggings and one of his garments on top—in this case a dark-gray denim shirt. Perhaps it was because he liked seeing her wearing his clothes, but even if he knew she would be looking differently had her suitcase actually made it, she was still gorgeous and stylish.

"What took you so long?" Sol's irritated tone took him out of his appraisal of her.

"I was in Long Beach. They have delicious pastries. Still no tea," Luke grumbled. The lack of a decent English breakfast brew had been one of his objections to Los Angeles since landing there. "But let's not get off track, should we? What the hell were you doing, talking to Jason Zit?"

"He's a colleague!" Sol said defensively, and she had the gall of pretending she hadn't been investigating Simon Smith's case behind his back. "I talk to journalists all the time. I didn't realize you'd assumed I would give you a regular update of all my professional dealings!"

"Now, cara, non facciamo i birichini," he told her but realized that Sol hadn't understood him. It happened sometimes when he spoke Italian to her. "Don't get sassy."

"Sassy! Sassy? One of my fellow critics is dead, and that's all you can come up with, really?" Her tone sounded strained.

"I'm doing my best to stay cool and not get angry at you, because we *both* know you weren't talking to Jason about your favorite films of the year or the increasing use of AI as a copyediting tool in your profession or whatever it is you talk about with your *colleagues*. Were you or weren't you asking him about Simon Smith's disappearance, even when we'd agreed you'd stay out of the case?" Luke had a smile on his lips, even if his tone was firm.

"I was," Sol admitted. "But I was going to tell you. Plus, we didn't agree I'd stay out of the case. You *decided* it."

"Because I was worried! I *am* worried." He was starting to lose his cool. "And look what happened?"

"Another critic bites the dust?" Sol said.

"If you want to *really* put it like that, yes," said Luke. "First Simon, then Travis, and now Jason. But tell me, what are we doing here?"

"An officer Tom Owens called me and told me to come at my earliest convenience. He wants to ask me about my conversation with Jason. Do you think I should have brought a lawyer?"

"Do you have a lawyer in Los Angeles?" Luke asked.

"I guess I could call my divorce lawyer. But I really hated his guts by the end. I suspect he was not-so-secretly siding with my ex." Luke could see she was pretending, even with herself, to be fine but was showing signs of anxiety. She was biting at her hangnails and pacing back and forth in front of him. "Wait, isn't Geoff some sort of lawyer?"

"No, cara, he's not a lawyer. Come here," he told her, his voice warm.

"What?"

"I think I need a hug. You do too." Luke surrounded her with his arms the moment she approached, and she rested her face against his chest.

"Aren't you mad at me for not telling you about Jason?" Her eyes closed as she breathed in his scent and calmed down.

"There's time to be mad at you *after* we talk to the police," he told her.

"We?"

"That's why I'm here. You have no lawyer, but your main squeeze, who's a sexy London detective with no idea about California law, is here."

"That'll do," Sol said, and then she processed everything he'd said. "My *main squeeze*?"

"A surfer chap taught me that today," Luke said as they slowly broke the hug and began walking closely side by side, their arms still touching. "After inviting me to bathe in coconut oil with him," he added, trying to lighten the mood as they entered the police station.

"Do I want to ask?" Sol lifted an eyebrow in his direction.

"When we're done with this."

...

"Isn't that Officer Hunky Dory?" Luke muttered to Sol in a whisper as they approached the same policeman who'd been at the entrance of Simon Smith's building the day Luke and Sol went looking for him.

"I think so," Sol replied, also in a hush as they were both now almost in front of an expectant officer Tom Owens.

"Officer Tom Owens?" Sol asked, making sure the man was the one who'd called her. "I'm Sol Novo."

"*Detective* Owens," the policeman corrected her. "And you'd be?" he asked Luke.

"Private Detective Luke Contadino. You stood me up this morning, *Detective* Owens," Luke told him. "And have been ignoring my calls since."

Sol frowned. "He was the guy you were meeting this morning? Oh, he's the one David put you in contact with …"

Luke's eyes were fixed on Detective Owens, only shy of intimidating. "Yes."

"Did David Sparrow tell you to stand Luke up?" Sol asked the policeman accusatively, and Luke had to suppress a smile. He liked it when she got fiery on his behalf.

"Now, now, ma'am, please," Detective Owens said. "I'm the one asking questions here. Why does your face look familiar?"

"Oh, I get that all the time. I have a very common face," Sol said, and Luke was almost unable to stop himself from snickering. The last adjective he'd use to describe her face was *common*. But it didn't look like Detective Owens had realized Sol had been the woman asking to get into Simon Smith's building the day he was reported missing.

"If you will please follow me," Detective Owens said, and he guided Sol and Luke through the maroon-carpeted second floor of the police station until they reached the door to a grim, small, windowless room with a table and some chairs in the middle.

"An interrogation room, really?" Sol said, and Luke heard the anguish in her tone.

"Standard procedure. We'll have more privacy this way. After you." Detective Owens indicated for Sol to get inside before him. Luke followed her closely.

"May I ask you in what capacity you're here, Mr. Contadino?" Detective Owens asked Luke as they all sat around the table.

"Mr. Contadino is my legal counsel," Sol said. Luke realized the anguish in Sol was probably only visible—and audible—to him. To people who didn't know her, she could be perceived as the confident and slightly intimidating woman who always took over in these kinds of situations.

"Your legal counsel?" Detective Owens looked unimpressed.

"That's exactly what I said," Ice Queen Sol said.

Sol's words about Luke's legal experience weren't completely misplaced or erroneous. She knew that Luke had taken three years to complete a qualifying law degree when he first went to uni. Of course, he'd never practiced or continued his education in that field, opting instead to intern in a private detective's agency. And he had absolutely no idea how different California law was from England's. Judging by what he'd witnessed so far, there was probably a law forbidding smart shoes from being worn at all times. And there was a statewide ban so that baristas never left any room for milk while brewing tea.

"What's happened to Jason Zit, then?" Luke said.

"You two are quite the curious duo," Detective Owens said, and even if he'd been affable and smiling from the moment they'd met him, Luke was starting to feel they were rubbing him the wrong way. "The police were called to the stretch of Beverly Boulevard between Detroit and Formosa at around noon today, as a Toyota RAV4 had crashed in front of the New Beverly Cinema. Mr. Zit, who had been at the wheel, was declared dead on the scene."

"He had a car accident?" asked Sol.

"He did, but we don't think the death resulted from the crash but the other way around," Detective Owens said cryptically.

"I don't think I follow," said Sol.

"We think something happened to Mr. Zit that left him incapable of driving," the detective explained.

"You think he was poisoned," Luke declared.

"And why would you make such an assumption, Mr. Contadino?"

"That's the kind of sharing of information I was looking to establish with you when we were supposed to meet this morning," Luke said.

"Ah, quid pro quo. I tell you things, you tell me things," Detective Owens said.

"Was that a *Silence of the Lambs* reference, really?" Sol protested.

Luke shrugged. "Sorry if I didn't get it. I don't think I've ever seen it."

"Kinda young, huh?" said Detective Owens, who was more around Sol's age, referring to Luke.

"Now I *know* David definitely asked you to give Luke a hard time," Sol said, and for the first time since she'd called him that day, it wasn't anguish that Luke heard in her voice but actual anger.

"Enough of the chitchat," Luke told Owens. He was starting to get tired of Officer Hunky Dory's brand of pretend friendliness. "Why did you ask Ms. Novo to come in today?"

"Because she may have been the last person to see Mr. Zit alive," said Detective Owens ominously.

"*One* of the last people," corrected Sol. "Emily was also there."

"Emily?" asked Detective Owens as if the name sounded familiar but he couldn't place it. He checked his notepad. "Ah, the wife!"

"Yes, Emily," said Sol, irritated. It occurred to Luke then —they didn't actually know Emily's last name. "And I suppose that a giant house such as that must employ at least two or three people to help run it."

"More like half a dozen between a housekeeper, two cleaners, one chef, one trainer, and a gardener," Detective Owens said.

"And they were all in the house?" Luke asked.

"Now, now, Mr. Contadino. You'll have to figure that out. I can't tell you everything, can I? Not when you still haven't fulfilled your part of the bargain. Quid pro quo."

"Not a bargain," Luke cut in. Detective Owens was grating on him.

"What were you doing at Mr. Zit's house, Ms. Novo?" Detective Owens asked.

"I went there on behalf of my editor in London. She's worried about Simon Smith's disappearance. Jason was Simon's editor."

Luke feared the policeman would realize then she'd been the woman who was at Simon Smith's apartment building a few days before. But he didn't, and Luke didn't know what to make of it. It didn't reflect well on the man's investigative abilities.

"Did Mr. Zit offer you any helpful information?"

"Not really. He thought Julie, that's my editor, was exaggerating and that Simon would probably be drinking in a bar somewhere."

"Was—*is* Mr. Smith a heavy drinker?" Detective Owens

asked. "See, I'm also tasked with finding that other peer of yours."

"Emily implied he drank like any other journalist." Sol shrugged, palms turned upward at her sides.

"Which, in your professional experience, means?"

"Anything from being able to hold his liquor exceptionally well in a professional setting to functional alcoholism, I guess," Sol said. "But please don't quote me on that."

"Swell. Journalist joke." Hearing and seeing his attempt at a pretend laugh was a bit painful. "Did you or Mr. Zit eat anything when you were at the house today?"

"Emily served some delicious Viennese biscuits and tea, and we all had a bite," Sol explained.

"Was the tea any good?" Luke managed to ask her.

"Best I've had in the city so far," Sol said, turning to look at him with a mischievous smile.

"And you really had to go there without me, right?" Luke returned the playful grin, and for a moment he managed to forget where they were and that they weren't alone.

"Ahem, hello! You two want to get a room, perhaps?" Detective Owens interrupted.

If only you knew.

"At what time did you leave Mr. Zit's residence?"

"A bit before eleven?" Sol answered.

"And Mr. Zit was feeling okay when you left?"

"As far as I could tell," said Sol.

"And you haven't been feeling unwell yourself?"

"Unwell?" Sol looked panicked.

"Mrs.—erm Emily said she'd felt nauseous and dizzy all morning," Detective Owens said. "We did some blood tests and can also do that with you."

"Right now I have a massive headache. But I'm sure it's all due to annoyance and hypochondria," Sol said.

"So no blood test?" Detective Owens pushed.

"Definitely no blood test," Sol said. "They can't force me, right?" She turned toward Luke and put her hand on top of his forearm.

"Absolutely not," he told her, trying to calm her with his eyes. He had literally no clue.

"That would be all—for now—but please do give me a call if you remember anything else," Detective Owens said as he gave Sol a card. "And don't get any ideas about leaving the county, let alone the country."

Luke's head jerked in the direction of Detective Owens.

"I'm sorry, are you saying she can't leave?" Luke asked, only moderately horrified.

"Not while we keep investigating. We may need to talk to her again," Detective Owens said. Luke thought the detective was enjoying being difficult. But Luke's worst nightmare seemed to finally be fully materializing in front of his eyes. That return flight back to London appeared to be further postponed.

"Breathe. Officer Hunky Dory said that I shouldn't leave the country, but you can still go whenever you want," Sol told Luke the moment they were out of the police station.

"Do you really think that I'm going to leave you *here*?" Luke said to her, halting abruptly in the middle of the street, his frustration palpable.

"You seem to forget this is also my home country. It's not like you'd be leaving me stranded in the middle of nowhere, Luca. I've lived here for ten years," Sol said, trying to elicit some calmness and humor.

"You have no clothes. You're sleeping on an inflatable mattress. You have no car. You can get sunburnt in January!

And there's no place to find decent tea," he argued. "And you're telling me that *I could leave you here!*"

"What if I told you there's actually places to get decent tea? It's just that I still haven't had time to take you there because this trip has been backward from the beginning."

"Well, what are you waiting for?"

"On it! But, before we go, let me say something." She had finally reached him, and there was a chance to talk about what had happened. "I can't help but think that we wouldn't be in this situation if I hadn't followed through with Julie's request."

"You mean if you hadn't gone to see Jason Zit behind my back?" Luke said. There was no way of mistaking how angry he was, even if Sol knew that he was making an effort to keep his voice down.

"Yes, and I'm sorry. I would still do it all over again, even knowing the consequences," she told him. "But I hate that it's also hitting you."

"I'm not mad because you were there for Julie. I'm mad because you didn't tell me about it," Luke said.

"And now I can't leave the country . . ."

"And now you can't leave the bloody country . . ." He pinched his nose and sighed in a gesture she knew he only made when he was nervous.

Luke's cell buzzed then, and he checked it exasperatedly.

"One can't even have an argument, it seems," he said. "I'm sorry. It's the client texting. Let me read it real quick."

"And we can go back to our argument?"

He lifted his eyes from his phone, recognizing the flirtation in her tone.

"We most definitely are going back to our argument," he said, but he no longer sounded so pissed off. "They want me to keep investigating Travis Wise's poisoning. They want me to check into Jason Zit's death—and they've even added Simon Smith's disappearance to the mix. But I don't understand. Didn't Jason and Simon work for a different publication than Travis?"

"They're all part of the same media conglomerate, Marquee Media," said Sol.

"So it makes sense that they ask for this expansion of the investigation, I guess. I'm glad you're here to help me untangle these things, cara."

For a moment it was as if he'd forgotten he was supposed to be mad at her.

"But you still don't want me getting involved in the case?" she asked him, one of her eyebrows raised.

"You mean *more* than you already are?"

"Come, I know just the place where we can have a proper tea and a bite to eat. We can keep talking there," she said. "And it's even walking distance from here."

"I *cannot* believe you."

She smiled as she grabbed his hand in hers and guided him through the most pedestrian-friendly—and photogenic —streets of Beverly Hills until they ended at the Urth Caffé on South Beverly Drive.

20

"**I can't believe** we're not here to board our flight back to London," Luke muttered through gritted teeth as he and Sol waited at the arrivals lobby of the international terminal at LAX.

"And I can't believe they still haven't found my luggage," Sol added. "Or that we still have no hotel room."

The lack of a room of their own had been aggravated by the fact that they had, indeed, finally found a perfectly nice place to stay that morning. Luke had even allowed himself to start anticipating everything he'd finally be able to do with Sol now that they were going to have a decently sized bathroom—not that a small shower room had ever been an impediment. But almost as quickly as they'd found the room, it was decided they would have to let it go. There was an excellent cause for it. But still.

A few minutes later, the reason for their trip to the airport—and for their loss of a much-needed hotel room—materialized in front of them. She was carrying two giant suitcases and wearing shorts, an *I Heart LA* T-shirt, slide sandals with socks, and rainbow-colored rimmed sunglasses. And she looked ecstatic.

She hugged Luke and Sol, holding one in each of her arms.

"I'm here, baby!" Divya declared.

"I can't believe you're so happy to be here," Luke told her. "Also, you realize you're wearing sunglasses indoors, right?"

"She's already blending in better than you," Sol teased him.

"Was it really necessary to bring two suitcases this huge!" Luke grumbled. "I hope we can fit them in the car."

"Stop complaining! One of the suitcases is full of stuff *you* requested!" Divya said.

"Did you have to bring stuff for the case?" Sol asked.

"The case? Signore Contadino here is morphing into the Maggie Smith character from *The Best Exotic Marigold Hotel*," Divya said. "He made me bring milk chocolate Digestives, Hobnobs, and tea bags. I had to check a second bag because of him!"

"No!" Sol couldn't repress her laughter.

"Yes!" Divya joined in.

"Are we done making fun of me? Because I may not share my biscuits and tea with any of you," Luke told them as he helped Divya with one of the suitcases and they headed to the parking.

"*Your* biscuits and tea? I paid for them and lugged them all the way here, mate!" Divya protested.

"She has a point, Luca," Sol told him, and he laughed as well. It was so good to see Divya. She brought a little bit of home with her.

Fortunately, Marquee Media had understood that Luke was going to need some help if they wanted three cases solved in any reasonable amount of time and had agreed to pay for the other partner at the Bakshi & Contadino Agency to travel to Los Angeles.

Luke hoped that with Divya there, things would get sorted out soon. Especially considering the situation between him and Sol was still *not* ideal. Even after the conversation they had the day before and even if he'd finally had the first good cup of tea since landing in Los Angeles, Luke was still sullen at what had happened with Sol—at his romantic partner hiding things from him. And yes, perhaps a part of him was also not happy at Sol for getting herself banned from leaving the country. But it was only a *tiny* part. He really was trying to be selfless.

"A silver Nissan Versa, really?" Divya complained as Luke and Sol stopped in front of the rented car. "Luke, mate, this is my first time in LA. Could you really have not splurged a little and rented a convertible Ford Mustang? Preferably in yellow."

"I don't think the client would appreciate any splurging on our side. Things are tight as is. We barely have the budget for your flight, the car, and the hotel."

"So where are we staying exactly?" Divya asked as they finished packing the car and made their way aboard, with Luke at the wheel.

"You're staying at a perfectly nice three-star hotel not far from here," Sol told Divya as Luke started driving. "I checked the reviews myself."

"Oh, and the rest are enjoying some romantic, luxurious resort that Sol must be paying for," Divya said.

"I wish," muttered Luke, and Divya turned in his direction, puzzled.

"Luke and I have been enjoying the generosity of some

friends and the discomfort of their hideous inflatable mattress," Sol explained.

"I don't understand," Divya said. "Why are you crashing at some friends' as if you were both in your twenties? Which, no offense, you aren't."

"No offense taken, believe me," Luke said morosely.

"Is the client not paying for everyone's hotels?" Divya asked.

"They are, within moderation," Luke explained. "But apparently, for some reason I *cannot* understand, everyone is in this city, and hotel vacancies are extremely rare. We've been trying to find a room for days. We finally did, and then a death was thrown into the case, and it was clear that you were needed here."

"And we really didn't think it was nice to make you suffer my friends' mattress," Sol explained. "Even if it comes with dinner included, and Geoff's cooking really is exceptional."

"So you keep the hotel room while we keep bunking in Los Feliz. Hopefully we'll find something tomorrow," Luke said, and he felt exhausted.

"I reckon that's why this one's in such a foul mood, then," Divya said, referring to Luke.

"Not entirely," Sol said. "He's also mad at me."

"I'm not cross with you," Luke said, but it didn't sound like he wasn't.

"He *is* mad at me. I went to talk to Jason Zit without letting him know, and then Jason turned up dead. And at the same time, Luke found out the poisoned food at the party had been intended for Jason all along."

Luke hoped his romantic partner had really grasped the dangers of that particular case and quit about his supposed crossness with her. "Oh, and now I've been instructed by the police not to leave the country."

"He's definitely mad at you," Divya agreed with Sol. "Don't worry, Luke. I'm here, mate. We're going to solve this thing in no time and be gone before you're even homesick."

"It's already late for that," Luke grumbled.

"Aye, I thought you'd say that," said Divya. "Still, we'll be out of here in no time. Especially with Sol helping us."

"Sol is *not* helping us. She's only here because she wanted to see you," clarified Luke.

"His overall reasoning is that I've done enough helping," Sol explained.

"He *really* is cross," Divya said.

"Yes, but he likes having company when he drives. So he may let me tag along if I promise to chat him up," Sol concluded.

 here did you leave Sol?" Divya asked Luke the following morning as he dropped by her hotel so the two of them could talk about the case.

"She dropped me off and headed to some Pilates class, if she's to be believed," he explained.

"Ouch! LA is not proving you well. You sound grumpy. You're never grumpy," Divya told him.

"Try being away from home without an end in sight, and then we can talk about grumpiness. Let's not make this about me, though. We need to talk about the investigation."

"Mind if we do it while we walk?"

"There's no walking here," Luke said, only slightly exasperated. The sooner Divya understood certain things about Los Angeles, the better.

"Don't be daft, mate. You just need to know where to go. Sol sent me a ton of recommendations about the area last night." Divya checked the maps app on her cell phone. "We're very close to Playa del Rey."

"Not another beach!" he protested.

"Since when do you have an objection against beaches?"

"Since now?"

"Ah, it's an objection against *California* beaches then," Divya pressed.

"Why is everyone so insistent on me enjoying my stay here? This is a work trip!"

"I was going to tease you, saying that it started as a pleasure trip, but I feel that would be rubbing salt in the wound," Divya said while she navigated them toward the ocean.

"Very much so."

No pleasure had, whatsoever.

"So let me tell you my theory about the case after I had a look at all your notes and updates."

"Please tell me you've cracked it," Luke pleaded. "The sooner we wrap this up, the sooner we get paid and go back home."

"I haven't really cracked it, and you're not going to be happy," Divya said.

"Why would I *not* be happy?" He turned toward her and, as he did, a couple of shirtless men came running in their direction. Luke rolled his eyes. Even runners looked like wannabe actors there. And, of course, they ran by the beach while sunbathing in January!

"You're not going to be happy because I don't think the incidents with the three critics are related. This is not one single case like we were hoping."

"You've got to be joking." Luke pinched his nose in exasperation.

"I wish I was."

"So we need to solve three cases now?"

"I don't know. I think so, though. Two at the least."

"It's too much of a coincidence—three journalists

writing or editing reviews, one of them disappears, one of them is poisoned, the other dies. And all of the incidents happened at almost the same time. You know I don't believe in coincidences," Luke said and then reconsidered. "*We* don't believe in coincidences."

"That's exactly why, if you have any other theory, I think we should pursue that one first."

"I think the director did it."

"That would be . . . ?"

"Victor Lago, the director of *Haughty Horizons*," Luke explained. "Simon Smith writes a terrible review about his film, the work he's been devoted to for more than ten years. A movie that's been ruined forever because of that review. People won't watch it, and it won't get any awards recognition."

"Isn't it a bit extreme? To kill because of a bad review?"

"You haven't been in this city enough, but *these people* are crazy about their work," Luke explained. "So Lago gets rid of Simon, but he's still not happy. He decides to go against Simon's editor as well, the person who enabled Simon to publish his rubbish review."

"That's the Jason chap?"

"Yes."

"Didn't Sol talk to him and wasn't he very ashamed of Simon's review?"

"Yes, but Lago didn't know that. So he tried to poison him at the party, only the waiter got high and confused and handed Jason's plate to Travis. Fortunately, because of Travis's nut allergy he didn't trust the food much anyway, and he didn't ingest enough poison, and he's still alive."

"So Lago almost gets the wrong person killed once, but he's cold-blooded enough to try and get Jason killed a second time?"

"Yes, he's avenging his masterpiece. And I do think my theory holds to that point," Luke said. "But here's where it has a few holes and where I could use your insight. How did Lago do it? How did he dispose of Simon Smith, and why did he get rid of him? Why did he switch to poison after that? I think getting the cyanide in the food at the party should have been easy enough, but how did he manage to poison Jason at his home?"

"Not sure how he got rid of Simon Smith, but he probably realized making someone disappear isn't easy. So he could have switched to an easier method, like poisoning, for his second attempt," Divya said, even if she didn't sound completely convinced about her working theory.

"I guess that could make sense. I mean, we still need to find Simon Smith . . ."

"Pesky little detail. But I think I know how Jason was poisoned."

Luke looked visibly puzzled. He knew his professional partner was good. She was the best. But even she couldn't magically figure out cases. She'd barely landed. She didn't even know the whole cast of suspects and persons of interest, and she already knew how the killer had managed to get to Jason?

"Yes, I do," Divya said, as if answering Luke's skeptical thoughts. "And you would, too, if you weren't such an idiot, and instead of being all touchy and offended, you'd taken the time to talk to Sol about her visit to Jason."

"I talked to her about it plenty!" he protested.

"No, you didn't. You were mad and felt insecure because she hadn't told you she was going to see Jason Zit. Guess what? You kept telling her to stay away from the case, so she decided not to tell you that she was tired of being told what to do!"

"I didn't tell her what to do!" Luke said.

"Yes, you did, Mr. Flawed Feminist. But not happy with that, you then went and never bothered asking her about the visit to Jason's house as you would have done with a regular person involved in the case."

"She's not involved in the case!"

"Stop grinding your teeth! Your blood pressure must be through the roof. I don't care if you like it or not, she *is* involved," Divya told him in a serious tone that took no exceptions. "The last time she was involved in one of your cases, you missed clues, ignored common-sense rules, and lost your job. Can you at least try and keep your cool this time? We're in LA, mate. This might be the capital of mindfulness and tree-hugger vibes. Let's hope some of that rubs off on us, eh?"

"Tell me what Sol told you about her visit to Jason Zit's place, then."

"Only if you promise to bloody calm down," Divya said.

"Fine, I swear I'll bloody calm down, alright?" Luke conceded. "What did Sol tell you?"

"That a box of chocolates with Jason's name on it had just been delivered when she was there the day he died. She saw it on her way out. My guess? Jason Zit had a sweet tooth, saw the chocolates, and couldn't help himself—probably scoffed a couple of them before heading out of the house and smashing his car outside a bloody cinema, of all places. Victor Lago could have easily sent those chocolates, lacing them with a fatal amount of cyanide."

"Why didn't she tell the police about the chocolates? Why didn't she tell *me*?" Luke asked.

"I don't know, mate. Did either the police or you bother to ask?"

22

"Why is he seething?" Sol asked Divya as she drove her and Luke to Victor Lago's home in the Hollywood Hills.

"I'm not seething," Luke grumbled from the back seat.

"He's still not over the fact that you went to see Jason Zit *and* didn't think of telling him about the box of chocolates," Divya explained, and Sol had the feeling the detective was starting to get tired of playing couples therapist.

"I didn't even remember about the stupid chocolates!" Sol protested. "I only recalled them because you're an excellent interviewer."

"And I am not?" Luke sounded offended.

"Enough!" Divya managed to say. "You two are extremely tiresome. I'm jet-lagged, and I want to wrap this thing up and maybe enjoy LA for a little bit before we can make Luke happy and go back to London. Can you please barter a truce of some sort until then?"

"*He* started it," Sol said, referring to Luke's foul mood of the last two days.

"No, no, no, cara. You started it when you lied to me."

"Don't call me cara if you don't mean it!"

"What do you mean, I don't mean it?"

"No truce then, I guess," muttered Divya.

They arrived at their destination a couple of minutes after that. A charged silence had taken hold of the car, and its occupants entertained themselves by admiring the house in front of them. The French Provençal-style mansion Victor Lago shared with his partner, showrunner Abbie Domingo, was perched over the Hollywood Hills. It had a swimming pool perfect for laps. It boasted views of the Hollywood Sign, the Griffith Observatory, and Downtown. And there was a For Sale sign in front of it.

"Don't want to get into nobody's business," Sol said as Luke and Divya were about to get out of the car.

"Really?" asked Luke, but Sol ignored him.

"Luke, mate. You're starting to annoy not only Sol, but me as well. And you promised you'd calm down," Divya complained. "What did you want to tell us, Sol?"

"I'd say based on location, amenities, and size, this house must be worth around nine or ten million. You may want to ask Victor and his partner how come it is for sale."

"Maybe they got tired of Los Angeles," Luke quipped.

"Maybe they need the money because someone's movie flopped," said Divya.

"Or maybe they're just upgrading. You never know with these people. I'm sure Abbie is making a very decent amount of money with her TV show. Especially with all the awards she's winning," Sol said.

"But it doesn't hurt to ask," Divya said.

"Exactly. So I trust you two will be able to make your way back when you're done with this, right?" Sol asked them.

"You're not coming with us?" Luke asked.

"You have to be fucking kidding me. First you tell me not to get involved, and then you find it strange that I don't join you for an interview! Get out of the car. We'll talk tonight." Sol looked Luke straight in the eyes.

"If I wasn't getting tired of being in the middle, I'd say that was extremely hot," Divya said as she and Luke made their ascent toward Victor Lago's home and Sol drove away.

"Who are you?" Abbie Domingo asked when she opened the front door of her house, dressed in a pinstripe, three-piece suit and wearing tortoiseshell-framed Prada sunglasses. She had to be the most elegant person Luke had seen since landing in that city, with the exception of the awards ceremony, of course. But it was almost as if Ange-lenos had only two modes: the most glamorous black-tie style or completely laid-back sportswear. Abbie Domingo was somewhere in between.

"I'm Luke Contadino. I don't know if you remember, we met at the party the other night," Luke told the TV writer.

"You're the younger fling who went to the party with the sophisticated journalist from Spain, right?" Abbie said, studying him from head to toe.

"That's me," said Luke. "And this is my professional part-ner, Divya Bakshi. We were hoping to have a chat with your partner, Victor Lago."

"You and me both, honey," said Abbie in a playful tone.

"He's not home, then?" asked Divya.

"He hasn't been home for weeks! I would let you in and tell you all about it, but I'm actually heading out. I have an appointment with my therapist to tell her all about Victor's betrayal!"

"I'm sorry to hear that."

The showrunner locked her front door and made her way to a convertible, burgundy Jaguar E-Type from the seventies parked in front of the house.

"Love your wheels!" Divya told Abbie.

"Thank you, it was a gift from Victor. One that I had to finish paying myself because indie filmmakers get all the glory, but most of them are broke!"

"So he had money problems?" Divya asked.

"He was hoping to get fame, glory, and *money* with *Haughty Horizons*, but then that wretched review was published, and he became unhinged. That's when he abandoned me and the dogs!"

"So he didn't like Simon Smith's review?" Luke asked.

"He detested it! *Haughty Horizons* is his baby, and Simon killed it!"

"A bit melodramatic, no?" Divya asked.

"Have a chat with Victor about *Haughty Horizons*, and tell me if I'm being melodramatic or not," Abbie said. "But, for that, you have to find him first."

"Do you have any idea where he may be?" Luke asked tentatively.

"I've checked the Bel-Air, the Peninsula, and the Four Seasons. If he's not there, I don't know where he could be! He's never been a fan of the Beverly Hills, something about the pinkness of the place that unsettled him, so I didn't bother to check there. You may want to give it a try though …"

"Got it, fancy hotels," said Luke.

"There may be something else. The second round of press for the movie didn't move the needle one bit, and people are falling asleep all over the country, watching *Haughty Horizons*! But he still doesn't seem to realize it. And he loves to party. So try the awards circuit. I'm sure he's convinced the movie still has a chance of becoming a cult classic."

"Fancy hotels and fancy parties. One last thing, and I promise we'll get out of your way and let you drive to your appointment," said Luke. "You made it sound as if he hasn't been here for a few weeks, but the other day you went together to the awards ceremony."

"He knew I was invited because my show had been nominated, and he *begged* me to let him go with me," Abbie explained. "And I'm silly and thought he wanted to reconcile when the only thing he wanted was to be photographed on the fucking red carpet with the hopes of someone talking about his movie!"

"I'm sorry about that." This time it was Divya trying to put the showrunner at ease, and Luke had the feeling both he and his partner felt for the woman and would have liked to meet her under different circumstances.

"Oh, don't be sorry! Nobody cares about the love life of a middle-aged, boring couple anyway! I don't think there was a single picture of him being taken or published. And they only took mine because I had too many nominations and won too many awards to be ignored. Plus, I'd been working out like hell for months and looked divine in that Armani dress. At least, that's what my publicist says! But I need to let you two go. Thanks for listening!"

"No problem, and thanks for your time," Luke said.

"Do you want us to let you know if we find him?" Divya asked.

"Please don't. Me and the dogs are moving on! I even put the house on the market. Too many memories, and I never liked the place," Abbie explained. "But chao, darlings. And Luke, maybe lose the frown. It doesn't suit you!"

23

"**A**re you thinking what I am thinking?" Divya asked Luke as Abbie drove down the hill and they waved goodbye one last time.

"That Abbie Domingo could do much better than Victor Lago?" Luke answered.

"No, the other thing."

"Ah, that Victor Lago didn't want to go to the awards *only* to be photographed. He wanted to have easy access to Jason Zit's food."

"I bet he knew the editor was going to be at the same awards ceremony as his ex, and he saw an opportunity that he couldn't miss," said Divya.

"Should we get to that hotel where Abbie said Victor probably would not be staying at, then?" Luke asked. "It sounds like a long shot."

"It's also not very convenient from here. Especially without a car," Divya said, checking her phone. "Reckon we should have a word with Sol first. Bet she'll have a few ideas about Victor's whereabouts."

"Ideas that Victor's own partner of many years couldn't

have had?" Luke's tone sounded growly in a way he hadn't exactly intended.

"You'd *think* that one member of a couple would know the other one better than everyone else. But sometimes we're ignorant to some of our own lover's—how should I put it?—peculiarities," Divya said. Luke thought the detective wasn't only talking about Abbie and Victor.

"If you think it could be beneficial to talk to Sol, we can talk to Sol," he conceded.

"Brilliant, I'll give her a ring now. In the meantime, and since we're here, mind if we do this as a hiking meeting?"

"What are you talking about?!"

"We call Sol to ask her professional opinion—that's the meeting part—and we do that while we're walking. My map says we're only thirty-five minutes from Runyon Canyon, and we can hike there. It's supposed to have views of Downtown and the ocean. We may even get a glimpse of the Hollywood Sign."

"I don't care about the Hollywood Sign!" grumbled Luke.

"But I do, so it's decided." Divya called Sol's number, setting her phone on speakerphone so Luke could also hear it.

"Hi, Divya. Has the grump behaved, or has he spooked Victor Lago?" Sol said. What exactly did she mean by *the grump*?

"Ahem, the grump is here with me right now, on speakerphone. So, yeah. He heard that," Divya said.

"Oh. Why are you calling?" In true Sol fashion, she was going to ignore the awkwardness of the situation.

"Victor Lago has not been living at home for a few weeks, according to Abbie Domingo. And she doesn't know where he is. You wouldn't know where we could look for him other than the Beverly Hills Hotel, right?"

"So you need my help?"

Luke rolled his eyes. Sol always left some things unacknowledged when it suited her. But others she most definitely didn't.

"Yeah, that'd be much appreciated," Luke told Sol.

There was silence at the other end of the line. Was Sol thinking? Was she driving? Was she coming up with a clever way of telling him to sod off?

"I have absolutely no idea what may be going on inside of Victor Lago's mind. There's a reason I couldn't stomach his movie. He's the kind of old-fashioned, straight, middle-aged, cisgender, white man who's dominated over Hollywood for years. But I tend not to empathize much with that kind of moviemaking, and fortunately there's a bit more diversity to choose from now," Sol explained. Divya and Luke glanced at each other with the softest hint of a smile, clearly used to her strong opinions.

"We totally understand," both Luke and Divya said in unison. Luke could sense there was an idea forming in the periphery of Sol's brain, but she was having issues grasping it because she didn't like Victor Lago.

"And he was a bit of an ass when I talked to him a few days ago," Sol continued.

Luke's gaze shot to the phone. There had been something unsettling in her words. "You didn't tell me about it."

"I think we were already living at Lola and Geoff's by then, and communication has been—"

"—lacking," Luke finished.

"Yes," Sol admitted.

"Going back to Victor Lago's whereabouts." Divya redirected the conversation. "Abbie says that Victor likes to party and be seen on the awards circuit."

"Ah," Sol said, and that really seemed to make her think of something. "I can't promise it's not going to be a total fool's errand—"

"—but," Luke prodded.

"There's this thing tonight at the Roosevelt Hotel, one of the many precursor parties ahead of the Oscars, where people go to be seen and photographed," Sol explained.

"Would he be invited?" Divya asked.

"Not directly, because his film hasn't been nominated or even considered for anything. But he has many friends who are probably invited. So I don't think it would be that hard to get in for him," Sol reasoned.

"Can *we* get invited?" Luke asked, and he knew he was threading a very fine line.

"*I* got an invitation to my email, which I'd completely ignored. But I think I can still RSVP, and I can bring one of you as my plus-one," Sol said. "Divya, I can pick you up at your hotel around seven, if that works."

"It works, but I thought you'd be taking Luke," Divya said, visibly confused.

"The grump and I will be talking tonight. After I come back from the party I have to attend for a case where I am most definitely *not* involved," Sol said. If Luke had any doubt—which he really shouldn't—whether she was mad at him or not, he no longer did. "Dress code is cocktail attire, but in California that's extremely relaxed. Especially because there'll be lots of press in attendance, and no one has the budget or the energy to make the effort. So just leave the slides at the hotel, and you'll be fine."

She was parking at Divya's hotel ten minutes after seven that evening, because if there was a place where Sol Novo managed not to be always on time, it was Los Angeles. Beating traffic just wasn't possible all the time there.

But when she reached the hotel lobby, it wasn't the wiry Mancunian detective waiting for her but a very dapper Londoner who had exhausted her patience lately.

"I thought I said I'd be taking Divya with me tonight," Sol told him.

She was furious not only at him anymore, but also at herself. She could feel butterflies in her stomach just because he was standing in front of her in all his manly magnificence, giving her one of his roguish grins. It was the same spiraling sensation she'd had when they'd started flirting—only they'd been together for months now. Shouldn't she be more reassured in whatever it was they had? Less dazzled, too, if her past experience had taught her anything.

Even if she loved Divya's company, the idea of spending a few hours with Luke was extremely alluring—regardless of what she may pretend. The fact that he looked gorgeous in the dark suit and white shirt open at the collar, contrasting with his bronzed olive skin, probably contributed to her need to be in his company. Sol may have picked up the expression "he looked like sex in a suit" in an Elsie Silver book and unfairly rolled her eyes while reading it. Luke had brought a new perspective to the meaning of those words.

But she was still furious at herself for thinking all those things. And she was resolved not to show any of that to him. *Because she was supposed to be mad at him.*

"Divya crashed half an hour ago. Bad case of jet lag after an extremely inadvisable hiking experiment," Luke said.

Why did he have to sound so sexy when he spoke? "Allora, solo io e te stasera, cara."

"Your Italian doesn't do anything for me," she said, and that was probably the biggest lie she'd ever told him. But what had her fuming was that Luke seemed to know she was bluffing.

"Would complimenting how sexy you look change that?" he said as he offered her his arm since she was perched atop the same very high shoes she'd gotten for the awards ceremony, and he knew her balance on those was shaky at best.

"You can compliment Lola, she lent me the dress," Sol almost barked as his gaze traveled the range of her curves, which were hugged in a strappy, dark-green dress. She could feel herself blushing under his inquisitive eyes. What was wrong with her exactly?

She was forty-three, twice divorced, mature, reasonably rational, and quite independent, yet she was literally melting because her lover—who'd been a complete ass the past few days—was shamelessly checking her out. His eyes were wordlessly telling her what he'd like to do with her if they ever found themselves in private again.

"If you keep looking at me like that, I'm going to head straight to the counter and beg for a hotel room. A storage closet would probably do as well," she finally told him, because she'd realized that playing cool was futile. She had given up. She took the offered arm and felt his muscular bicep under the fabric of his suit.

"That doesn't sound like such a bad idea," he said, still fucking her with his eyes.

"I think there's a damn party you need me to drive you to," Sol reasoned, against all her instincts. "The sooner you get this thing solved and wrapped up—"

"—the sooner you quit being on Officer Hunky Dory's

no-travel list and we get back home," he said, and that seemed to sober both of them up.

"Plus, I'm still quite mad at you," Sol said as they walked toward the hotel's exit. She was still holding his arm tight as they moved, clinging to him for balance. "Even if the prospect of some angry sex sounds quite—"

"Please don't finish that sentence," Luke begged her. "I checked at the lobby before you arrived. Unfortunately there's not a single storage closet available at the hotel, let alone rooms."

"Calmémonos entonces," Sol said, and she sounded as disappointed as he was.

"Yeah, let's get our heads straight."

24

"So, are we good?" Luke asked her as they entered the already packed lobby of the Roosevelt Hotel in Hollywood. Perhaps she was just tired of being mad at him—or maybe it was the way he'd whispered those words in her ear, sending shivers down her spine—but she no longer remembered what had irked her so much.

"We're good," she said. She was normally quite adept at talking things over and analyzing whatever had happened so the relationship could continue to thrive. But she was perfectly aware that what she and Luke needed at the moment weren't more words.

"I think I know why you didn't want to come to this thing," Luke told her, his arm around her waist and his lips close to her ear, looking ahead of them. Her hair was gathered in a simple knot at her nape, and she could feel his breath and each one of his words on her exposed skin.

"I hate parties. Plus, I wanted to have an early evening to scour the internet in search of a hotel room for us," Sol told him.

"That, and you probably didn't want to see her." Luke

pointed to Claudia a few meters in front of them. But before Sol could make a sudden one-eighty-degree turn and avoid her, the editor was already walking in their direction.

"Sol Novo! I wasn't expecting to see you here," Claudia said in her high-pitched voice.

"Well, I wasn't planning on coming," Sol told her in what she thought was probably an equally high-pitched tone, but she was feeling a bit nervous.

"You never got back to me about that job offer," Claudia said, her tone only slightly reproachful, and she stared at Luke. "But, of course, in the end I guess you decided to leave me for such a gorgeous man."

"Can you blame me?" Sol decided there was nothing else to be said. Not to Claudia, anyway.

"Luke, I know your case has been keeping you busy with new commissions. But we're so absolutely devastated about Jason," Claudia seemed compelled to say, even if she didn't necessarily look devastated. "It's completely heartbreaking. A terrible loss. And now that he'd finally found the courage."

"The courage?" Sol asked, both because she was curious and because she knew Luke also wanted the answer to that question.

"To divorce her! It was no secret his marriage had been in shambles for years. Rumor around town," Claudia said, lowering her voice and leaning closer to them, "was that he'd met someone else. You remember him from his days at *Performance Weekly*, right?"

"Barely," Sol said, and it was true.

"He's been a miserable grouch for years! Absolutely unhappy with her—and everybody else because of it. Very open about it too," Claudia explained.

"Why didn't they divorce before if the marriage was so

troubled?" Sol genuinely couldn't comprehend why someone would stay in a relationship that made them miserable.

"She's loaded. He liked the money," Claudia said.

"Ah." Sol felt a bit naïve for ever thinking that a senior editor's salary could stretch to a house like Jason and Emily's in Hancock Park.

"Ah indeed," echoed Claudia. "But, sadly, I need to let you and Luke go momentarily. I see that Ryan Gosling just arrived, and I have to harass him so that he gives us an interview for the home page."

"Good luck," Sol told Claudia as the editor walked toward Ryan Gosling like a predator in search of dinner.

"She offered you the job again?" Luke asked Sol when they were alone.

"She basically told me the job was as good as mine," Sol admitted. "But I don't want to work with her again. And I don't want to move here again." A mere month before, she would have also added *And the last thing I want is to live in a different neighborhood than you. There's no fucking way I'm going to live in a different country and one ocean away.* But she didn't.

She rationalized the decision not to tell him. They were hardly in a private setting. Those were words better said alone and in confidence. But not that deep down she knew that she was also starting to have too many doubts. And all the chatter around her about divorce wasn't helping her. Remembering her last failed relationship wasn't helping. Luke's attitude the last few days wasn't helping. So she hardly felt like exposing her feelings for him even further—especially when she didn't really know if she truly had the energy for another Relationship with a capital R.

"Victor Lago is at the bar," she suddenly told Luke as she

got a glimpse of the director drinking alone. And she felt vindicated in her decision not to have told Luke all that she was thinking. They were there for a different purpose than having a heartfelt chat about the state of their partnership.

They made a fast approach in the direction of the bar, or as fast as humanly possible, considering Sol's shoes and how packed the room was. "I'm going to make an introduction and be all nice with him so that he talks to you, but promise me you won't leave my sight," she said.

"Why would I leave your sight?" Luke then seemed to remember something she'd said. "What happened when you interviewed him?"

"He asked me where the magazine had been hiding me all this time, because he hadn't seen me around before," she explained. "And that was a pity."

Luke stopped in the middle of the room and stared at her. He seemed to be grappling with what she'd told him, struggling to find the words to express whatever crossed his mind.

"Does that happen often? Do random blokes try making advances with you in a professional setting?"

"You'd be surprised," Sol said. "But less and less since I turned forty, I guess. So I hope by the time I'm fifty, I'll be completely transparent."

"Not to me." Her knees went weak at his words. "Is it possible I saw him checking you out during the party? I've never been one for violence, but do you want me to, I don't know, punch him or something?" He sounded serious.

"Gods no! That would solve nothing, and we still need to talk to him about his possible involvement in the case. But would you just keep me very close to you the whole time you talk to him?"

"Gladly," he said, and he tightened his grip on her waist.

"Victor, how are you doing?" Sol asked the director when both she and Luke stood in front of the filmmaker.

"Marvelous!" the director said, a glass of an amber-colored beverage in his hand as he directed his gaze to Sol. "So good to see you!"

It all happened in slow motion then. Victor Lago, who Luke would have said was quite drunk, recognized Sol. He probably couldn't remember her name, but he appraised her figure with a mixture of letch and amusement in his eyes. Victor made a move toward her, his free arm extended in what looked like an attempt at a hug. Sol's expression shifted to horror. She recoiled, attempting to take a step back, only to stumble into someone else standing at the bar. That's when Luke cut in. He threw his body between Sol and Victor, extending his hand to the director in a firm handshake.

"And you probably remember me as well," Luke told a somewhat-puzzled Victor.

"Uh," Victor replied.

"This is my partner, Luke," Sol told Victor, sheltering behind Luke's body and peeking only part of her head around him. "I don't know if you remember him from the awards ceremony."

"Not really . . ." said Victor, as if he was now realizing Sol hadn't been alone at the party the other night.

"I was hoping to have a chat with you," Luke told the director.

"I see. You're a fan of my work, are you?" Victor's whole face lit up.

How do you politely tell someone that you haven't seen a single one of their movies and don't feel like it because your partner fell asleep watching their last film? But also, why did Luke have to be polite with Victor after what he'd told Sol?

"Not really," Luke said. "I'm investigating the disappearance of Simon Smith, the poisoning of Travis Wise, and the death of Jason Zit."

"Good for you, I guess!" Victor said. Why did his accent sound different all of a sudden? It was now giving less artificial British notes, more broad New Yorker. "But I have no clue who any of those people are."

"Two of them were seated with all of us during the awards the other night," Luke said, and he could smell the lie in Victor's words.

"Look, mate, I don't recall you and pretty much anyone else from the other night. The only one I remember seated at my table is her," Victor said, directing his gaze toward Sol in an admiring way. Luke had to restrain himself from growling at the director. Victor Lago had managed to awaken his most basic, primal side, and he wasn't sure how he felt about it. He still drew Sol closer to him.

"You don't recall the person who was taken from the table on a stretcher?" Luke asked. He knew such a direct approach tended not to yield good results. Especially since Victor Lago seemed to be the only person in Los Angeles immune to Luke's accent and his charms. But the filmmaker was grating him the wrong way. And he wanted him to stop looking at Sol. He also knew Victor was lying.

"That's one of the chaps you're investigating? I thought he had a heart attack!" Victor said, and why did he have to keep using British slang?

"He was poisoned," intervened Sol. "I told you about it when I interviewed you a few days ago."

"Food poisoning?" Victor kept playing confused.

"Cyanide," said Luke, and he watched Victor's reaction. First there was the processing of the information, then the understanding of what had been said, and finally . . .

"What, you think *I'm* the one who put the cyanide in his food?" Victor's accent sounded once again New Yorker.

"What makes you think such a thing?" Luke feigned ignorance. "I was just wondering if you saw something unusual during the party or someone getting close to Travis's food."

"As I've already mentioned, I don't recall much from that night."

Convenient. Also, that wasn't exactly what Victor Lago had said, not recalling when they'd first started talking, but Luke still wanted to ask about something else. Someone else.

"And are you sure you don't know who Simon Smith is?"

"The name sounds familiar." Victor pointed upward, making a circular motion with his finger. "But nothing more than that."

"We also talked about him during the interview," Sol told him.

"The only thing I remember about our interview is you, darling." Victor was clearly making Sol uncomfortable. Luke had always considered himself patient and calm, but the director was irritating him to no limit.

"So you don't know the man who wrote the review that destroyed your movie?" Luke said, and *again*, he knew he was approaching the conversation the wrong way. And yet he couldn't stop himself from antagonizing Victor Lago.

"My movie is not *destroyed*," Victor said. His words came out strained, and Luke felt the thrill of victory. He'd finally managed to aggravate the filmmaker as much as Victor Lago was aggravating Luke.

"What Luke meant to say is that Simon Smith was one of the really small group of journalists who had access to *Haughty Horizons* when no one else had," Sol said.

"As I'm sure I've mentioned before, the PR team takes care of that sort of stuff," Victor said, as if promoting a movie was a dirty business beneath him. "But perhaps you should talk to Claudia."

"Claudia?" Sol said.

"Claudia Hopkins. I think she did some freelance media consulting for the movie. She advised the team on how to promote it. Not that it had any positive outcome." Victor chuckled. "If you'll excuse me now, my glass is empty, I need a refill. And I'm really *bored* with this conversation." With that, he made exaggerated gestures to get the barman's attention.

...

"That man is a consummate liar," Sol told Luke ten minutes later when they were both snugly seated in a more secluded part of the Roosevelt, going over everything Victor Lago had told them. "He pretended he didn't know anything about things I'd already told him or asked him about in our interview. He told me he never forgot a face."

"Either he was lying to you then or he was lying to me now. But he clearly was lying to someone," said Luke. "Abbie said he hated Simon Smith. Yet he's feigned indifference and even ignorance when we've both asked about the critic."

"You think he did it?" Sol asked him. "All of it?"

"I think I don't like him one bit."

"Yeah, but is it because he's a potential killer or because you didn't appreciate how he checked me out?"

"Both," declared Luke.

"I have to say, I've never been into the whole possessive alpha thing," Sol said, moving her hand in a wide circle in front of his chest, "but it's sort of—perhaps—mildly turning me on."

"Mildly?" Luke arched one of his eyebrows.

"Considerably." Her lips parted, and she inched toward him. Her eyes were filled with desire. And that would have been the perfect moment and almost the perfect place for a kiss.

But it wasn't.

"Look at you, all cozy in a private corner. Am I interrupting something?" Claudia's voice filled the space.

This fucking city. Never a bloody moment alone.

"Not really," Sol said, although he could see that she was as disappointed as he was. "We actually wanted to talk to you."

"Really?" Claudia said. "I'd have said you've been avoiding me for the past week, and now you—and the beau—want to talk to me?"

"We just wanted to ask you about something Victor Lago mentioned," Sol started tentatively. "He said you advised on reaching out to Simon Smith to review *Haughty Horizons*? And that you did some freelance media consulting for the movie?"

Claudia's complacent features faltered for the briefest of instants, but the editor efficiently pulled her façade back on.

"You know as well as I do that would be a conflict of interest, as my employment as an executive editor at *Performance Weekly* prevents me from getting paid by movie studios. My objectivity as a journalist could be perceived as breached," Claudia said.

"As a veteran journalist and a smart, *old* woman, I also know that this city is fucking expensive and some consulting jobs pay well," Sol said, a pleasant manner never abandoning her demeanor.

"I can trust that you'll be discreet," Claudia continued.

"You know I am," Sol said.

It looked like they were understanding each other, and Luke realized once again how much Sol helped him whenever she got involved in a case, interpreting the entertainment world for him. He still didn't want her getting entangled, nonetheless.

"Oh, whatever!" Claudia finally gave up, and her manner relaxed. She made Sol and Luke scooch over and sat next to them. "I knew I should have said no, but can you blame me? There's constant chatter about layoffs, and I can't be sure I'll have a job next week! So I decided to make myself a bit more of a comfortable mattress to fall back on, just in case. I watched *Haughty Horizons*, realized that it was a slog that was only going to attract a very annoying kind of straight man who thinks himself intellectual, and I advised on showing it to exactly that type of journalist. I even made a list for them."

"I'm sure it wasn't a very difficult list to make," Sol said, a smile tugging at her lips.

"It wasn't. And yes, Simon I-think-Sofia-Coppola's-movies-are-just-for-women Smith was at the top of it."

"Would you mind sharing the list with us?" Luke asked the editor.

"If you promise discretion, and only because I can't really say no to someone as pretty as you," Claudia said.

"We won't say a word, but Claudia, perhaps you should talk to Victor Lago. He's drunk and doesn't seem as devoted to secrecy as we are," Sol said.

"Ugh!" Claudia sighed. "Let me go talk to that fucking haughty know-it-all."

"Were you lucky? Did you get Ryan Gosling?" asked Luke before Claudia left. He was genuinely curious.

"I did. And not even Victor Lago is going to ruin my buzz," said Claudia with the most triumphant of smiles.

"You think she told us the truth?" Luke asked as Claudia strutted back to the lobby of the Roosevelt in search of Victor Lago.

"I think if she was testy, it could be because she knows this information makes her vulnerable with her employer," Sol said. "Does she make sense as the poisoner/killer?"

"I can't see a motive," Luke admitted. "But this case keeps getting more and more complicated. I don't like it when things don't make sense."

"I would agree with you about the lack of motive, but I need to tell you something that may add to the pile of things that keep complicating your case—and perhaps throw some light about that motive." Why did it sound like things were about to go sideways? "I haven't told you this before because, honestly, we haven't had any time alone to talk. The occasion didn't arise. So don't get even *more* mad at me."

"I'm not mad," he said, but he kind of sounded like he was.

"The day I was talking to Jason and Emily about Simon, when I left, Emily gave me Simon's manuscript," Sol said.

She has the book written by one of the people whose disappearance I'm investigating, and she only thinks about telling me that now!

"I see," he said, and he thought he was doing an excellent job at not losing his cool and sounding nonexasperated, which he was anything but. "And?"

"What do you mean *and*?!" It was clear that if he was making an effort not to escalate that conversation and remain not mad with her, she was not extending him the same courtesy.

"I'm sorry. Is there anything in the book?" he asked, trying to sound as civil as possible, given the circumstances.

"I've just skimmed through it, but Simon talks about Claudia in the book, and her less ethical habits."

"Like doing consulting jobs for studios even if she shouldn't?"

"Yes. If that gets out, not only could she lose her job, but her reputation as an editor would be ruined," Sol explained.

Claudia Hopkins was suddenly not only an extremely obnoxious editor with the ability of always importuning Luke, she had also found herself with motive for Simon Smith's disappearance.

"Anything else you may want to share?" Luke asked.

"I haven't had time to finish it yet!"

"Of course," he said, and he sounded furious, even if he didn't want to.

"I guess there went our two full hours of not being at each other's throats."

"Why don't we make it three hours of truce while we drive to Los Feliz, and we can go back to rowing once we're back in the discomfort of our old friend, the inflatable mattress," Luke said. This time he did sound as conciliatory as he was attempting to be.

"The problem is that there we don't argue," Sol said, her tone defeated. "We simply fume at each other in silent frustration. Plus, driving back to Los Feliz should be a breeze from here, not a full whole hour!"

"You wish, cara, you wish."

25

"I think Sol just forwarded me the list of critics Claudia made," Luke told Divya as he drove them to Travis Wise's apartment in Westwood the morning after the party at the Roosevelt Hotel. He handed Divya his phone so she could take a look at it.

Divya skimmed the list, scrolling over it a couple of times. "Simon Smith's name is there, as well as Jason Zit. But no other name sounds familiar."

"Can we trust the list, considering Claudia could have a reason to get rid of Simon herself?" Luke asked.

"We're still working under the assumption she never read the book, right? Not that many people did, really," Divya continued. "But we should definitely *not* forget about her."

"Going back to the list, why did Claudia include the name of an editor there? Jason was an editor, not a critic."

"Claudia made a note next to Jason's name: 'Interested in being a critic again. He thinks his talents aren't fully used as an editor.' It's such a pity Jason Zit is dead!" Divya sighed.

Luke's gaze flicked to Divya's face briefly before returning to the road. "I'm afraid to ask, but why?"

"Because he's perfect as the person behind Simon Smith's disappearance. Isn't he? He hated him, and apparently he wanted to do his job. Probably thought he'd do it better. But his death doesn't look like a suicide by chocolates to me . . ."

"Unless . . ." Luke said, because he liked where Divya's thought process was bringing them.

"We're dealing with two different cases," Divya finished his thoughts. "One person who made Simon disappear—and right now that person looks like Jason Zit. And a different one who poisoned Travis by mistake and then killed Jason. It's unfortunate that we can't talk to Jason and test our theory about him getting rid of Simon."

"Most definitely unfortunate, especially for him, as he's dead," said Luke, amused.

"Alright, alright, I get it. But can you really blame me for wanting to sort this mess out? The sooner we're done with the case—"

"—the sooner we go back home." Luke was already daydreaming about the first thing he was going to do when they were back in London. He'd probably have the strongest English breakfast tea, followed by a long walk by the Thames.

"No, mate. The sooner we get paid," Divya corrected him, bringing him back to reality.

"Is it that bad?" Luke asked.

"We've got no office, so at least there's no rent to worry about there. But unless we get some cash in soon, I've no idea how I'm gonna pay the rent on my crap little studio flat."

"I've been so wrapped up in the case and being away

that I've completely forgotten about the bills and rent. But I'm skint too," Luke said, and he marveled at how he'd managed to almost forget about it. It was as if the change of context and being away from home had made him forget about many details of his daily routine. Was that why people loved traveling so much, perhaps? Because it facilitated getting away and forgetting everyday life problems?

"Can you shack up with Sol? In a more permanent way, I mean. I know you sleep there almost every night," Divya said.

"I've been thinking about asking her to officially move in together but don't know how she's going to take it. Everything was so good between the two of us before coming here that I almost want to keep it just the way it was. And I don't want her thinking I'm only bringing the subject of moving in together up because I can't pay the rent," Luke reasoned.

"So we better solve this case—or cases—soon."

...

Luke liked Travis Wise. He was a nice man. Sol had told Luke only good things about her former colleague and all the ways in which he'd mentored her when they'd worked together. And the poor man had been poisoned just a few days before! But the detective resented Travis a bit right now, nonetheless.

The critic had been kind enough to see Luke and Divya at his apartment in Westwood to answer their questions. He'd even offered them tea, since the detectives were British and he thought that was the appropriate treatment. But was it necessary to serve a lukewarm cup of water heated in the microwave with a powdery tea bag next to it? Divya gave Luke a glare meant as a warning: He'd better dunk that tea bag in the water and drink whatever light-brown concoction came out of it. They needed Travis to talk to them.

The thing was, the journalist was eager to like Divya and Luke from the start, and he was eager to talk to them.

"I'm so sorry I couldn't see you before," Travis said. "I wasn't ready to receive anyone. I looked awful!"

The man was wearing a silk, short dressing gown over elegant wide-legged trousers, all in navy blue. His curly black-and-white hair was perfectly cropped. Luke doubted Travis Wise had looked bad a day in his life. But the detective also understood that the journalist had just undergone a very dramatic experience and hadn't been ready to talk—until then.

"I'm so glad you folks are looking into this," he said while his trembling fingers stirred the milk in his tea. "But I'm afraid I'm not sure I'll be able to be of much help."

"Why don't you tell us what you remember from that night," Divya started, and Luke saw that his partner's easy manners put Travis at ease.

"A very boring, very long show," Travis said. "Every year we complain that awards ceremonies are tedious, and every year we keep producing the same overinflated show. Fortunately, I wasn't reviewing the ceremony because I would have given it two out of five stars."

As Luke had taken out his notebook to start jotting things down, he thought it looked like *all* entertainment journalists tended to live in their heads and pretend the world of Hollywood was of the utmost importance to everyone—not just Sol.

"Did you eat or drink anything while you were at the show?" Divya asked.

"Lots and lots of bottled water, but no booze for me. I had an early spin class the following morning and wanted to be fresh for that. Been trying to lose a couple of pounds," Travis said, patting his waist. "Who knew what I needed wasn't a membership to SoulCycle and an iron will to achieve that but to be poisoned!"

Travis laughed nervously, and Luke decided to let Divya continue with the questions. He didn't want to add to the journalist's discomfort.

"Was that why you barely touched the food on your plate?" Divya asked.

"Yes, that, and I have a severe nut allergy. Not your typical Californian being picky with their food just to be difficult. But an *actual* allergy. My eyes get watery and itchy, my lips get puffy . . . I'd been reassured my food was carefully prepared and hadn't been in contact with any nuts. After two hours of the ceremony, I felt hungry and nibbled on some hummus and grapes," explained Travis. "Of course, I didn't have to worry about nuts, but cyanide!"

"And you didn't notice anyone approaching the table and adding some stuff in your food before you ate it?"

"I'd have noticed if someone did," Travis said with a reassurance that Luke couldn't help but question. In the chaos of a packed, hectic event like the awards show, it was easy to miss many things—even someone, stranger or not, slipping a few drops of poison into your food.

"Did you see anyone who may have been suspicious or out of place?" Divya asked.

"Everyone was either in black-tie and one of the guests or strictly dressed in black and working. But anyone dressed the right way could have easily sneaked in, I think," Travis said.

"I thought the security was a bit lax," Luke contributed, nodding in agreement with Travis. "Can I ask you about Victor Lago? He was seated at our table."

"He was, but I didn't see him anywhere next to my plate with nefarious intentions, if that's what you're asking." Travis laughed nervously again.

"And you have a good relationship with him? Never reviewed one of his projects negatively?"

"I doubt he even knows who I am, as I'm a lowly television critic and he's been very vocal about the superiority of cinema," Travis said, a bit dismissive.

"Doesn't Abbie Domingo work on TV?" asked Divya, confused.

"As if that would stop him from being a total snob. But I hear Abbie has finally kicked his ass to the curve and moved on. She deserves much better," Travis said.

"She does," Divya and Luke agreed in unison.

"I think Sol told me your review of *Slowing Down* was quite positive, but have you ever reviewed one of Abbie's other shows negatively?"

"Not that I can recall . . . She's one of my favorite showrunners. Why do you ask?"

"We believe you weren't the intended victim for the poisoning but are trying to tie all the loose ends," explained Luke.

"They didn't try to kill *me*?" said Travis. He stopped his teacup midair to his lips and spilled its contents all over his gown. He didn't seem to care—even if Travis Wise didn't look like a man who walked around with stains all over his clothes.

"We're quite certain you got handed the poisoned food by mistake, and someone else was the target," said Divya.

"You may think I'm crazy and completely selfish, but that would be such a relief!" said Travis, visibly shaken. He left the teacup on top of his coffee table, stood from the sofa where all of them had been seated, and started pacing up and down his living room. "I think I need a drink, and to hell with the fucking diet! Anyone else feel like a bourbon?"

Both Divya and Luke politely declined as Travis poured himself a generous shot.

"Here's to not being wanted dead," Travis said, and he downed the liquor in one swallow, then served himself a second glass. "Who was the poisoner trying to get, then?"

"Jason Zit," answered Luke.

Travis immediately drank the second shot when he heard that name, and he ended up coughing nervously.

"They really got him the second time. I read the article in the *LA Gazette* about his death. The police don't think it was an accident, right?" Travis said.

"It didn't look like an accident, no," Luke confirmed.

"Fuck!" Travis sighed as he collapsed on the sofa.

"We know this is hard, but from your professional perspective, is there a reason why Victor Lago would want any harm to Jason Zit?" Divya asked, tentatively, as she pried the empty glass of bourbon out of Travis's hands and placed it on the coffee table, next to the discarded teacup.

"Like in my case, I highly doubt Victor Lago had any idea who Jason was," Travis said.

"He was Simon Smith's editor when he wrote his review of *Haughty Horizons*," explained Luke, and he could see the shock in the journalist's glassy eyes. It looked as if Travis was having a full inner conversation with himself, parallel to the one he was having with the detectives. He was probably realizing what a lucky chap he'd been.

"No one cares about editors in our profession in that way!" Travis dismissed Luke's words the same way Sol had done when he'd run his theory by her. "They rarely get credit. Have you met Victor Lago?"

"Briefly," said Luke.

"He's a self-centered, pompous ass. But murder isn't his style. Lawsuits, on the other hand . . . He's sued Marquee Media, the company that owns *The Showbiz Reporter* and that owns the publication I worked for—and that is employing you folks. He's alleging neglect in the editorial oversight of *The Showbiz Reporter* as they defamed *Haughty Horizons*."

"Does he have a case?" asked Luke.

"Probably not, but he'll still try to make as much noise as possible and will get a few headlines. That's much more his style than actual cold-blooded murder—even by poison."

"What can you tell us about Claudia Hopkins?" Luke asked, although he wasn't sure that was a good idea.

Travis tried composing himself, arranging his silk gown and looking at the tea stain. "I can tell you that she fired me."

"Would you say making someone disappear under bloody circumstances is her style?" Luke had decided that was a perfect enough moment to also inquire about Simon Smith.

"The woman is ruthless and lacks any compassion, but she's the most squeamish person I've met. I've seen her faint at the office every time there has been a blood drive. And she's never even donated herself or gone anywhere near it!" Travis said. "Poison, on the other hand, could perfectly be her weapon of choice."

Luke was intrigued by that last part, but could he believe Travis's remark? Or was the journalist simply reacting to the fact that he'd been fired by the unsympathetic Claudia a mere few days before?

Luke and Divya talked to Travis for a few more minutes, making sure the journalist had recovered from the shock of learning he was never the intended target of a killer still on the loose. When they left the apartment building, Luke received a phone call he'd been expecting for a few days.

"Officer Tom Owens, thanks for calling me back," Luke answered. Even if he knew he shouldn't be irritating the police agent, he just couldn't avoid it.

"*Detective* Tom Owens," the policeman corrected him. "I'll admit I had no intention of returning your call. But something happened."

"Someone else died or disappeared?" Luke hadn't been able to shake the feeling that Sol could still be a target as there had already been three entertainment journalist victims in that case.

"Not that we know of," Officer Hunky Dory said, and Luke felt an instant relief. "But I expect you to report to me immediately if you find out something."

"Of course," Luke said. *As if.*

"Cool beans." Officer Hunky Dory seemed oblivious to Luke's somewhat irreverent tone. "This is more of a warning call."

"Warning call?" Was the policeman going to tell Luke he knew he had access to Simon Smith's manuscript? That he should have shared his findings about Claudia Hopkins's list, perhaps?

"Stay away from Victor Lago," Hunky Dory said instead. "He doesn't like you. He's a vindictive fellow and doesn't appreciate being accused of murder. He says you harassed him yesterday night and implied he'd been the one to poison Travis Wise and to make Simon Smith disappear."

"Really, and he could remember both those names and mine?" Luke said, chuckling—and relieved he'd been wrong in his presentiment about another journalist in trouble.

"Look, pal, I don't like you either. The only reason I tolerate you is because I know the media company hired you, but I still don't have to be nice to you. I talked Victor Lago out of filing a restraining order against you because that would be a lot of paperwork, and this case is already a bureaucratic mess. I'm buried in lab results, background checks, and the online clippings of three very prolific journalists because my boss believes the key to all this mess is in someone's writings. But stay away from Victor Lago," warned Detective Owens.

Luke grunted to signify he'd gotten the message. He'd been convinced Victor Lago was behind Jason's and Travis's poisoning incidents, but after talking to Travis and thinking about the case more objectively, he realized he simply didn't like Victor Lago because of how he'd talked to Sol. But he needed, once again, to leave his personal feelings aside and keep a cold mind for the investigation.

"You still there?" Hunky Dory asked Luke.

"I'm still here," Luke answered.

"So that you see that I am a good person, I'm willing to start that quid pro quo with a first offering. In exchange, I only ask that you think of me if you find anything that may help me in the case." Luke grunted again. He wasn't going to promise anything, but he still wanted to sound compliant. "The autopsy found cyanide in Jason Zit's system. He'd been poisoned with the same substance as Travis Wise."

"What about Emily?" Luke asked.

"The wife?" asked Owens, a bit confused, and Luke thought the detective still couldn't remember the names of all the people involved in the case. Was it that hard? It wasn't like it was such a great cast of characters. He was having more issues telling apart all the middle-aged journalist men.

"Yes," Luke said.

"We also found very small traces of cyanide in her body

when we did the labs. Apparently she'd eaten a small amount of what we think was the source of the poison. Not enough to kill her, but she was indisposed for a bit."

"And do you know the source of the poison?" asked Luke.

"I'm afraid you'll have to figure that out by yourself." Detective Owens chuckled. Little did he know, Luke had already done that. Thanks to Sol and her observational skills.

26

"Calm down, we'll be there in no time." Luke heard Divya talking on the phone as soon as he hung up with Detective Owens. He didn't like the tone of that sentence. Divya sounded distressed, and she *never* lost her cool.

"What happened?" he asked the second she ended the call. He had a very bad feeling.

"Sol rang me because you were on another call, and your number kept sending her to voicemail," Divya explained, and Luke really couldn't care less why his lover hadn't called him directly but had called his colleague. He wanted to know if she was okay. "She's just got a letter."

"A letter?"

"Someone left it at her friend's house, the place where you two are staying," Divya explained, and Luke was losing his patience. Why was she being so slow in telling him what he needed to know? What had happened to Sol?

"What does the letter say? Is Sol alright?"

"She's fine. She's at the friend's place, and she told me the friend and the husband are also there, and even the kid has taken the whole thing extremely seriously. He's been going through all the footage from the security cameras, trying to figure out who dropped the letter off."

"I love that kid!" Luke couldn't avoid saying. "What does the letter say?"

"*Stop sitting on your fucking ass and start reading Simon Smith's book*," Divya said, her face completely serious.

"What?"

"Apparently it's a very short letter that contains only that sentence."

"They want her to read Simon's book? Is there any direct threat of what would happen if she doesn't do it?"

"No, just those words."

"How does the letter writer know Sol has Simon Smith's manuscript? I didn't even know until last night!"

"Could someone have been following her and saw her leaving Jason Zit's house with the manuscript?"

Luke had told Divya that morning about the conditions under which Sol had come into possession of Smith's manuscript.

"Or could the killer have been watching Jason Zit's house, and they saw Sol leaving it, and now they're also onto her and she's in danger!" Luke's heart pumped exaggeratedly fast, considering he was simply standing in the middle of the street and not involved in any strenuous activity.

"It's weird though, innit?" Divya said.

"What is?" he almost barked, even if he didn't mean to be curt.

"We were at the point where we believed that Simon Smith's disappearance and the two poisonings were unrelated . . ."

". . . but now there's something else pointing to both cases possibly having something in common," Luke completed Divya's thought as they used to do while working on a case together.

"There's something that still doesn't completely feel right. I don't like it," Divya said, and Luke also had that feeling, just at the edge of his mind, telling him something didn't fit. He knew he needed to listen to that feeling to crack the case. It was how he'd cracked all the cases before that. But he wasn't paying attention to that feeling because there were other, more important things—like making sure Sol was safe.

"What I don't like is someone sending Sol letters, even if there's no direct threat in them. They're still telling her what she should do. I knew she shouldn't get involved in this bloody case, but the woman is the most stubborn person I've ever met!"

"Luke, mate, I know you're worried. I'm worried too. But she's alright. Breathe," Divya said. "I've never seen you like this."

"This city is doing my head in!"

"I don't think it's just that you miss London. You're worried," Divya said, compassion in her eyes in a way Luke had witnessed before when they were interviewing people in need of solace. He'd never before been the one to need that extreme kindliness from her.

"Of course I'm worried! She could be in danger, and it would be because of me. I know she's been trying to help me, us, with these bloody cases! We've been cross with one another for days, and now this happens! What if something had happened to her?"

"It hasn't," Divya told him, and that made him snap out of it. Sol was alright. Nothing had happened, but it could have.

He was just now starting to realize what would happen if

he ever lost her. Had he even told her how much she meant to him? He hadn't even told her that he loved her. It had been implied, but he'd almost felt Sol's reluctance to hear those words. As if her past two divorces prevented her from believing them ever again. So he'd preferred to not tell her that and just show his feelings and regale her with plenty of other words. He thought now that he was a complete fool, and he should be telling Sol, and everyone who listened, how much he cared for her, that he *loved* her.

"Are you alright?" Divya asked, taking him out of his inner thoughts.

"I am, yes," Luke said.

"Want me to drive?" Divya offered.

"Don't worry. One Brit driving on the wrong side of the road is enough. No need for you to also experience the sensation and be traumatized for life."

"Okay, mate, let's go see Sol."

"Let's," he said, and he had never wanted to see his lover more than at that moment.

...

Of course, what Luke hadn't predicted when he and Divya headed to Lola's place, was that he'd never have the chance to have a moment alone with Sol—and to tell her everything that was eating him up inside.

When they got to Los Feliz, Lola's family had rallied around Sol. Alex kept scanning the security footage and had promised Luke and Divya to send them anything he could find. Lola kept fussing and offering her friend hot tea and hugs. Luke had the feeling that both were equally comforting for Sol as they were for Lola. And Geoff, of course, was cooking a delicious dinner to make everyone comfortable and even invited Divya to join them. How Lola's husband had managed to roast to perfection a whole leg of lamb with carrots and sweet potatoes, Luke didn't know. There was even some apple galette for dessert.

"I think you should go back home to London," Luke told Sol when they were finally alone after dinner. Divya had left half an hour before, and everyone else had gone to sleep. Luke and Sol were now both brushing their teeth in the guest bathroom. He was wearing the pants from the black-and-green plaid flannel pajamas his family had given him for Christmas. Sol had claimed the notch-collar top.

"Wha'?" Sol said, her mouth full of toothpaste. "Why?"

"It would put my mind at rest."

"You seriou'?" she asked, still brushing.

"Very," he told her, and he was bracing for a strong reaction from her.

She simply finished brushing, rinsed her mouth, dried the few drops of water around her lips in a motion that he found both elegant and sexy, and looked him straight in the eyes through the mirror. Her eyes were feisty.

"It's not a matter of putting your mind at rest, though. Is it?" The remark was full of bite. "I *am* the one who got the letter. I am the one who should be trying to put *my mind at rest*," she added, turning toward him, no longer looking at him through the mirror but now meeting him face-to-face.

"We don't know who sent you that letter, and you could be in danger," Luke said through gritted teeth. He tried keeping his tone down; he didn't want to disturb the whole house. He also needed Sol to understand that this wasn't a game. She had to stop putting herself in harm's way. The sooner she was out of Los Angeles, the better for everyone— and the sooner he'd be able to finally stay focused and solve that case.

"I think precisely because I received the letter, it's quite clear that I am not in danger." She had the gall of trying to reason with him. "Think about it. One critic disappeared. Another one gets poisoned by mistake. The third one gets poisoned on purpose and dies. If I was also part of this line of tortured critics, something else would have happened to me. Something far worse than getting a rude letter."

He wasn't going to admit to her that her arguments were sound, and he'd probably have reached them himself if he'd been thinking clearly. But there was no way he was going to stay sharp with her there. He needed her gone. She was too much of a distraction.

"Please don't try and play detective, will you?" It pained him when he saw the hurt those words caused her. But he really wanted her out of danger. "You're no more than an amateur, pretending she knows what she's talking about. Dating a detective doesn't make you one."

"You fucking bastard," Sol said in a surprisingly measured tone. He knew she, too, didn't want to wake anyone up, even if, judging by her bulging eyes, she'd be screaming at the top of her lungs if they were alone. "Can you stop playing mind tricks to get rid of me? How many times do I have to tell you? I don't do overprotective men. I can't leave the fucking country, remember?"

Luke cursed under his breath. He'd forgotten about Officer Hunky Dory telling Sol not to leave until Jason Zit's death case was closed. He was completely unhinged and not thinking straight. What was worse, he'd enraged Sol, and it had been for nothing. Even if he'd managed to convince her to leave Los Angeles, which he knew now he had zero chances of achieving, she'd still not be able to do it.

"I know you're under a lot of stress," Sol continued, her tone icy. "And it's the middle of the night, so I won't be asking you to leave now. But you'll leave this house tomorrow morning. And you'll be on the mattress alone tonight. I'm taking the fucking couch, which I know is way more comfortable because I slept there before. I've been only sleeping on the fucking mattress with you instead out of fucking solidarity because we both didn't fit on the sofa. Don't." She raised her hand in front of her when he tried getting closer. "I'll call Divya tomorrow, because I have been reading that book, and I think I found something else— besides the allegations about Claudia. I'll tell her all about it. But don't even think about calling me or reaching out unless it's to fucking apologize. And *maybe* I'll think about giving you another chance."

And with that, she left the bathroom, leaving behind a hint of her intoxicating fragrance. Luke had really messed up.

27

The following day, he was knocking on Divya's door before seven in the morning.

"I blew it with Sol," he told his colleague and friend when she opened her door, fresh-faced and with her short hair still wet from the shower. Luke had to admit jet lag had at least one advantage: Divya was already up and ready.

"What now?" she told him, implying that he'd been blowing it with Sol for days. And he had.

"I told her to go back to London," he said as Divya let him inside, and he collapsed on top of one of the chairs in the hotel room, which may have been full of discarded clothes in varying degrees of cleanliness, but he didn't care. Fortunately, neither did Divya.

Divya breathed deeply, her eyes darting upward. "Let me guess, she didn't take it well?"

"She threw me out of her friends' house and told me not to contact her unless it was to apologize," he explained, raking his hand nervously through his messy hair.

"And what are you waiting for?" Divya said. She sounded a bit impatient.

"I can't apologize."

"Are you serious!?" She definitely sounded cross at him. "You can't tell a grown woman what to do, mate! And I can't believe that I am really having to explain this to you. I had you pinned for a feminist ally. I'm sure Sol had too. Not sure any of us would want *anything* to do with you otherwise."

"I still think she should go back to London. But even if she wanted to, which has been plenty clear to me she won't do if only to go against me, she still couldn't because of that stupid Detective Tom Owens!"

"So tell me again why you're not apologizing, then? She can't return to London, and it's out of your control and *her* control. And by the way, she already has one man telling her she can't leave the country. She doesn't need her partner telling her she has to leave it."

"I mean, when you put it like this!" he said, defeated.

"Luke, I really thought you were better than this." Divya sounded genuinely disillusioned. It was as if he'd let his favorite teacher down. "Men, mate. You always have to disappoint, don't you?"

Luke didn't like the sound of those words. He wasn't just *another man*, certainly not one who was simply a disappointment to women. His two sisters and his mom could vouch for that, right?

"Go on then, off you go back to Sol," Divya told him, as if realizing he'd finally seen his mistake and was ready to correct it. "Considering it's rush hour, it's going to take you a good hour to get there. Plenty of time to practice your apology. Because the first words you're going to tell that woman are, 'I'm an idiot. I'm sorry. I won't pretend to tell you what you have to do *ever again.*'"

"She won't want to talk to me yet. She's too mad. The only reason I'm not too worried that I'm not there is because the friend promised me they'd look after her and make sure she was safe. But Sol doesn't want me around," he tried reasoning, but Divya was already grabbing him by the elbow, ushering him to stand and leave.

"*'I'm an idiot. I'm sorry. I won't pretend to tell you what you have to do ever again,'*" Divya repeated as Luke was now in front of the room's door again and she was opening it. "She'll be happy with those words, to start with. You'll still have to do a full mea culpa after that and try explaining such a stupid lapse of judgment. But I trust you'll be able to figure out what else to say, right?"

Divya gave him a pointed stare. He'd better start saying the right things.

"Right," he muttered, still not completely sure what had happened. His colleague was already closing the door to her room on his face when he remembered something else that needed mentioning. "Wait, she told me she'd found something in Simon Smith's manuscript and is going to call you and let you know. Please pick up when she rings you."

"Luke, *mate*, since when do I not pick up the phone when it's Sol or anybody else?"

"I wasn't trying to tell you what to do." He put his hands up as if to plead blamelessness. "I was only giving you the last update on the case."

"Yes, yes. Off you go. Can't say I'm particularly fond of you at the moment."

Luke tried giving his colleague his best puppy-eyed expression in the hopes of regaining some of her sympathy. But as he was going to say goodbye and leave, he got a phone call.

"It's Marquee Media," he told Divya as he picked up the call and put it on speakerphone.

"Luke, good morning. How are you? Claudia Hopkins here." Luke recognized the unmistakable voice of Sol's former editor. "I know it's early, but I'm an early-morning person. My bosses wanted me to give you a call. They'd like to know if you have any updates."

And to think, he'd heard somewhere Americans weren't direct. It wasn't as if Claudia had actually asked him how he was doing and meant for him to give her an answer.

"So?" Claudia's impatient tone cut through the morning air as Luke and Divya looked at each other, interrogating themselves silently and deciding what they could offer.

"We had a very interesting chat with Travis yesterday," Luke said after a nervous, throat-clearing cough. "And we're almost prepared to confirm filmmaker Victor Lago had nothing to do with either the poisonings or the disappearance of Simon Smith."

"Pity," said Claudia, and she did sound genuinely upset. "It would have made for such a juicy story. The headline writes itself: *Has-Been Director Kills Editor, Makes Critic Disappear Because They Dishonored His Snoozefest of a Movie.* Or something like that. Shorter, of course . . ."

"Right," Luke said, and both he and Divya were rolling their eyes in disbelief. Luke's colleague seemed to be telling him, *Showbiz people, mate.*

"So." Claudia's tone changed to businesslike once again. "Victor Lago is out. Who's in? What else have you *sleuthed*? Is that even a verb?"

"I think it is," said Luke. "We're following several leads at the moment."

"Yeah, that won't do. You need to stop exploring and start wrapping this whole thing up," Claudia said, and it was as if Luke was having déjà vu. Every time he was entangled in some sort of Hollywood investigation, they reached a point when the client lost their patience and wanted things solved quickly. "My bosses at Marquee Media aren't happy. Between you and me, they're thinking about firing you if you don't come up with a culprit soon."

"Investigations take time. If they are unhappy, we can send an invoice for services rendered," Luke said, and he hoped the bluff in his tone wasn't audible. "But we know there's not simply one culprit."

"What do you mean?" Claudia asked, and her tone had turned from ominous to genuinely curious.

"We think Simon Smith's disappearance and the poisonings are unrelated."

Luke could almost hear the wheels turning in Claudia's brain.

"Interesting," she finally said. "I'm thinking how we could use this information."

"Use it?" Luke didn't follow.

"As I've said, Victor Lago as our man was the perfect story. And we need some sort of favorable story. My bosses aren't happy with so many of their employees at the media company biting the dust. They think it reflects badly on Marquee Media, which is why they hired *you*. But there can still be other ways of spinning this. One of my writers is going to be calling you in a few minutes. Would you be so kind as to answer their questions about the case?"

"You want to quote me in an article?" Luke asked. He'd never say so to Sol, but he didn't like talking to journalists. He still knew it was a necessary thing to do for certain high-profile cases. And the publicity they'd gotten from past cases had brought Divya and him some new clients. He still felt trepidation every time he had to speak to a reporter.

"Yes, we'll write something about the threat to the press when journalists are silenced," Claudia said, and Luke thought she was saying those words out loud as she thought them.

"Silenced for what reason?"

"Doing their jobs. Obviously! Can you think of something clever to say?"

"I'm sure I can come up with something." What was it that day that all women wanted him to say the right words but didn't appear sure he was able to do it?

"And leave Simon out of this, okay?" Claudia said.

"What do you mean?"

"I mean don't talk about him in the story. Even if Jason was an absolutely mediocre editor with not the best manners—the man would never remember anyone—he and Travis were still pretty well regarded in the industry. Simon, on the other hand . . ."

"Nobody seems to like him much," Luke said, almost as if to prove he wasn't such a simple man, after all, and could deliver what was being asked of him.

"Exactly. It doesn't suit our narrative of sympathetic journalists being censored. Let's leave him out, yes? You said the two cases weren't related, anyway."

Luke had said that, and he probably wouldn't have thought of mentioning Simon if someone had asked solely about the poisoning case. But being told not to do it made him feel queasy, nonetheless.

"You know Simon mentions you in his book, right?" Luke asked the editor.

"And I'm sure he only had awful things to say about me," Claudia deadpanned, and she sounded as calm as usual. "Tell me, does he have *good* things to say about anyone?"

He needed to ask Sol, but he had a suspicion that the

answer to Claudia's question was going to be no. When he hung up with Claudia, Divya didn't wait to let him know what she thought of the situation.

"I'll call Sol now and ask her whatever she found in the book. We need results soon. It sounds like we could find ourselves without a case unless we come up with something."

"Good idea," Luke agreed. There was no need to speak the words *And we really need the money*. They both were plenty aware of it.

"But you still need to go and apologize to her," Divya declared.

"Seriously? Shouldn't I be prioritizing the case? We want the client to like us and pay us—"

"We both know you won't be prioritizing the case if you're all worried because you had a row with Sol. Go talk to her, fix this, and then you can start thinking about the case."

"You're probably right," Luke conceded.

"You know I am, and you've finally started sounding reasonable and likable this morning," Divya teased.

Sol saw Divya's call as she was about to leave Lola's house that morning for an early Pilates class. She needed to do something other than fume about Luke, and nothing calmed her more than a good, strenuous activity like exercise—or sex, but that was not an option at the moment. Hence the early Pilates class.

"I was going to call you after my class," Sol told the detective, picking up the call.

"Good morning to you too," Divya answered, and Sol could hear the playfulness in her tone. "Did you sleep well?"

"You know perfectly well that I didn't," Sol said. "You

have that supersonic detective thing where you always know everything. You could probably hear the lack of sleep in my grumpy tone."

"Yeah, that and Luke was just here and told me what happened," Divya said. "The idiot is heading in your direction as we speak. Ready to apologize."

"Tell him there's no need. I don't want to see him." Sol tried sounding as unequivocal as possible, even if she wasn't sure she really didn't want to see Luke.

"He knows he really messed up," Divya continued.

"Because you told him," Sol said. She wasn't going to fall for that. She wasn't going to be convinced by Divya of how awesome Luke was.

"I did have to do a bit of explaining, yes. I'm so glad I'm not into men. They're all a bunch of troglodytic, immature, emotionally unavailable simpletons. I don't know how you stand him."

"I mean, he's not like that," Sol said, and why had she disliked those words so much when describing Luke? Wasn't she hating Luke at the moment?

"Isn't he now? Does that mean you're ready to forgive him?"

"Are you playing tricks with me?"

"I would never do such a thing!"

"I won't be here to listen to his apology, anyway. I have a class and then an appointment," Sol said.

"Are you taking safety precautions?" Divya asked, and Sol realized if it had been Luke who asked her that, she'd have called him an overprotective ass. But coming from another woman, it was endearing.

"Lola is running an errand, but she's picking me up after that, and we're both going together to Pilates. And then she'll drop me at the appointment. It's in Santa Monica, and

I'll probably grab an Uber from there. I'm sharing my phone location with her, so she'll know where I am at all times."

"Sounds good. Mind sharing your location with me as well?"

"Do you think it's really necessary?" Sol wasn't particularly big on privacy, but she was starting to feel not really independent with so much scrutiny in regard to her whereabouts.

"It would put my mind at rest," Divya said.

"You do realize the last time someone said those words to me, it didn't end well, right?" Sol fumed.

"Yes, but you'll still share your location with me because I'm not him."

"You're bossy!" Sol argued.

"I'm not, I just want to make sure you're alright while we investigate."

"Okay," Sol said as she put Divya on speakerphone and changed the settings on her device to share her location with the detective. "But only because you asked nicely."

"And because I'm not Luke," Divya said, and Sol hated that she was right. "Want me to tell him you won't be at Lola's?"

"No, let him look for me."

"Your wish is my command. But listen, believe it or not, I didn't call you to talk about Luke."

"Really?" Sol saw Lola approaching in her car and exited the house, heading in her direction. She jumped into the passenger seat and gave her friend an apologetic look as she kept talking to Divya on the phone.

"Really. He told me you'd told him you've found something in Simon Smith's manuscript."

"Oh, that," Sol said.

"Yes, that. Some of us still have a case to solve." Did the detective sound a bit flustered?

"It may be nothing, it's just the manuscript came with an acknowledgments section at the very end. I thought it was a bit odd. It's nothing you include at that stage in the writing process," Sol explained. "I read it mostly because it's one of my favorite things to read in books in general. It can be a window into a part of the author's life and their network of family, friends, and professional relationships. But unlike what happens in most books, Simon doesn't have a word of thanks for anyone."

"Charming."

"Very much in character. Plus, it almost sounds as if it was some sort of riddle." She reached for the last pages of Simon Smith's manuscript inside her bag and proceeded to read to Divya. "*I scorn the echoes of my final act. Think I'm silent now? Look past these lines. If you seek the truth behind this page. Look beyond death—beyond the final stage.*"

"Oh bloody hell! What's all that about?"

"I guess you didn't crack the riddle in one go then," Sol said.

"Of course I didn't. I'm good, but I'm not *that* good. Send me a picture of those lines, will you?"

"On it. And I'll let you know if I find anything else in the book."

"Good, and Sol," said Divya, and she sounded worried.

"Yes?"

"Be careful."

28

Even after fifty-five minutes of sweat, pain, and strength training, Sol was still furious with Luke. And she was furious at herself for giving him so much headspace. As if that wasn't bad enough, she wasn't exactly looking forward to her appointment in Santa Monica.

"You sure about this?" Lola asked her for the umpteenth time.

"I made you drive me all the way here. You bet I'm sure," Sol told her friend.

"I wouldn't mind if you changed your mind. We could go grab something sweet at Sidecar Donuts and have a chat about that eviction you forced at my place in the early morning," Lola said.

"Luke had been a total ass," Sol said defensively.

"I'm on your side, remember?" Lola said. "I'm just curious how you got mad at your perfectly supportive—and, let's not forget, extremely pretty—boyfriend and decided he needed to leave *my* house. But you're about to meet someone who we know for a fact is the total villain in this story."

"I hate it when you make so much sense," Sol said as the car approached the Palisades Park overlooking the Pacific Ocean in front of the Santa Monica Pier and as she recognized the person she was meeting. "Can you drop me off here, he's already waiting. I'll call you once I'm done, okay?"

"Okay. Don't forget to share your Uber ride link with me. And call me and tell me what happened!"

"Of course," Sol said, and she kissed her friend on the cheeks before getting out of the car.

As she saw Lola's car merging into traffic and getting farther away, her heart shrank. She felt a deep apprehension for what was coming ahead. She still knew she needed to do it.

She eyed the man she was meeting a few meters ahead. He was dressed in a tailored navy suit, and his dark-blond locks were perfectly styled. For the first time in almost four years, she surprised herself by having one thought: He was so good-looking. No wonder she'd married him.

"Ah you came. I thought you would stand me up," the man told Sol in a reproachful tone, and it was as if she was hit by a cascade of ice water. And that was it. She no longer saw any kind of attractiveness or felt any appeal. No wonder she'd divorced him.

"Nice to see you too, David," she answered, a smile plastered on her face.

"Is it really? Nice, I mean? I thought you hated my guts."

Sol had already been dreading the meeting even before getting there, but she now felt vindicated in her reluctance. It was going to be hell.

"You see, that was part of the problem. You're incapable

of even trying to appear mildly agreeable for the sake of peacefully co-living with someone else," Sol said.

"We're no longer co-living, in case you had forgotten," David told her.

She breathed deeply to appease her nerves and exasperation. There was no way she was going to make him understand anything. She hadn't achieved it during the ten years they'd been together. One conversation years after the worst divorce in the history of separations surely would not accomplish it.

"Actually, I don't understand how you could have forgotten about us no longer co-living. Aren't you screwing some British bimbo now?"

"Respectfully, none of your fucking business," Sol said. A smile was still on her lips even if her eyes were now murderous.

"No, no, no, no, ma'am. You made it my business when you gave your fucktoy my phone number, which I thought you had lost because you never answer my calls or texts!"

"Luke is not my fucktoy, he's my partner," Sol said, seething. And, of course, David knew she hated being called *ma'am* and did it anyway. "He needed help while investigating a case, and I naïvely thought you could assist him. I know it was a mistake. Your buddy Detective Tom Owens has been giving him the cold shoulder. I hope you're happy."

"I couldn't care less," David told her, and she believed him. It would have been easier to understand him if he'd been just jealous, but then again, David had never aimed for ease.

"What do you want, David?" she said, no longer smiling and in a tone that had sounded a bit hostile. But the idea of meeting had been his, and she wanted to know his purpose.

Also, she needed that rendezvous to be over. The sooner the better.

"The gloves are finally off. Happy to be with the real Sol. You know I never like it when you filter yourself."

It had been amply discussed between Sol and her closest friends that one of the things that had precipitated her toward divorce had been discovering David's tendency toward doing everything in his power to enrage her and then trying to spend as much time as possible with unfiltered, bitchy Sol. It was exhausting. So she breathed deeply again, reminded herself that he wanted to see her being mean, and made herself smile.

"The gloves are back on. I agreed to a fifteen-minute conversation, and the clock is ticking. Perhaps we could take a beautiful stroll along the park while we watch the views and you tell me what's on your mind," she said, and she didn't even know where that pleasant, fake persona had come from. But the important part was that she knew it did nothing for David. He got off on pissy Sol, not pleasant Sol.

After a few minutes of silent walking where Sol could guess all of David's frustration, he finally said, "You left me without giving me a second chance. I would have tried to make it up to you, but you decided it was over and left."

For the first time since she could remember, her second ex-husband, whom she had learned to despise, seemed not only inclined to have a civilized conversation about the reasons for their divorce, he even had said something that wasn't plain odious.

"I know I made a mistake," David continued, referring to the fact that when they were still married, he'd made Sol believe he'd had an affair with a younger woman with the misguided intention of rekindling their romance. "I wasn't cheating."

"I know."

"Then why?"

"I had stopped loving you," Sol said.

"I hadn't," he told her.

She was tempted to tell him that one of the parties still being interested wasn't reason enough to continue a marriage. She opted for something a bit more constructive in that situation: "Why don't we put aside all the bad moments and the bitterness and focus on the good moments we had? Because there were some great moments, remember?"

"There were," David admitted, and for an instant Sol thought that perhaps she'd been too harsh in judging her second ex-husband, and she felt guilty about it. Until he proved her right in her harshness and talked again. "So, is this how things work with ex-husband Number One? I know you're still all lovey dovey with Miquel. I wonder how the fucktoy takes that."

"David, you're exasperating!"

"Thank you, darling. I'm happy to see I can still elicit something in you."

"Can we at least try and be civil?" she asked, not ready to be riled so easily. "We spent a decade together, and I hate having to pretend it never happened just because I can't cope with how things ended. I think that's why you asked to see me today."

David seemed ready to reply with one of his sharp retorts.

"Don't," she told him, before David could say anything. "Just think about it. Let me know when you decide. I promise to unblock your number and answer the phone. But David," she warned, "unless you show some maturity and give me an acceptable answer, I'm blocking you right back. For good."

And with that, she left him standing in the middle of the park and walked away.

When Luke had first met Sol, he'd been assigned to a case where she'd been one of the suspects. He'd surveilled her for weeks without her knowledge. He'd fallen for her then. But he'd also felt like a total creep, stalking a woman who had no idea she was being watched and following her every move.

He was at present reliving all the dread from those days. By the time he'd driven back from Divya's hotel—while being interviewed by one of Claudia's journalists—he hadn't found Sol at Lola's place. The house had been empty. He'd called his colleague, who, after a bit of haggling on his part and his insistence that Sol could still be in a somewhat dangerous position, had finally disclosed Sol's whereabouts to him.

When he finally got to Santa Monica, he was ready to approach Sol on the streets of the busy coastal city and intone the wise words Divya had ordered him to say.

I'm an idiot. I'm sorry. I won't pretend to tell you what you have to do ever again, he kept repeating to himself in his mind like some sort of mantra.

He saw Sol getting out of Lola's car and was walking fast in her direction when he realized she was meeting someone else there. Sol's appointment in Santa Monica was actually a chat with David. Luke recognized the ex from some pictures she'd reluctantly shown him, and he crumbled under the discovery.

He stopped in his tracks and watched Sol from a distance while she had what looked like an extremely pleasant conversation with the man who'd been married to her. Could Luke have fucked things so gloriously with her that she was thinking about getting back with David? Was that why she'd been acting so distant since they had landed in Los Angeles? Was she garnering second thoughts and realizing she made a mistake when she left California—and David? And then she made another mistake when she started shagging Luke?

Of course not.

But why was he having all those absurd feelings? Since when was he insecure in his relationship with Sol? Since they'd landed in that bloody city, that's when. And why did Sol look so utterly pleased and enchanted with the ex? It was as if she couldn't stop smiling!

He got several texts from Alex then and was glad for the distraction. Anything would be preferable to watching Sol be delighted in the company of her ex-husband.

ALEX MARTÍN

sending a ton of screengrabs from the house sec cams

that's def the dude who left Sol's note yday

Luke opened the pixelated pictures Alex had sent with the texts and saw what looked to be a person of medium build and height, dressed all in black and wearing sunglasses and a cap. It was hard to see any distinguishable features or traits, but it was the person who'd left Sol the note urging her to read Simon Smith's manuscript. They could be seen delivering the note to the house in one of the images, slipping it into the mail slot by the front door.

A couple more messages from Alex arrived then.

Luke opened that last picture nervously and recognized the same person from the previous screengrabs.

"Fuck!" he muttered and started walking in Sol's direction.

He didn't care if he was going to interrupt a cozy chat with the ex; he needed to make sure Sol was safe.

But in his haste to reach her, Luke hadn't realized she was no longer standing in the same spot she'd been for a while and had already left David and started walking decisively in Luke's direction. It was only after she was almost on top of Luke that he grasped she'd been walking toward him.

"I'm so sorry," a distracted Sol, who was checking her cell phone, said when she almost crashed into Luke. It was as if an invisible thread had pulled them together, like the two opposing poles of a magnet. She then lifted her eyes from her device and recognized him. "What are you doing here?"

Before she could say anything else or realize that he had been following her, he blurted out, "I love you."

Sol stopped in her tracks and remained immobile in the middle of the street, her eyes wide open, her mouth agape.

"The only reason I haven't told you before is because I'm an idiot. I'm sorry," Luke continued, taking advantage of her being totally stunned. "I'm also sorry for pretending I had any right in telling you what to do yesterday. I just want to make sure you'll be fine. I'm terrified at the idea of something happening to you . . . because I love you."

After what felt like an eternity in which Sol remained

immobile, looking him in the eyes, her lips still parted in astonishment, Luke said, "Sol, I need you to tell me what you're thinking."

"I've been trying to say those words to you for weeks," she told him, her eyes not moving one millimeter from where they were pinning his.

"What words?" he asked, even if he knew the answer.

"I love you."

"Why didn't you?" he said, a smile tugging at his lips.

"Because I'm the idiot here. Because I've been hurt too many times. Because I didn't want to say those words ever again and then have to take them back."

"Let's make sure we don't ever have to take them back then," he said, and he could see the emotion in her when she heard him.

"I've just had a somewhat unpleasant conversation with the most obnoxious of all my exes, and I really never want to have a chat like that with you," she told him. If it wasn't because he'd never seen her crying, he'd say her eyes were welling up. "Ever."

"We won't." And that was a promise. "But as happy as I am about this turning point in our relationship, we need to leave."

"What do you mean, we need to leave? I thought you were gonna kiss me and sweep me off my feet!" she complained.

Luke couldn't contemplate that possibility for even a second as he was receiving a new message from Alex that he didn't want to ignore.

"Are you seriously checking your phone *now*?" If a second ago, she'd told him that she loved him, she sounded like garnering completely opposite feelings at present.

"Please, let's not row five seconds after we've said I love

you," he told her, his eyes still on his cell phone. He grabbed her arm to start moving. "I promise to kiss you and be my most deviously charming self soon. But we need to move."

"What is going on?" she protested as they both walked at a brisk pace.

"Is there any other friend whose generosity we could abuse?" Luke asked. "I think it's better if we don't go back to Lola's home."

Sol looked at him intently for a few seconds. Then she grabbed her phone and made a call.

"I know exactly where we're going. Forget that it's going to be a fortune. I should have tried moving us there days ago!"

29

"Anytime now would be fine," Sol told him the moment they had closed the door to their suite overlooking the ocean at Casa del Mar. She sensed Luke's shoulders relaxing.

"Thanks for getting us a room," Luke teased her.

"That goes directly to the Sol Novo Trust as an emergency expense. But I didn't mean that." She scrunched up her nose in exasperation. "What the fuck is going on? What were you doing, following me?"

Luke made a face, trying to deny the accusation, but she cut him off.

"Shush." She took her right index finger to his soft lips. "I *know* you were following me. I'd also like to know why we couldn't go back to Lola's."

"Other than the fact that we've needed to be alone in a space outfitted with four walls and a bed *for days*?"

His tone was pure insinuation, and she knew he was doing his best to make her questioning hard. He wanted her to give up, but she wouldn't, even if it was almost impossible to ignore how hot he looked with that sexy smile on his face and those hungry eyes that kept eyeing her like the most delicious prey.

"Yeah, other than that," Sol said, trying but not completely succeeding at playing it cool. "Everything I have, which isn't much because my suitcase is still missing, is at Lola's. We have absolutely nothing with us here."

She was slightly preoccupied about her skin care routine, even if she knew she probably had more important things to worry about. But then again, she was forty-three. It wasn't as if she had the luxury of any oversight when it came to sunspots, wrinkles, and dryness.

"I think we have exactly everything we need here," Luke said, his voice velvety, his arms around her waist, and his fingers already under the sweater she'd borrowed from him, tracing a descending line from the small of her back directed to her ass.

She needed to intervene.

"As much as I want, *and need*, this to happen," she said, reluctantly intercepting those rogue fingers on her body and stopping them, "I need you to start talking first."

"You need me to start talking *more* than you need *this*?" he whispered in her ear as he urged her against the wall, one of his legs pushing between hers.

"You're making this extremely difficult," she said, relaxing against his touch and letting his lips caress her neck and shoulders. Just feeling his breath on her skin made her shudder. "Okay, I surrender," she said, allowing her eyelids to close and her body to simply feel.

"Are you sure?" His voice alone could make her tremble.

And it wasn't lost on Sol that he'd said those words in his huskier tone, after unapologetically getting her out of his sweater, and with his lips trailing a path of utter heat and destruction on her upper body.

"Your mouth is already on one of my nipples, and that hand you've so masterfully gotten under my leggings is headed in one direction." She whimpered all the reasons she was sure she was his to do as he pleased.

"It could technically be headed for more than one place. But yeah," he told her as he pinched her nipple with his lips, her clit with his fingers.

"I can't think rationally," she said. No, she moaned.

"So how do we want this to go on, then?" he asked because, of course, he'd guessed she had requests. He knew her that well.

"I know you're going to have objections. But I really need this to be *fast*," she said, and while Luke started groaning, she interrupted him. "Don't complain, Luca. You've already managed to get the order in which things are happening altered. We're fucking first—and talking after."

"Can we shag first, do all the talk you seem to need after, *and* make slow unhurried love after that?" He looked at her with a raw yearning in his eyes.

They were so close to the ocean that she could hear the sound of the waves washing against the Santa Monica coast. She could even smell the saltiness of seawater in the room. Or perhaps it was Luke's labored breathing that she was smelling. His fragrance had always reminded her of the sea.

She didn't reply. Not with words. She simply returned his stare. *Whatever you want.*

He looked at her with eyes that said *Your rules* and then he took his T-shirt off. His smirk never left his lips.

If asked about it before meeting Luke, Sol would have said that after so many months into a relationship, she'd see herself immune to many of the charms in a lover. That wasn't the case with him.

Her heart still skipped a beat and raced ahead, her face blushed, and she felt the need to fan herself every time he stripped. She was ashamed to admit that she'd probably only felt that deeply hot and enthralled by someone's body walking among Greco-Roman marble sculptures depicting athletes, and the time in Florence when she just couldn't take her eyes off Michelangelo's *David* and didn't leave the Uffizi Galleries for hours.

Luke was breathing, moving, human marble sculpted to perfection—or at least to some of Sol's ideals of what a male body had to look like: athletic and slender, toned but not bulky, olive-skinned, and with a few dark hairs grazing his chest. And he was completely aware of the effect he had on her. He took his pants off next, and she allowed her eyes to drink in all his beauty. But he was still not completely naked. Her eyes searched for his, slowly traveling down his body until stopping on his boxers, arching her eyebrows in urgent demand.

His smirk grew even more pronounced, and he took the garment off.

She bit her lower lip, allowing herself one glimpse at his erection and proceeding to also undress.

"I can help you," he told her, moving closer and leaning forward over her as her back was still against the wall. The saltiness in his smell hit her even harder.

He unclasped her bralette first, his forehead glued against hers, his chestnut eyes on Sol's, his lips hovering a few millimeters from her mouth. His left arm firmly clasped around her waist.

"You're gonna kill me with the fucking anticipation," she told him in between breaths as the fingers of his right hand traced her collarbone, the lines of her shoulder, pulling down one of the straps of her bra, then the other. Slowly uncovering her breasts completely and getting rid of the garment.

You need to start taking the need for fastness seriously, she almost complained, but she didn't as he kneeled in front of her, pulling down her leggings and thong and tossing them aside. When he took his mouth between her legs and indulged her clit with the urgency she required, she arched her back against the wall. Her eyes closed. One of her hands went to his tousled hair, and the other one searched the wall for balance—her legs were starting to feel wobbly. She loosened and got lost in the utterly sensual position.

"As much as I missed this," Sol whimpered after what

had felt like an instant of bliss but she was sure it had been actual minutes, "I need more."

"So bloody impatient!" Luke grumbled and started standing up, his tongue tracing a hot, wet line along her body in his ascent.

He grazed her hip bone with his teeth, explored her belly button, tasted the whole contour of her breast, and licked the most sensitive area at her neck and behind her earlobe.

He kissed her lips then, his body pushing into her against the wall.

When she finally came up for air, her mouth disentangling from him momentarily, she decided to voice her complaint—even if there was no dissatisfaction but simply the urge to mess with him.

"Too much, "she started as he bit her lower lip and pulled at it, "fucking foreplay," she continued in a laborious exhale. And she knew she was moaning, partly because those lips of his were lighting her skin on fire. But mostly because two of his fingers were relentless, taking turns against her clitoris and inside her.

He smirked at her remark. "Liar."

And, okay, perhaps she'd been a bit deceitful, but she loved provoking him when they were fucking.

"Turn around," his smokey voice told her.

"Finally," she sighed and could hear his protesting snicker as she turned and his greedy hands clasped at her hips, pulling her ass against his body.

She reached behind her, finding his cock and bringing it to her opening. As he sank inside her, they both cried out in pleasure.

"Harder," she pleaded. He thrusted inside her again,

pressing her against the wall, and she felt him deeper this time.

His fingers circled her clit, and she felt rapt. Her eyelids dropped, and she simply—felt. Luke's breath on her neck, his chest raspy against her back, his cock plunging against her in a delirious, intoxicating rhythm.

Right then, pinned against a wall in one of her favorite hotels in the world, she would have had difficulties answering common questions like what was the name of said hotel, what she did for a living, or where she lived. She would fail at telling someone her name even.

Because then, she was just a woman getting exactly what she needed most at the moment from her lover, in the most delicious, unrelenting way.

"Voy a—" she started saying, and the first notes of release had her screaming.

"Posso sentirlo," he said, his lips on her ear, a chill racing down her spine. And she could hear his pants—and the smile on Luke's lips.

As they both orgasmed, rammed against the wall, Sol couldn't help but realize she'd never been so thoroughly fucked in Los Angeles.

"So much for needing a bed, eh?" she told him while he rested his forehead on her shoulder, his lips already kissing her there.

"But we definitely needed the walls, cara," he said, and they both started laughing.

...

"Is this the moment when we talk, then?"

"Should we do relationship or case chat first?" he answered. They lay in bed, naked, facing each other, their legs intertwined, their profiles aligned—noses touching, lips practically meeting. She was well aware that he'd managed to modify yet again the order in which things had happened. Since fucking against the wall had been followed by some slower-paced lovemaking on the bed.

"I thought you were going to keep pretending like I wasn't involved in the case and just keep me in the dark," she said, only slightly reproachful, as her fingers traced the outline of his collarbone.

"Since when have I kept you in the dark? You've managed to inveigle yourself into plenty of my cases whether I've liked it or not," he said, searching for her eyes.

"Please. It's just been two cases, and in the first one it was you who implicated me." Her hand had moved to play with the dash of hair on his chest, tickling him.

"Let's not row again," he pleaded.

"Agreed." She sighed. "Why were you following me?"

"I wasn't following you. I wanted to find you and apologize. I needed to mend things. And then Alex texted me pictures of the guy who delivered that letter for you yesterday?"

"The one saying I should stop sitting on my ass and read Simon's book?"

"Same guy was lurking near the house again this morning," Luke explained.

"Oh my god! Are they going to be okay? I need to call Lola!" Sol sat up and searched around for her clothes and phone.

"Relax, they're alright. Alex texted me right before we checked in at the hotel. They were all at the house, tucked in for the day, ready to watch a movie. Geoff, of course, was cooking something that sounded delicious." His words relaxed her a bit. He'd also sat up and reached for her searching hands, enclosing one of her wrists in his fingers and trying to appease her.

"And what happens tomorrow?" she said, turning to face him.

"Let's worry about right now. We don't even know if the mystery delivery person is dangerous." Luke tucked a strand of her disheveled hair behind her ear.

"It must've been worrisome enough for you to have us promptly moved out of Lola's place!" she objected.

"That was just an excuse to get you finally alone and naked."

Even though she knew he was turning up the charm to the fullest to soothe her, it was still working.

"Did Mystery Delivery Person leave another message for me today?" Sol asked.

"They did," Luke admitted. "Alex also sent me a picture of that."

He stood from the bed, finding his cell phone inside his discarded trousers on the floor. She followed his every move while he was doing it, not because she was anticipating whatever the new message said, but because she liked watching Luke's elegant moves—especially if he was naked.

"*Done any fucking reading yet?*" he read from his cell phone. "*Don't be afraid to skip a few chapters.* Any idea of what they bloody mean?" Luke asked her, visibly confused.

"I think I do." She bit her lower lip. She loved it when she was able to surprise him.

"One, that's *very* sexy," he said, still standing on the other side of the room. "Two, please tell me."

"I'm sorry, but I've been told I can't get involved in this case," she said, crossing her arms over her chest and trying her best at seriousness.

"You've got to be joking me!" He groaned.

"Uh-huh, I have a very stubborn partner who thinks I must stay away from all this investigating business. Apparently, and I'm quoting here, I'm an amateur and *dating* a detective doesn't make you one," she continued, running her fingers through her hair and sweeping it to one side to look sexier.

Luke groaned again in a mix of regret and anticipation. She knew he wanted to know what she'd figured out about the case. But there was something Sol wanted first.

"Please don't hold my foolishness against me. I didn't mean what I said yesterday. I just wanted you safe and stupidly thought that was a good strategy," he said.

"So you're ready to admit that you were a total ass," Sol said.

"An idiot. An arse. Someone who most definitely doesn't deserve you."

"Okay, okay. Don't overexaggerate. But I'm going to need you to sweet-talk me. A lot."

He returned to the bed, grabbed her waist, brought her back against the mattress, and pressed himself on top of her, brushing but not quite touching her neck with his mouth.

"We said we'd talk *before* the lovemaking. In the end it was the other way around," she whispered. "And now you're trying to make me lose focus *again*."

"This is no lovemaking attempt. This is sweet-talking and me trying to extract information from you. Information that you clearly want to be tortured for," he said, grinding his hips against her body. His tongue took a slow, thorough trip along the length of her neck.

"Okay, okay, okay," she gasped. "You win. Let's wrap up this conversation quickly."

"Gladly," he said, rolling to his side and propping his head over his muscled, flexed arm.

"There was no need for the whole pinning me down and tortuous neck play since I've already divulged the information you're so interested in."

"Huh?" Luke asked.

She had to admit that toying with him was fun. Plus, a confused Luke was an even sexier-than-usual Luke.

"I had a chat with your work partner this morning, remember?" Sol said. "I told her about what Simon wrote at the very end of his manuscript."

When Luke returned a blank stare, Sol continued talking. "I guess she still hasn't told you about that since you were probably pestering her so that she'd give you my location . . ."

"What does Simon say in the book, Sol?"

31

"Can somebody please explain the need to go bloody sock-less in January! It's rainy. It's not even that hot today!" Luke grumbled as he saw a man dressed in a paradoxical mixture of a woolen hat, down jacket, shorts, and clog Birkenstocks with no socks. He was walking an enthusiastic, tail-wagging golden retriever.

"I reckon you should eat," Divya said.

They sat side by side inside their rental car, parked a few houses down from Lola's home and hoping for a sighting of Mystery Delivery Person.

"Here y'are, mate—take some of these," Divya said, handing Luke the half-full packet of milk-chocolate Cadbury Fingers she'd been eating. "If you are feeling summat healthier, there are pistachios and chia seed crackers in my backpack."

"Chia seed crackers?" Luke argued in disbelief. "California's a bad influence on you."

"I can't wait to be back in London!" Divya grumbled.

"Me neither." Luke sighed in agreement while eating a

biscuit and keeping his eyes trained on Lola's house across the street.

"Oh, I know, believe me," Divya said. "But the reason I can't wait to be there is so you stop being a pain in my arse!"

"Alright, fair enough," Luke admitted.

"Looks like we're gonna be stuck here for a while, so how'd that chat go with Sol, then? Did you tell her you're an idiot?"

"I did," Luke said. Why did he have the feeling that his colleague and friend was enjoying herself at his need to admit his shortcomings?

"Good on ya! And I take it she forgave you?"

"I'm very persuasive." Luke flashed a smile at her.

"Don't get cocky. You've forgotten all about how to be persuasive since you landed in Los Angeles," Divya admonished him. "I think both me and Sol are losing our patience with you."

"Sol doesn't have any patience," Luke said. "Never has."

"You made my point. Tread carefully with that newfound grumpiness of yours."

"Told you I saw her talking with the second ex-husband yesterday?"

"You didn't," Divya said, and as she did, she turned to face him. Her interest was piqued.

"Not sure what they talked about. One thing got to another yesterday, and then she told me about that bloody riddle. And here we are," Luke said. He felt relieved just by having shared his worries with Divya. "Never asked her about the ex. Not sure if it's a good idea to do it . . ."

"Considering what she's told me about him, she's as interested in him as she is in having someone sneak into her place and steal all her clothes. And we both know how attached she is to all the contents in her closet."

"You're telling me not to worry," Luke said.

"Aye, that, and stop being so grouchy and go back to your usual charming self. You're prettier when you smile."

They went back to a reflective silence while they both munched on biscuits and chia seed crackers, which Luke had to admit were actually not bad and—according to the nutritional label—packed five grams of protein per serving.

"Does that look like Mystery Delivery Person to you?" Luke said after a few minutes pondering the surprising nutritiousness and taste of Californian snacks. He pointed to a pedestrian advancing in the direction of Lola's house.

"Same height, same build. Wearing black trousers, black sweater, black cap, and the most hideous sunglasses. It could be them," Divya said, her eyes traveling repeatedly from the street to the picture on her cell phone in front of her. "Unless you're a celebrity, no one wears ultra-skinny early-2000s-style sunglasses anymore. And they hardly look like an It Girl."

"Same glasses they were wearing yesterday and the day before," Luke said. He was also checking the pictures Alex had sent.

"Should we have a chat with our Mystery Delivery Person, then?"

Divya and Luke got out of the car and crossed the residential street, heading in Mystery Delivery Person's direction.

"Hey, mate, can we have a chat?" Luke asked when the cap-wearing, letter-delivery person was a mere couple of meters away. But that was exactly when they started running.

"Not bloody again," Luke muttered under his breath as he bolted after Mystery Delivery Person. Divya was already ahead of him, always the most explosive runner of the two of them.

Fortunately, Mystery Delivery Person didn't seem to be in as good shape as surfer chap Vinny Green had been. The letter writer started showing signs of tiredness two houses down the street. Divya and Luke crashed into him at the edge of Lola's neighbor's front yard, the three of them tumbling into a hedge. As Divya pinned Mystery Delivery Person down, Luke yanked off his cap—and exchanged a glance with Divya. They knew that face.

"We've been looking for you all over town." Luke gave the sweaty runner a smug, knowing look. The detectives weren't even panting. It had been a short, easy run, and Luke suddenly felt happy and decided he was in good shape after all.

...

"So, guess who's not only *not dead*, but he didn't even really disappear?" Luke told Sol. She was his first call after the conversation with Mystery Delivery Person and a brief pit stop at Lola's house. Luke wanted to let Sol know there was nothing to worry about.

"Let me guess. Simon Smith?"

"Same. Divya and I just talked to him. He assured us he never meant any harm to you or Lola's family. I already talked to them to let them know all is good and no more mysterious people would be delivering strange messages to their home. Alex sounded a bit disappointed, to be honest. I think he liked playing assistant to the investigation."

"I'm sure he'll find something else to do! And I'm so glad everyone is okay," Sol said, and she sounded relieved. "What are you doing with that information now? Are you going to tell Officer Hunky Dory?"

"We're going to talk to Marquee Media first, which basically means calling Claudia, as she is our intermediate. We'll let her know that at least part of the case has been solved. And we'll go from there. I'm glad she's no longer a suspect now that we figured out she had nothing to do with Simon's disappearance. Because it was weird to be feeding her updates while fishing for possible clues," admitted Luke.

"She's going to want to publish something juicy about this," Sol said, and did she sound excited about the idea?

"What? No! That would be crazy. And why do you sound so thrilled about it?" Luke asked.

"It would be great publicity for the agency, obviously."

"Your mind works in very bizarre ways when you're in your journalist mode." Luke chuckled. "But, sadly, I need to let you go. I just wanted you to know you're safe."

"I already knew that," Sol said.

"Well, I didn't. Or at least I wasn't sure, and I'm so relieved to finally have that sorted out. Let me ask you something. What would you have felt if I was the one getting mystery messages from a possible murderer?"

"I'd be terrified," Sol said, and Luke could almost hear her thinking on the other side of the phone. "And I may have asked you to ditch whatever case you were investigating—Shit!"

"I'm not sounding like such a total arse all of a sudden, eh?" Luke said.

"Shush! You're still not off the hook and have plenty of sweet-talking to do," Sol protested.

"And I'll gladly do it. Sweet-talking you is one of my favorite pastimes." His tone was honeyed. "But I guess I managed to make myself look a little bit more charming now that you understand better the reason behind my misguided actions?"

"You've always been charming," she said. "Now go and call Claudia. And Luca—"

"Yes?"

"Don't be late tonight. We have a lot of catching up to do."

And with that promise, he hung up and couldn't suppress a smile. Was it possible that, for the first time since landing in that car-centric, hostile-to-pedestrians, obsessed-with-seasonal-vegetables, Hollywood-fascinated, beauty-venerating metropolis, he was happy? Why shouldn't he be? They'd just cracked part of the case, the client should be satisfied, they would get paid, and—most importantly—he and Sol were flirting on the phone again.

He went back to the car, still smiling. He found Divya already inside. She was most definitely turning into a total Californian and doing some frantic typing on her phone while drinking a giant iced coffee with a straw.

They called Claudia from the car, but Luke took care of the conversation since he'd been the one to talk to her from the beginning—and Divya had expressed her desire not to have to deal with the snappy editor.

"Luke, I'm terribly busy," the editor answered her phone with a too-important-to-deal-with-you-right-now tone, and Luke finally understood why Sol was so adamant about not wanting to work with her as a manager again. She wasn't exactly the nicest person, even if she pretended otherwise. He also understood why Divya was happy letting him take care of that conversation.

"You requested results, and we are ready to deliver," he said.

"Finally! Hold on a second," she told him and then

proceeded talking to someone else. "*No, not there! Over there! Careful. Careful! Those are some Heath Ceramics vases, and I don't want them smashed!* Sorry about that, a package is being delivered, and of course *I* need to take care of everything. Tell me about the case. My bosses will be thrilled."

"We know what happened to Simon Smith," Luke said, feeling bad for whoever had delivered that package and had just been yelled at.

"An overzealous fan of *Haughty Horizons* and Victor Lago's filmography kidnapped Simon and is asking for a retraction of his review or they'll start cutting his fingers off one by one so that he's never able to write again," Claudia said.

Luke wasn't sure if the editor was joking or if that had been her hypothesis all along.

"I'm afraid it wasn't that," Luke said.

"Don't tell me he did something foolish!" said Claudia.

"Depends on what you mean by *foolish*," Luke said. "My colleague and I just talked to him twenty minutes ago. He's perfectly fine. No one kidnapped him. All his fingers seemed intact—not that missing a few would stop him from writing. He basically faked his own disappearance—"

"Oh my god! This is genius!" Claudia interrupted him, laughing.

"Do you want to know why he did it?" Luke asked while he and Divya exchanged a look of incredulity.

"Oh, but I know why he did it!" Claudia said, and the laughing evolved into some sort of cackling. "Fame, of course!"

"He told us he faked the whole thing with the hopes of getting some articles written about his, and I quote, *mystifying enfant terrible persona* and that it would result in the publication of his book."

"Genius!" Claudia continued, and she was certainly not having the reaction either Luke or Divya had anticipated.

"But with the poisoning of Travis Wise and then the death of Jason Zit, the headlines have been elsewhere," Luke continued explaining. "And Simon felt left behind. He didn't like the article you published yesterday with my quote in it and absolutely no mention of him. So he decided to be proactive and sent anonymous notes to Sol."

"What does Sol have to do with this story?" Claudia sounded surprised for the first time in the whole conversation.

"She managed to get her hands on a copy of Simon's unpublished manuscript," said Luke. And why did he feel weirdly proud about his partner—not his professional one but his romantic one—for being extremely resourceful in the resolution of a case? "There's a riddle written in the book that Simon left with the hopes of readers suspecting that he wasn't actually dead *dead*. And Sol found it."

"So he's sour at Travis for being poisoned and Jason for being dead and decides to accelerate the process and make the announcement that he's not actually disappeared by sending notes to Sol. I love it!"

"Right. My colleague and I are drafting the full report, but do you want to inform your bosses while we do the same with the police?" He wanted to at least wrap up that part of the case soon.

"The police?" Claudia said, as if the concept of talking to the legal authorities sounded completely preposterous and bizarre.

"We can hardly hide this from them, as they have an open investigation on Simon Smith's disappearance," explained Luke.

"Oh, okay, okay. Can the sharing of information with the

authorities be put on pause for, let's say, a couple of hours? We need to get an article about this story published ASAP, and I don't want to get scooped by a competing outlet," Claudia explained.

These people!

"Are you sure about giving it this kind of publicity? This is exactly what Simon wanted when he started this ruse," Luke said.

"But it's such a well-crafted ruse! The headline—"

"I know, it writes itself." Luke sighed. And he didn't even try to persuade Claudia any further, because the truth was that Divya and he could not only use the money resulting from that case but also all the publicity. Of course, Sol had been right, and he'd have to let her know.

While Luke was having a surreal conversation with editor Claudia Hopkins, Sol was dialing the number of editor Julie McQueen. The Londoner picked up after two tones.

"You found Simon?" the editor answered. Fortunately, Sol had much better news than the last time the editor had used that line on her.

"I mean, I didn't, but Luke and Divya did. I helped a bit, though," Sol said. "But Simon is well."

"Sol, hon. That's such a relief. So what happened to him? He got the director from one of the movies he's trashed over the years to drug him and keep him in their basement while they force fed him brussels sprouts and chicken liver, right?"

"That's weirdly specific, but no." Sol realized she didn't exactly know how she was going to deliver the information. She'd never done well when it came to empathy. "He pretended to disappear in an attempt to get publicity and get his book published."

"Oh, the rascal!" Julie laughed.

Sol couldn't believe what she'd just heard. "Rascal? Aren't you upset that he had you worried sick and nothing happened to him?"

"I'm glad nothing happened to him, hon."

"Of course you are, but still, aren't you infuriated?"

"I mean, it's just such a clever plan. Don't you think?" Julie continued. "And I see now that I may have been crucial to its whole development. I was the one to insist from the beginning that something had happened to him. I'm sure he counted on my friendship, and my tenacity, to stir some trouble."

"When you put it like this . . ." Sol said. Maybe she really had tried to empathize and see things from Julie's perspective. Or maybe she'd just been working too long in an environment where all kinds of publicity could be seen as good publicity. Either way, she thought Julie was right.

32

"**O**fficer Tom Owens?" Luke had called the number of the detective in charge of Simon Smith's disappearance.

"*Detective* Tom Owens," a frustrated Hunky Dory told Luke.

"Luke Contadino here. I thought you'd be interested in some of that quid pro quo."

"If you called to tell me that Simon Smith is not dead, I've already read the article at *Performance Weekly*, thank you very much, buddy."

"It looks like your boss was right, after all," Luke said. "The key to some of this mess was in someone's writings."

"The fucking book," Owens said.

"Look, I called because the *Performance Weekly* article didn't mention all the details. But if you're not interested in some friendly exchange of information, I can just hang up and let you go back to your open investigations." He was only slightly bluffing. There was some minor information he'd give Owens, but he needed the detective and couldn't afford not getting access to whatever he had.

"Hold on a second. What details?" Hunky Dory sounded mildly nicer.

"Well, he obviously staged his own kidnapping or whatever the scene at his flat was supposed to imply," Luke started.

"The lab results for the blood at his apartment came back as a mixture of corn syrup, food coloring, and cocoa powder. It's the kind of ingredients used by practical effects and makeup teams in movie sets," Hunky Dory explained, and Luke thought that the whole thing sounded preposterously Hollywood *once again*. "So we were a bit puzzled by that."

"Yes, his intention was never to be believed completely dead but to surround himself with lots of mystery and get himself a book deal and some headlines out of it," Luke explained.

"I would have preferred not to have been sent on the wild goose chase of a missing journalist when there were other, more important things to investigate. But I'll be glad to mark this whole thing as solved," Hunky Dory said, a hint of frustration in his tone. "Any chance you know where we'll be able to find Simon Smith? I'd like to have a friendly chat with him. Don't want him getting any ideas and pulling another fake disappearing act in case he doesn't get to sell the screen rights of his book—which I'm afraid he might."

"That's why I'm calling you, actually. To tell you his whereabouts. He's not home. He got it into his head that the press are going to be looking for him there," Luke said, and he sighed. "So he's booked himself at a place called Chateau Marmont because he told me he was feeling like entering his celebrity era. If that makes any sense to you . . ."

"I guess you need to be an Angeleno to get it," Hunky

Dory said. "Thanks for the information. Tracking him down has proven *not* easy. And I want to put that case to rest, for good."

"No problem," Luke said and then proceeded to state the real reason behind his call. "So how's the Jason Zit investigation going? Any leads? We heard he may have been seeing someone—"

"The girlfriend rumor?" Hunky Dory asked, and Luke was glad the detective seemed to have warmed up to him and was in a chattier mood. "I'm starting to believe it was just that: a rumor. We've poured over all of Jason's emails, chats, phone calls, and text messages. There's nothing there to indicate he was having an affair or even an office bromance! I don't think he was even mildly flirty with anyone, to be honest. All our interviews with his work colleagues seem to indicate that. And we haven't been able to locate any friends who'd seen him in the last few months."

"Could the person having an affair with him have lied to you?"

"Yes, but some other colleague would have told us about them. I'm sure you've noticed, journalists—"

"Are nosy and love to babble," Luke said. He'd never let Sol know he'd said such a thing about her profession, even if he knew she shared the belief. "Could Jason have had any device you haven't checked?"

"Like a second cell phone for booty calls?" Hunky Dory said. "We haven't found anything. Unless he bought a burner with cash and kept it extremely well hidden, I'd say the man was faithful—and utterly boring."

"Let's see if I got this right. Julie is too happy to have been kept in the dark about Simon's behavior, because she feels she was instrumental to him in getting this investigation going. And that's why he didn't pick up her considerably more and more anxious phone calls," Sol said. She and Luke were having dinner at Felix Trattoria that night, and they were going over the latest development in Simon Smith's case. "Claudia is thrilled to have been the editor in chief at the outlet that first reported Simon's story and declared him not only not dead but a genius. I won't read you the headline, because I'm sure you've seen it."

"I have. Claudia called me and read it to me," Luke said, savoring a glass of Frappato and then handing it over so that Sol could taste it as well, as she'd ordered something different.

"That thing is clickbait gold," Sol said, then tasted Luke's light-bodied red wine. "And Officer Hunky Dory is thrilled to have one less case to worry about. Oh, and of course, Simon Smith is now hunkered down at Chateau Marmont, thinking himself the next Hunter S. Thompson."

"You're disappointed," Luke said.

"You're making it sound as if I'm sad that the man is alive. But it makes you think about the survival capabilities of white, straight men of his generation. The man has been absolutely abusing the works of others for years. Nobody likes him. He feigns his own demise and now is rewarded with headlines and most probably a book deal, according to what I'm reading and hearing." Sol sighed and sipped some more wine. "The whole thing has made me wonder—"

"About what?"

"Are those the lengths people have to go to get their works published these days?" Sol distractedly twirled the tonnarelli cacio e pepe on the plate around her fork. And she questioned the prospects of her yet unpublished book.

"Do you mean do you need to fake your own death to have some agent or publisher show interest in your book?" Luke looked at her with those warm chestnut eyes that always made her stomach flutter.

"Of course not. But is there any other way?" she wondered.

"I know you don't like being reminded of this," Luke said, and he appeared to be tentative. "But just be patient. I know something will turn up. It's just a matter of time."

"You know I'm not a big fan of patience!"

"Believe me, I do," he said with his most smoldering smile, and she managed to almost forget about everything else. Even that she was still a person of interest in a murder investigation, or that unpublished book of hers. But the moment was interrupted by the arrival of an annoying text message.

"Sorry, I thought I had silenced it."

Her cell phone had been lying on top of the table, as she'd taken it to show Luke a message from Lola when they'd been seated at the candle-lit table facing Abbot Kinney.

"I can't believe it!" she said. "It's from David. He says he's *ready to be a* nice *ex.*"

"Is that what you talked about yesterday?" Luke asked her, and did he look a bit hesitant?

"In a way, I guess. I think we both needed some sort of closure."

"And you got it?"

"At least this way I get to think about the ten years I spent here and not pretend like *he* never happened," Sol said. Even if she had a hard rule preventing her from talking about past relationship failures with present lovers, she somehow didn't feel awkward sharing that with Luke. "I still won't call him to go for a drink when I come to LA like I do with Miquel in Barcelona. But it's nice to be on good terms."

"Glad you managed to get it sorted with him," Luke said, and he did look genuinely glad. "Basically because it looks like you won't be ditching me for him."

"What? Of course I won't be ditching you. Certainly not for him!" she protested. That had to be the most ridiculous idea. "I thought you were the one contemplating taking some time off."

"Time off?" His eyebrows knitted together. He sounded genuinely confused—and a bit offended. "Why would I want to take *any* time off from *you*?"

"We had the most hideous Christmas break!" Sol finally came clean. And it was only after she said those words that she realized it had probably been the wine that gave her the courage—or lack of common sense—to do it.

"What? It wasn't hideous! It was great!" Was he being serious? "Okay, perhaps it was a bit cramped," he admitted when she didn't say anything. "And an absolutely different experience than when we traveled alone this summer. But I'm still glad we got to spend the end of the year together. Not sure your parents share my enthusiasm . . ."

"I'd like to tell you that they'll warm up to you, but I wouldn't get my hopes too high if I were you." She sighed. "Don't take it personally, though."

"So you hated Christmas?"

"A little. Didn't you?"

"Not really," he said, his eyes fully on her from across the table. "You know I don't like prying. But how have the holidays tended to be in the past when you were in a relationship?"

"By the end of both my marriages, utter misery and reproachful hell," she admitted. "I think I've been divorced too many times, and now I'm scarred for life!"

"There's no such thing as having divorced too many times!" He sounded genuinely sincere. And that was one of the reasons Sol had allowed herself to fall for him. Even if she was still terrified about what the future could hold for them. Because one thing was sure: She didn't want to go through a separation again. Not from him. He listened, he always knew what to say, and he looked like an Italian model.

"In any case, it's ridiculous that you were thinking I was going to leave you, for David or at all. I actually wanted to ask you—"

"Se . . ." he continued her unfinished sentence, speaking in Italian and with anticipation. But was it really the right moment to open herself to him even more and say those words?

Fuck it!

"Si querrías venir a vivir conmigo," she told him.

"You'll have to tell me if I'm getting ahead of myself and totally misunderstood you. You know my Spanish is still limited. Ma sì, andrò a vivere con te."

"Seriously?" she asked him, surprised. "Now it's me who is wondering if my limited Italian is deceiving me."

"It's not," he said.

"We've just had some very shitty days, and you still want to live with me?"

"Perhaps that way people will stop thinking I'm too young for you and this is just a fling that will soon run its course," Luke said. Sol was looking forward to people not correcting her while she referred to him as her partner. She normally didn't care what others thought, but she realized she, too, was tired of some folks around them deeming their relationship only temporary. "But these last few days haven't been so shitty. And I recall, once we've been finally able to find some time for ourselves, they've been actually remarkable. All we needed to smooth things over was shagging and talking."

"You make it sound so easy," she said.

"Isn't it easy?" His eyes were still pinned on her. Had he blinked at all since telling her the secret for a working relationship? Shagging and talking.

"My past experience indicates that it's definitely not easy," Sol explained.

"I'm not talking about past relationships, cara. I'm talking about *us*," he said, and she could feel her insides melting.

"If it wasn't that I already told you that I love you, I'd probably be telling you after what you just said." She was blushing, and her heart rate had spiked.

"You still can tell me." He smiled, and she realized how much she'd missed this flirty version of him.

"I'm going to admit that *we* have something special," she said, and she was loving the food, the wine, the conversation, and most especially the company. "But, for argument's sake, I don't think it's as easy as simply shagging and talking to sustain a relationship. There's more than that."

"Of course, but those two are necessary pillars."

"You should have given Jason Zit your advice the other night. Perhaps saving his marriage was just what he needed not to have ended up poisoned," Sol said, and she regretted the words the moment they came out of her mouth. She'd tried being clever, but the joke felt ill-timed and in poor taste.

"What makes you think so?" Luke's demeanor had

changed. He no longer was a lover thinking of all the ways to seduce his partner. He was in his detecting mode.

"Forget about it. I'm obviously a bit tipsy. Not sure why I said what I did."

"You may be tipsy, but I think you've been spot on. It was the obvious first conclusion. Why didn't we think about it before?"

33

"For a woman who is supposed to *not* be involved in this case of yours," Sol told Luke and Divya the following morning as they knocked on Travis Wise's apartment door, "I sure am quite the hands-on collaborator."

"And we both really appreciate it," Divya said. "But we reckon Travis'd be more open if the ask came from you. As the whole thing could be—"

"Potentially dangerous and triggering for him. Sure. I'm convinced coming from me, he'll say yes, no questions asked." Sol couldn't avoid the sarcasm.

Travis opened the door a mere few seconds later wearing a two-piece pajama-like suit in dark-green silk.

"Oh my god, you look divine!" Sol told him the moment she saw him. She kissed him on both cheeks in a friendly gesture Luke knew she reserved for people she genuinely liked. And Luke couldn't avoid smiling. The woman couldn't resist a tasteful garment even if she had other, more pressing things on her mind. "You *need* to tell me where you got it."

"This?" Travis said, absolutely pleased but with a tone

that feigned he was just wearing an old rag. "One of the vintage stores on Melrose."

"Argh!" Sol protested with passion.

"Don't tell me you don't like vintage stores?" Travis said, and Luke thought the outcome of what they'd come to do there, and their success, depended on Sol's answer to that very random question.

"Of course I do! I love vintage stores! But I'm hopelessly lost in them. Can't ever find anything," Sol said.

"Let's make a date, and we can go together. I'll help you sort through the mess," Travis said, and Luke breathed out. He saw Divya also relaxing by his side. They both suspected their chances with Travis were good. "But let's all get in. The kettle is already on." Luke perked up. If Travis was using an actual kettle instead of the microwave this time, perhaps there was hope of the tea being steeped at the right temperature.

"This place is wonderful," Sol said as they walked inside the open-concept living-dining room featuring herringbone wood floors, treetop views from a wall lined with windows, and a low-profile tuft-cushioned modular sofa. Perhaps it was because the first time Luke had been to Travis's flat, Sol wasn't there to notice its beauty, but he had missed many of its tasteful details then.

"I got it in the nineties, and it was a steal. Of course, back then it didn't look like it. But now I would never be able to afford a two-bedroom in Westwood," Travis explained, slightly frustrated. "But make yourselves comfortable. I'll bring the tea."

"Let me help you," Luke managed to say.

But before he could follow Travis to the adjacent kitchen, Divya glared at him. *Don't you dare go telling him his brew is not right.* Luke got the message and simply helped

Travis, bringing cups to the tea table in the living room. Sadly the whole "kettle on" comment had been a figure of speech, as the water had been once again warmed in the microwave.

He sat by Sol's side on the sofa, dunked his tea bag in his lukewarm water resignedly, and was only happy because this time the tea was also being served with biscuits. He took one of the Oreo-like ones from a packet with Paul Newman's face on it and once again had to marvel at the ability that place had to make everything Hollywood related.

"I'm afraid this isn't exactly a social visit," Sol started, sipping her own tea and seemingly unaware of the many sins Travis had committed in its making. Luke had long suspected that Sol wasn't as discerning in her tea consumption as he was. Not that he had any desire to ever tell her. But he'd witnessed her drink the blandest of things since they'd left London.

Or perhaps that was what seasoned travelers were resigned to do: they just ate and drank anything.

"I imagined as much when you told me you weren't coming alone but bringing the detectives in tow," Travis said, his tone friendly, as usual.

"Well, the detectives have asked me to help them and ask you something. I didn't want to say no to them because I really like them. But please feel free to tell me no," Sol said.

"Why would I want to say no?" Travis said, his interest seemingly piqued.

"Because you'd be potentially dealing with a killer—and the person who poisoned you."

...

"Luke, mate, we should take this," Divya said as they

exited Travis's apartment building half an hour later. Divya's cell phone had started ringing. "It's Moon," she added, referring to the person she'd been dating for a few months and an employee at a streaming service that had brought them lucrative work in the past. "I think Meshflixx may have more work for us."

"Can you take it?" Luke said, holding Sol's gaze. He wasn't pleased.

"He wants to tell me how I let him down," Sol explained to Divya.

"Alright, I'm going to be in the car taking care of this." She pointed to her buzzing mobile phone and then their car parked right in front. "You two can do all the rowing you need on the street, I guess."

"Fancy a walk?" Luke asked Sol, making an active effort not to show all the wrath he was feeling.

"I mean, this area isn't necessarily the most charming for a stroll. If we were just North of Wilshire, it gets a bit more pedestrian friendly—"

"I don't care about pedestrian friendliness." Luke fumed.

"Really? Since when?" Sol teased him.

"Just let's please start walking so that Divya—and the prospective client—don't hear us rowing." Luke ran a hand through his hair, his voice edged with frustration.

"Are we going to argue?"

"Why did you tell Travis that you'd join him?" Luke finally blurted out.

"You couldn't expect him to visit a potential killer by himself, no?" Sol asked Luke as they began walking along the tree-lined street filled with low-rise apartment buildings.

"Why not?" Luke said under his breath.

"Travis is obviously still processing what happened to

him. He was poisoned. We believe he wasn't the intended target, but the fact remains he's only alive because of a very annoying nut allergy he's had—and dreaded—his whole life. And that conveniently saved him. We're asking him to have a conversation with the person who could be responsible for his poisoning, and we're arguing he has nothing to worry about. If he has nothing to worry about, I have nothing to worry about," Sol said. "And I know Travis will feel better if I'm there."

"Your bloody reasoning is bang on," Luke admitted. "But, and I know I am going to sound extremely selfish, could you perhaps have thought about me?"

"Who do you think I was thinking about?" Sol stopped in the middle of the street, moving her hands and arms exaggeratedly while talking, the way she did when she was being funny—or starting to get angry. "You need this case solved. I did everything I could to guarantee Travis's collaboration and, with it, hopefully we'll get a resolution and a fast return date to London."

"I didn't mean to think about me because I want to go back to London—which I want," Luke said, but his tone was no longer angered. "Or so that we could wrap up this case quickly. What I meant is that I'm going to be worried about Travis the whole time he's with the suspected killer. The last thing I want is to also be worrying about you. I really don't think straight when I'm worrying about you."

"But you and Divya told me there was nothing to fear when you persuaded me to come with you folks and talk Travis into helping you," Sol argued.

"And I really think there's nothing to fear, because I genuinely think our killer is someone who only had one intended victim in mind and won't want to get rid of anyone else," Luke said. "But if you're mixed up in it, that's when I start fretting, and my head's all over the place."

"Got it," Sol said. "I promise next time I end up inexplicably entangled in one of your investigations, I'll show less initiative, and I may even listen to you if you ask me not to get myself in the middle of all the action. But you have to ask nicely."

"Thank you," Luke said, and he felt a big relief.

"I think we've been extremely good these past couple of days when it came to shagging, but there was still some more talking we could have done," Sol said. "And just to be completely transparent, I worry about you too. I worry when you work until late at night or if, like in this case, you're investigating a murder."

"This is an exception. The cases I normally work on involve cheating, labor disputes and very inoffensive stuff," Luke almost dismissed her, but then he thought better. "But I understand. You worry too. I think it's part of this loving business we've gotten ourselves mixed into."

They locked eyes for a few seconds, as if grasping all the new implications of their commitment, what they'd admitted feeling for the other, and what that would entail going forward.

"I get why you're anxious. But I've already promised Travis that I'd be joining him this afternoon, and I'm not one who stands up her friends," Sol said then. "Especially not when this friend in particular has promised to go shopping with me and show me all the secret spots from the Melrose Avenue vintage scene . . ."

"Sol," Luke pleaded.

"I promise I'll be extremely careful, Luca," she said in all seriousness. "And even if the most delicious things are offered to me, I won't eat or drink anything."

"Don't even sip anything. We can't risk a repeat poisoning even if we think it's highly improbable," Luke said, and he realized he was repeating those words more for himself than for her. He *knew* she was well aware of what she should and shouldn't do. "And Divya and I will be right outside, available if you need us."

"We know what the safe word is," Sol said.

"I really hope you don't have to use it." Luke stared at her, his eyes searching for hers, and his hand went to her face, tracing it tenderly. They stood in the middle of the street in silence for a few seconds. He hoped his eyes were able to tell her everything he hadn't been able to convey with words. In the end, he decided there was still something he needed to say. "I really love you. Please don't get poisoned in bloody Los Angeles."

34

Travis and Sol sat nervously on the luxurious couch Sol had found so incredibly comfortable the last time she'd been in that particular Hancock Park mansion. But now it was somehow not such a cozy experience. Had the sofa's upholstery always been this scratchy? She even found the house uglier this time around. During her first visit, she'd admired the dark hardwood floors, built-in bookshelves, and fireplace. But she now found the place slightly old-fashioned and stuffy, and the bookshelves were suspiciously devoid of many books, considering the house belonged to an editor.

She kept thinking about their earlier visit to the chocolate boutique Cacao Vieille, which had confirmed some of the suspicions she and the detectives had been garnering. The fact that they seemed to be onto the right person made her feel even more uneasy.

She was also feeling a bit insecure in her casual style—her suitcase was still missing. But next to Travis, clad in a well-fitting tweed suit, she looked like a total Lululemon mom with her yoga pants and Luke's sweatshirt.

"Almost there," they heard their host from the kitchen down the hall. Sol and Travis looked at each other, worry etched in both their faces.

"You sure you don't need any help?" Travis hollered to their host. He had tried for friendliness, but his tone had come out a bit nervous and strained.

"I have everything under control," Emily finally said from the living room. Jason Zit's widow brought in a tray with a teapot, cups, saucers, and giant chocolate chip cookies. She placed everything with ease on top of the coffee table.

"This looks delicious," Sol said, and she really hoped Luke and Divya, who were parked nearby and were listening to this whole exchange thanks to the recording device strategically placed in Sol's belt bag, would not decide the mention of food and beverages was reason enough to intervene and barge in.

"I got the cookies from Levain on Larchmont," Emily explained as she served some fragrant black tea in the three delicate china cups she'd brought. "With everything that's happened . . ." Emily continued, sitting in an armchair in front of Sol and Travis. Her eyes were red and puffy, her voice broken. "There's a nonstop flow of people coming and going, making questions and inquiring about how things are. And I like being prepared."

"I think everyone would understand if you didn't offer them anything," Sol said tentatively. She, for sure, would have preferred it.

"It actually keeps me occupied if I have to run to the store to buy some baked goodies, and I can offer tea to visitors," Emily said, grabbing one of the teacups. She sipped from it.

"And how are you? Travis and I just wanted to come and

make sure you're holding up," Sol said, grabbing the closest cup of tea and taking it to her lips but not tasting it. She knew if she so much as made a sipping or slurping sound, Luke would be pounding at the door.

"I've been better. But surprisingly not as bad as I thought I would be. Not sure if that makes me the most terrible person ever," Emily said, and Sol couldn't think of what to say or how to react while Travis kept looking suspiciously at the tea offerings in front of him. "I mean, it was a terrible accident. But, of course, you know we were separating. Everybody knew. So it's not as if I lost the love of my life. I simply lost an extremely annoying person. It's still devastating—"

"I didn't know about the separation," Sol said, and she was tempted to ask Travis whether he did, but her colleague's gaze was fixated on the food and drinks in front of them. "But I think I understand."

"You have two ex-husbands, right?" Emily asked. It always annoyed Sol when people remembered every single detail about her life, but she couldn't remember a single remarkable thing about them. That lack of knowledge was exaggeratedly true when it came to Emily, and she couldn't understand why.

"I do. I only ever wished one of them to disappear from the face of the earth, though," Sol said. She knew for that chat to be mildly successful, she was going to have to pay her dues and share more than she'd normally be comfortable with. "But I think I understand what you're saying."

"Do these have nuts?" Travis blurted, referring to the cookies in front of him, and Sol thought her former colleague was definitely nervous and on the jumpy side.

"They have walnuts, yes!" Emily said. "Sorry about that.

I keep forgetting you're allergic. Oh my god! I could have killed you! Couldn't I?"

"It takes more than a few cookies to get rid of me." Travis chuckled. "I never trust cookies."

"I'd say we could all agree Travis has been extremely lucky with this allergy of his," Sol said, leaning back on the sofa and trying to relax in the situation but not missing a detail in Emily's reaction. "And his mistrust in certain foods."

"How so?" Emily asked, and she did look genuinely confused.

"Well, because obviously I'd be dead otherwise," Travis said. "Whoever wanted Jason dead tried getting rid of him during the awards ceremony, and I got handed his plate by mistake."

"Is that what happened?" Emily said in horror, and Sol had to hand it to her. The woman's performance was flawless. Or could she, perhaps, be telling the truth? If that was the case, Sol and Travis were being the most atrocious, nosy guests.

"We really don't know," Sol intervened, still set on reading as much as possible from Emily's facial expressions and body language. But if she had been riled up by the chat of almost killing the wrong man, Emily wasn't showing it. "But I think that's one of the possible scenarios."

"I just thought it all had been a terrible misunderstanding," Emily said, sounding genuine again. "And some fan had sent Jason some poisoned chocolates by mistake."

"By mistake?" Travis said. He sounded a bit judgy.

"I know, it sounds so silly. But who could have any reason to kill him?"

"Other than you, you mean?" Travis said. Sol had doubted his presence up until that moment, even if he had more of a relationship with Emily and gave them the perfect excuse to visit her. But he'd been completely out of it until then. On the other hand, Sol didn't think she'd have been able to pose such a prickly—yet relevant—question as Travis had just done. It was clear the job Divya and Luke wanted done was a team effort, and she was happy to be paired with Travis for it.

"Why, because of the affair rumor?" If Travis's question had been a blow, Emily's face barely showed it. "The police already cleared me of that. He didn't have a girlfriend!"

"I didn't know about the g—" Sol started but interrupted herself. It was better not to lie if she really wanted to get something out of that conversation. "Why was there a girlfriend rumor?"

"He started it," Emily said, and for the first time, she sounded bitter. She'd quit being the nice, sweet woman for just one moment, showing a different, fiercer face.

"He pretended he was having an affair? What's wrong with men!" Sol couldn't avoid saying. "No offense, Travis." She took her hand to Travis's sleeve.

"None taken," Travis said with an understanding smile.

"My second ex-husband did the same thing to me! He thought that would help him lure me back!" Sol raised her eyebrows. She was so enraged, reminiscing about the whole situation and empathizing with Emily, that she almost forgot she wasn't supposed to drink any tea. But she was able to stop herself before doing it. It wasn't that she thought there was any chance of Emily having poisoned the cups in the kitchen before serving the tea in front of them. She just didn't want to give Luke a heart attack.

"Jason didn't want to rekindle anything. He wanted me to leave him!" Emily said, and there was a hint, again, of that fiercer side of hers.

"I'm sorry if I'm prying," Sol said. "I'm trying to understand how some men's minds work, since I've also been on the receiving end of a fake affair. But couldn't he just have asked for a divorce instead of playing such a hurtful game?"

"He should have, but that would hardly have gotten him anything," Emily said cryptically, but she left it at that.

They all either drank or pretended to drink tea for a whole uncomfortable moment of absolute silence. Sol's mind was spinning, throwing options on what to say next, but nothing seemed to be appropriate or smart, considering her task. She was starting to understand that Divya's and Luke's job was, indeed, more complex than she'd ever given them credit for—not that she had any intention of letting them know that. But her tried and true technique of falling silent so that her interviewee subject would continue talking, and hopefully reveal something about themself, wasn't exactly working on Emily. The woman had been married to a journalist, after all.

"So, you two have the afternoon off work, I presume," Emily said in a not-so-subtle change of subject.

"My afternoons are perpetually off," Travis started. "Didn't you hear I was forced to retire?"

"I think I may have heard something. Sorry about that." Emily was, once again, a model in politeness and empathy. "What about you, Sol?"

"Huh. I'm supposed to be writing this article from the interview I did with Victor Lago," Sol said. The events from the last few days hadn't allowed her to focus on work much. "But I somehow haven't gotten to it yet. I honestly don't know what to say about it."

"About *Haughty Horizons*?" asked Emily.

"Yes, I mean. I guess I've never been like Simon Smith," Sol said, in all honesty. "I don't find any pleasure in publicly destroying someone else's work. But the thing is, I hated the movie. And I don't really like Victor Lago."

"So you don't think critics can be nice?" Emily asked. It almost moved Sol to realize that the woman—who she was there to see for entirely calculating reasons—had actually hit a nerve and put into words something she'd been thinking for a while but hadn't fully articulated.

"Travis has always been a nice critic," Sol reasoned.

"I still got booted. Perhaps I'd still have a job if my writing had been a bit harsher in some of my views," Travis lamented. "It surely seemed to work for Simon Smith. I've heard he's getting a seven-figure book deal."

"Seven figures? Are you kidding me?" Sol scoffed.

After a few agreements from Travis and Emily and some backchanneling sounds, they found themselves once again in perfect silence, except for Travis's pretend slurping of his tea.

"And are you taking a few days off work, then?" Sol finally thought of asking Emily. She didn't know what Emily did professionally. They'd now officially reached the point in the relationship in which it was bad not to know and almost even worse to admit it. But she thought she needed to ask, nonetheless.

"Oh I've been taking the whole day off for the last"—Emily said, squinting as she thought—"fifteen years?"

"So you don't work?" Travis asked, and it looked like he was also clueless when it came to Emily's occupations. "Good for you. If you have any advice on how to spend my mornings, and afternoons, please do tell. So far, the only thing I have on the calendar, besides SoulCycle, is hot yoga and power walking. I'm exhausted just thinking about it. "

They left half an hour after that, when they'd run out of ideas for new topics of conversation. The chat hadn't exactly cracked the case, or gotten a confession, but Sol was certain about three things, and she made sure of sharing them the moment she got into Luke and Divya's car.

"She feels no remorse, not even when we mentioned the poisoning of Travis—but that could be because nothing awful happened to him. There has to be a prenup. And you should probably find out what Emily did when she was working."

35

"We've been in this bloody place a day short of two weeks," Luke grumbled. "But let's start looking for return tickets, because we're wrapping up this case today."

"It would be fantastic to no longer be on Officer Hunky Dory's no-leaving-the-country list. I really need to go back to London," Sol said.

"Because of the appointment with your colorist," said Divya, as she had also heard Sol complaining about the unmissable rendezvous.

"No, because my editor really wants me back in London. I've been neglecting work for way too long. Plus, I miss home. And yeah, the appointment with the colorist," Sol admitted.

The three of them were enjoying an outdoor breakfast of frittata, pastries, tea, sun, and the odd celebrity sighting—they'd seen one of the original cast members from *CSI* on their way there—at Gjusta in Venice.

The sunglasses were on, the weather was a temperate

seventeen degrees Celsius—even if Sol was still wearing one of Luke's cozy knits (it smelled like him: lavender and smokey wood)—and their return home looked closer. Although she had always loved traveling, she cherished her time at home every bit as much. Right now, Sol was starting to feel tired of so many meals eaten out, and she was missing her cozy Georgian cottage South of the Thames River.

"You sound as if you're also a bit homesick for London," Luke told her with his most seductive grin.

"I *am* homesick," Sol admitted.

"I thought you loved traveling," Luke said.

"I do, but like you said, we've been out for almost two weeks for a trip that was supposed to last four days. I'd like to go back to the comforts of my own house, my own closet, and the city I learned to love," she said.

"After that, I think he's even more in love with you than he already was," Divya said.

"What she said," Luke agreed with a smile.

"Alright, people, let's pack you back to London soon, then. Let's make it possible," Divya said, getting into her working mode.

"Aren't you also coming once we wrap up the case?" Luke asked, furrowing his brow.

"He's worried you may find yourself alone in such an inhospitable place," Sol joked.

"I won't be alone. Moon is coming for a couple of days for work, and I'll stay with them. They'll show me around since you two have been very inconsistent hosts," Divya explained.

"I'm sorry about that. I promise to do a better job next time," Sol said.

"Next time?" Luke said in horror, but he was only half joking, and Sol and Divya couldn't avoid laughing out loud.

But the moment of perfect happiness felt like the calm before the storm. They still had a suspect to catch, and Sol couldn't help but wonder if Luke was being too optimistic in thinking the case was nearly done. Emily had proven to be an extremely smart person who got away with murder because everyone either ignored her or failed to recognize her existence

They shouldn't do the same and keep underestimating her.

"Officer Hunky Dory is returning my call," Luke said then, and he put the police detective on speakerphone—there were no people at the tables around them. "Detective Owens, good morning."

"Morning, pal," Hunky Dory said. "Everything good?"

"Yes, we're focusing on the Jason Zit investigation and were wondering if he and Emily had a prenup. Would you happen to know?" Luke asked.

"I do happen to know. Do you want to share anything?"

"Not right now, but I promise you'll be the first one I ring if we unearth anything," Luke said. It wasn't lost on Sol that Luke had never been a big fan of the police detective, which was probably why he was approaching the chat in the wrong way. He had been too straightforward and hadn't even asked if the officer was doing okay.

"Yeah, like you did with Simon Smith? That's not gonna cut it, pal," Hunky Dory said.

"We still got your job done for you," Luke replied, and Sol thought he sounded as patience-deprived as she normally was.

"My, my, my. And to think, I always believed the saying

about British people being blunt and too direct was just a cliché." Sol could practically hear Hunky Dory rolling his eyes.

"Detective Owens, Divya Bakshi here, Luke's more reasonable and nicer colleague. Nice meeting you," Divya intervened before Luke could further importune the police officer. "How are you doing?"

"Nice meeting you, as well. Doing fantastic, but I'm afraid the answer is the same, even if you sound much more tolerable than your colleague," Hunky Dory said. Luke opened his mouth to protest, but both Divya and Sol glared at him in a way that shut him up. He raised both his hands in surrender.

"More tolerable and more generous," Divya countered Detective Owens. "You see, we happen to think Emily could have been the person poisoning Travis Wise and Jason Zit. And forgive me, because we don't seem to have a last name for her. Is it also Zit? Not to be rude, but it does sound proper daft that someone'd pick that last name on purpose."

"Uh, I think so. Not sure, though," Hunky Dory said absentmindedly, as if rummaging through his notes. "Of course, we checked into her. The spouse or partner always makes for the most probable suspect."

Sol went back to two nights before, when she and Luke were having dinner and she made an unfortunate comment that had finally jogged his mind into realizing Emily was probably the killer. *It was the obvious first conclusion. Why didn't we think about it before?* he'd said. All that time, they'd all been paying no attention to Emily. Sol couldn't remember having met her years before. She didn't know what Emily did, what she liked, or even her full name. Had Emily simply gotten tired of being the transparent woman married to Jason Zit?

"And you ruled Emily out?" Divya continued her conversation with Detective Owens.

"She, herself, was also poisoned by the chocolates that killed him. She ate a minimal amount but still enough to put her out of commission for a couple of days. She had no reason to get rid of the husband. The money was all hers already, some family inheritance. It's not like she had to kill him to take it. There could have been no crime of passion, because there was no cheating and she knew it," Owens said. "And I don't know if you've met her, but the woman is nice and pleasant. I don't think she could hurt a fly, honestly."

"We still think she could be our killer, and we think we've been underestimating her this whole time," Divya said. Sol realized she wasn't the only one to have reached that conclusion. She knew Luke was thinking exactly the same, the way he was looking at his colleague and nodding. "Now, chances are we're going to look into this and reach the same conclusions you already have. You're the veteran LA detective here."

Luke rolled his eyes, and Divya sent him a threatening stare. Yes, some strategic flattery was crucial if they wanted to get the information they needed, her eyes seemed to tell him.

"That I am," Hunky Dory said, and Luke rolled his eyes a second time. Sol had to admit she was having way too much fun observing her partner in such a bizarre professional setting. It was as if he couldn't think completely straight since they'd landed in Los Angeles, and he wasn't his most proficient and efficient self at the job. No wonder he was so adamant about getting back to London.

"But would you mind sharing some of the details about the situation between the Zits? We believe there was a prenup," Divya continued tentatively, trying to confirm what had only been a suspicion on Sol's part.

"There was, but like I said, it didn't change things for Emily. She was rich when she married, she remains rich now," Detective Owens said.

"What would have happened in case of divorce?" Divya asked.

"She'd still have kept everything. I think the only way he had to get some of that money was if Emily left him. But not if he was the one asking for the divorce," Detective Owens said. "But that's hardly of any relevance now."

"Of course," Divya conceded something everyone at the table knew wasn't true. "And, by any chance, would you happen to know what Emily did before she stopped working? I'm sure you did a thorough interview with her, and that may have come up. We've got a bit of friendly betting going on among ourselves. My mate Luke thinks she was a librarian. I say political aid."

"Neither." Detective Owens chuckled. "I think she was a journalist, same as the husband. They worked together for a time."

"Thanks so much," Divya said. "That's been incredibly helpful. And like I said, I'm sure this will be nothing. But, if it is, we'll make sure to ring you and let you know. Have a nice rest of your day, Detective Owens."

"And you, too, Miss Bakshi. No need to give my regards to that curt colleague of yours."

Divya hung up, and only then she put her full attention on Luke.

"What's your problem with the *charming* Detective Owens exactly, mate?"

"Let me see . . . He stood me up, he implied I was too

young for Sol, he told Sol she can't leave the country." Luke ticked each item off on his fingers. "Oh, and he's basically an arse. Thanks for dealing with him, though."

"Any bloody time," Divya said, smiling. "We got what we needed."

36

"Am I the only one who feels conflicted about this and thinks we should let Emily . . ." Sol let the thought hang. The three of them had moved from Gjusta and were now strolling alongside the more commercial stretch of Main Street in Santa Monica.

"What? Get away with murder!" Luke said.

"That's what happens when you let civilians get involved. They're soft," Divya said, shaking her head in disbelief.

"I mean, you have to feel for the woman a little bit, no? She meets Jason in college, falls in love," Sol argued, enumerating some of the findings they'd unearthed about Emily after a bit of precise online research guided by the conversation with Detective Owens. "They start dating, get married, move to Los Angeles, pursuing their dream of becoming critics. I guess sharing the same exact professional dream was on the chancy side of things, but whatever. They move here, both get miraculously hired by the same publication, and then, of course, things start getting ugly."

"Still no reason to let a killer go," Luke said. "What if she marries again, and she also gets annoyed with the second husband."

As a woman who had gotten annoyed not by one but by two husbands, Sol could understand Emily's predicament. Then again, she hadn't exactly poisoned any of her former spouses—not even the second one.

"I think it should be me talking to her," Sol said.

She wasn't sure what she expected after saying those words, but it certainly wasn't what happened next.

"I bloody agree," Luke said, teeth clenched. "Any objections, Divya?"

"Objections? Me? None at all. Sol is perfect for the job. She shares the same profession as Emily, they knew each other previously, and they both had proper shite husbands. But my question is, are you feeling alright, mate?"

"I probably have sunstroke, but I basically agree with everything you said," Luke told Divya and then stared at Sol. "I think Emily likes you. Let's take advantage of that."

"Okay, but I have to warn you. I also like her. Depending on what else I find out and what she tells me about her motives, I may sympathize even more with her." Sol felt queasy after saying that out loud.

"As long as you don't end up poisoned or enable Emily's escape in some way, there's no crime in liking a killer here and there," Luke said. How he had the ability of always saying exactly what she needed to hear, she still couldn't comprehend.

Sol was only certain of one thing: She was a very lucky woman. And that knowledge made her feel even more for Emily somehow.

...

Sol and Emily shared a table for two by the floor-to-ceiling windows overlooking La Brea Avenue at République, and Sol wished they hadn't chosen such an iconic place. It felt intrinsically wrong—and bizarre—to hope for a killer to confess in a neo-Gothic 1928 building commissioned by Charlie Chaplin. But as Luke kept repeating over and over, the whole thing was just too Hollywood. They were in Los Angeles, after all.

"Ma'am," a waiter addressed Sol as they brought the order of Genmaicha tea and kouign-amanns. People needed to stop with that! She really wasn't that old.

"I wasn't expecting your call," Emily told Sol after the waiter left. "Not so soon after the visit yesterday."

"I'm not sure if you're going to believe me when I tell you that, after getting to meet you a little, I'd have loved to be friends," Sol said. "But I'm afraid this isn't a friendly call."

"What kind of call is it, then?" Emily said, and once again Sol saw the nice woman transform into someone fiercer in front of her eyes.

"We believe it was you who poisoned Jason," Sol said. Saying those words out loud had been much harder than she'd anticipated. *This is the last time she got herself entangled in one of Luke's cases.* She allowed herself a microscopic glance at him and Divya, who were perched atop stools at the restaurant bar, pretending to be a couple of influencers, judging by the amount of selfies they were taking. Luke was disguised in such a way—long, wavy blond wig, Hawaiian shirt, and colorful shorts—that it was difficult even for Sol to recognize him. But she felt better by having them so close, and she knew that even if it looked like they weren't paying attention to her, *they were.*

"*We?*" Emily questioned.

"You know my partner is a private detective," Sol said.

"He and his colleague were hired by Jason's employer to investigate what happened to him."

"I know," Emily said, no longer the amenable, nice woman. "Marquee Media, of course, called me to let me know. I found it strange that they'd chosen a couple of out-of-towners, to be honest."

"They have a knack for Hollywood affairs, even if they don't always advertise it," Sol said, unable to disguise the pride she felt when she said those words. "We know that you and Jason got hired by the same publication years ago and started working first as entertainment reporters and then as critics. We don't know exactly what happened, but you stopped being a contributor. I have my suspicions."

"Which would be?"

"I'm gonna go out on a limb and say layoff," Sol said.

"Easy bet in this field, but yes," Emily said. "But so that we're clear, I've admitted to having been let go, not to having killed my pitiful husband. I'm still not sure what exactly you think you know."

"Understood," Sol said. "But I think your pitiful husband was even more pathetic than we give him credit for. I did some reading this morning, everything I could find online from your writings back in the day and from Jason's articles. You were funny, down-to-earth, compassionate, and a joy to read."

"Thank you," Emily said. Sol knew the easiest way into a writer's heart was to show them you appreciate their work. But she'd been sincere in her words about Emily's writing.

"But Jason was a self-important blowhard who didn't seem to care if all the words in his reviews were comprehensible," Sol continued. "Of course, he was the one to keep the job."

"I don't have to tell you how this profession works,"

Emily said, and she really didn't. It made some kind of twisted sense that the better, more straightforward writer had been the one to lose her job.

"Did you try to find another job after that?" Sol continued, and she would normally have never asked someone that. She was big on not pressuring people into having to feel purposeful all the time. But in this case, it was pertinent.

"I did," Emily said, and Sol could hear it in her voice—she hadn't appreciated the accusation. "I'm sure you know I didn't necessarily need the money."

"That doesn't mean you didn't need the thrill, right?" Sol said with a genuine smile. "What I can't understand is why, at some point, you started doing Jason's writing. I couldn't help but notice how his clippings got much better after you no longer published under your own byline."

"He certainly could use my help," Emily said, not even trying to deny the fact she'd been doing Jason's writing for him. It was almost as if she needed to tell the story, and Sol was giving her the chance to do it. "I found the thrill again, even if it was under Jason's name. It was very Zelda Fitzgerald of me, if you want. We were in love, we were married. Everything was a partnership, even our writing."

"So what happened?" Sol asked, and she really wanted to know.

"The idiot got tired," Emily said, and there was so much exasperation and disappointment behind those four words. "You know how it goes. Writing is so draining. And even if *I* was doing most of the actual writing, he said he was getting tired of pitching and fighting his editors every single day."

"So he switched into an editor position."

"And he thoroughly hated it. And it wasn't as if having to deal with someone else's writing wasn't draining as well,"

Emily said. "Of course, I told him that was going to happen, but by then he'd stopped listening. He'd stopped loving me too."

If, when she had boarded a plane headed to Los Angeles almost two weeks before, someone would have told Sol that the trip was going to force her to confront her past relationship and divorce multiple times, she would have laughed at them. She'd been that good at avoiding recalling anything that had to do with David. But there she was, hearing some words that ringed too close to her not-so-distant past life.

"My second ex-husband also managed to stop paying attention to an incredibly annoying degree," Sol recalled. "I think that tipped the scales for me and helped me fall out of love with him."

"Oh, I fell out of love, alright," Emily said, seeming almost offended by the insinuation in Sol's words.

"But you didn't want to be the one who left him, because that would have meant he'd get to keep part of your money," Sol said, and again, she dreaded that conversation and promised herself never to offer her services as an amateur sleuth ever again. Let the professionals deal with the could-be killers who also happened to be extremely sympathetic.

"Can you blame me?" Emily inquired, and Sol didn't want to have to answer that question. "But you have it wrong. You believe this whole carnage was because of money. It wasn't."

37

"Why don't you tell me what it's about then, Emily," Sol said, purposely using Emily's name to create rapport.

"A few days ago, you didn't know my name," Emily told Sol. "Even if we've met at several work functions. For years, I've been either *Jason's wife* or simply no one because people couldn't remember me. You certainly didn't."

"Oh, come on! Don't measure anything by my inability to remember a name!" Sol replied. "I'm the fucking worst. I'm a self-centered, selfish brat who gets upset if her hair-stylist is running late or if she can't secure the hottest restaurant reservation in town."

"Yet you still get people to like you and remember you. You have friends. You managed to get yourself a boyfriend who looks like the love child of Daniel Day-Lewis and Monica Bellucci!" Emily said in an almost reproachful tone.

Sol had to recognize that Emily had managed to describe Luke in an alarmingly concise and accurate way.

"Partner," corrected Sol. "But believe me when I tell you, I also don't know how that last part came to be possible. A part of me still thinks I banged my head against a wall, and he's just a figment of my imagination. Any moment now, I'm going to wake up and realize I made him up."

"Only you didn't, *honey*," Emily said, and Sol remembered Emily using that same word without meaning it in the past, with her now-late husband. Cold sweat ran down her back.

Sol stopped eating right away, even if she knew it was impossible for Emily to have tampered with the food while it had been in front of her that whole time. She didn't allow herself to look up and give away the location of her two accomplices, but she was almost sure Luke's vigilant stare was on her. And she felt relieved just knowing it.

"Since you're no longer eating, are we done?" Emily finally said.

"I feel you still have things to tell me." Sol tried to persuade Emily, but she knew she'd probably lost her and Emily was already planning to leave.

"Only things you probably know: Be extremely protective of your byline and what bylines you decide to publish under," Emily said. "I heard you wrote a book. Don't wait for others to tell you what to do with it."

Sol was tempted to ask what Emily meant by that. She wanted to have a nice conversation with a potential friend and a colleague. But she was there for other reasons.

"I saw that Jason won several journalistic awards during his career," Sol said. "I'm guessing those were actually for your work."

"Regardless of who wrote what, he was the one to get the accolades. And the one whose last name people remembered. What's my last name, Sol?"

Shit.

"Zit?" Sol guessed.

"As if I was *ever* going to take that ridiculous last name!" Emily said.

"Okay, so you got tired of people not realizing you were the only actual talent Jason had." Sol had run out of time and needed to ace her next lines. "And, on top of that, he dares concoct a fake girlfriend to see if you'll leave him so he gets to keep some of your money."

"I've told you, money has nothing to do with this!" Emily said.

"But humiliation does. First, he embarrassed you by giving up on a career at which you were excelling for him. Then he never gave you the credit you deserved. He shames you in front of everyone, telling them he's being unfaithful—"

"Since the girlfriend ruse hadn't worked out, he was planning on incapacitating me, declaring me medically unfit, institutionalizing me, and getting the fucking money," Emily said.

Sol couldn't believe her ears. Her arched eyebrows attested to that, as did her saucer-like eyes.

"Fuck! Could he do that?"

"Let's say by that point, I was too pissed to figure out whether he had any chances. I wasn't going to risk it," Emily said, her tone calm and collected. "So yes, I may have laced his food with cyanide. I felt bad for Travis, though. I never meant for him to get hurt. I'm so relieved nothing major happened to him."

"Oh, he knows," Sol said. "But what happened at the party?"

"I found a way of distracting the waiter serving our table, and I tainted Jason's food while the waiter was otherwise occupied. I never predicted he was going to switch the plates! But, in hindsight, I guess that's what happens when you offer someone weed. Their senses get impaired."

"And then you realized it was Travis who'd been poisoned and raised the alarm." Sol tried following Emily's tale.

Emily looked Sol straight in the eye. "I don't believe in collateral damage."

Sol nodded. She believed Emily.

"Which is why the second time around, you chose a much more private place."

"I bought the chocolates, with cash obviously. Injected them with cyanide and posted them to the house. I was well aware that Jason had such a sweet tooth, he would not be able to resist eating the whole thing, even if he didn't know who sent them." Emily chuckled, shaking her head as if still in disbelief. "His ego was so over inflated, he thought they were from a fan!"

"Was it always the plan to eat some of the chocolates yourself?" Sol asked.

"The spouse is always the main suspect, honey. But no one could suspect poor me, could they?" Emily said, her eyes fierce, almost menacing. "So how did you get me, then?"

"A hunch," admitted Sol. "And a visit to Cacao Vieille. There's a shop person there who remembered a redheaded woman buying a big box of chocolates one day before Jason died."

"No one ever remembers me!" Emily argued, her features stern.

"They are one of those people who never forget a face."

Emily chuckled. "Oh, the irony!"

"Is it wrong to say a part of me thinks Emily was too kind and should have probably opted for a more painful way of getting rid of Jason?" Sol said when she, Luke, and Divya finally got in the car after Emily's arrest. They'd been interviewed by Hunky Dory for hours and had given him the recording of the conversation where Emily had confessed.

"Are you sure you're okay?" Luke asked her from the driver's seat. He took one of her hands, which lay limp in her lap. He was a bit worried about her.

"He tried incapacitating her!"

"He was a right piece of shite!" Divya agreed from the rear seat of the car.

"He was," Luke said. "And this is why I've been insisting that you shouldn't get involved. You look like you've been run over by a bloody train."

"Delightful. Apparently, I feel like shit and look like shit," Sol said.

"I didn't mean it like that." Luke tried a smooth left turn on Santa Monica Boulevard. Whoever had designed intersections like this deserved his utmost antipathies. "You look beautiful, you always do. But I can see this bloody case has taken an emotional toll on you."

"I don't think I had realized before," Sol said, and she kept her eyes lost on the horizon, not looking at him. "How hard this profession of yours can be."

"Oh, it's never this bad!" Divya said. "You just picked the wrong case to be all nosy. The last thing we did in London involved finding a sixty-something-year-old woman who had argued with her brother twenty years ago, and the two of them had lost touch."

"In the end, they reconciled and it was quite heartwarming," Luke said, his hand still holding Sol's.

"Can we all go have dinner—something simple and

yummy like pizza or burgers—and get very drunk?" Sol said. She'd finally broken out from her staring-at-the horizon bad spell to turn first to Divya, then to Luke.

His heart eased as he locked eyes with her. His gaze silently promised her love and worship.

"Absolutely," he told her.

"Sounds dreamy," Divya agreed.

Sol inputted the address of Burger Lounge in Santa Monica on his cell phone so that the car navigation system guided them there, and the three of them sat in perfect comfort and silence, still mulling over the case.

"Is the client happy?" Sol asked Luke and Divya.

"I talked to the people at Marquee Media before getting interrogated by bloody Hunky Dory," Luke said. "They did sound happy. Claudia especially. But I'm starting to understand why you were so adamant about not working for her again. The woman is *not* nice. She dressed down one of the writers with me on the phone. Had absolutely no problems telling them they were the most mediocre reporter she'd ever worked with."

"Ai! I feel for them. She really can be the worst." Sol was reminded of some of her own bad experiences with the editor. "But, tell me, she wants to write about Emily, right?"

"I'm afraid she does," Luke said.

Sol chuckled. "She'll have to figure out her last name first."

"I think that's probably the reason nothing has been published yet," Luke said. "But she said she'll put in a good word for the agency."

"And mention you in all the articles?" Sol asked, and did she sound chuffed about the idea of the agency getting loads of publicity?

"Something like that, yes," he conceded.

"And the best thing is, we can finally send all those invoices. And we're going to charge them extra for working out of town," Divya contributed.

"Yeah, let's make that extra hefty," Luke agreed. The whole away-from-London thing had been extremely uncomfortable.

Sol interlaced her fingers with his, as his right hand was still on her lap, and he smiled. They were going home, and they'd survived that bloody city. Not only that, she'd asked him to move in together. Perhaps Los Angeles hadn't been such a terrible experience, after all?

38

"So then the conclusion you've reached—" Lola asked Sol in Catalan the next day over a breakfast of toasted levain bread with orange marmalade at Superba Food + Bread in Hollywood. Sol had left Luke at the hotel ready to go for a run and seemingly integrated in Los Angeles—wearing a tank that showed lots of arms and shoulders, and a pair of short shorts displaying muscly legs. He was even more tanned than when they'd first landed.

"That I'm too old to drink and that one should *never* order wine if it comes out of a can," said Sol, who wore sunglasses indoors.

"No, no, no. We already knew that." Lola dismissed her. "You just decided to ignore it because you were feeling thirty or something. And you're now paying for the consequences, by the looks of it."

"If you only knew," Sol admitted. "My only solace is that Luke and Divya are also quite messed up. And they're much younger. They also drank a lot more than me, so. We had to take an Uber back to the hotel!"

"Weren't you just going out for some burgers?" Lola stared at Sol with wide eyes.

"Don't judge me, but we went to Cabo Cantina after dinner," Sol said, referring to a Mexican bar famous for its signature margaritas served by the liter. "It gets blurry after the strawberry concoction that we shared."

"I bet it does. But let's not get distracted with your wild tale about yesterday night. What I meant was, what have you decided about Luke? Are you going to propose?" Lola asked.

Sol flicked a hand dismissively. "Oh that, I already did!"

"Sol Novo! You never told me!"

"Well, I had no time with the whole being chased down by a delusional, media-obsessed lunatic," Sol argued. "I'm sorry to have gotten you and your family involved in the whole mess, by the way. And thanks for providing us with a roof and a mattress for so many days."

"I hear it's a very uncomfortable mattress," Lola admitted.

"You don't even know. You should get rid of that thing. But seriously, thank you." Sol hoped her eyes conveyed everything she didn't know how to put in words.

"No problem. We loved having you at home. Geoff was delighted with all the extra people telling him his cooking is delicious. And Alex really likes Luke," Lola said. "It was a great visit."

"It was," Sol said. Now that she no longer had to sleep on the discomfort of Lola's mattress, she could look at the past and recall all the ways in which it had been a great experience.

"But you haven't finished telling me about your proposal." Lola's nosiness took Sol out of her musings.

"He said yes, obviously, or I'd be crying on your

shoulder and wondering why everyone hates me," Sol deadpanned.

"Please," Lola dismissed her, and it wasn't lost on Sol that of all her close friends, Lola was the one who took her less seriously. And she loved her for that.

"Anyway, I think I realized something," Sol continued.

"That you can't keep pretending anymore that you are thirty," Lola teased her, gesturing at her general hungover state. "And that touristy bars with colorful decor and gigantic drinks should be reserved for *tourists*?"

"No, not that. I already knew all of that! But I realized Luke's main flaw is probably his aversion to travel," Sol said, in all seriousness. "But I can live with that."

"I mean, he was here for two weeks, so it's a mild aversion," Lola tried reasoning.

"Uh," Sol objected. "I wouldn't describe it as *mild*, but—"

"Something you can tolerate?"

"Definitely. The moment I realized he's not perfect, even if he looks the part sometimes, but that I didn't mind this particular quirk, I proposed."

"Congratulations." Lola reached over the table in a hug. "And you're still sure you don't want to marry again, right?"

"Give me a break!" Sol protested, even if *perhaps* she no longer felt so strongly as before about that particular topic.

"You know who's not having such a great day as you, right?" Lola asked.

"No clue who you're talking about," Sol said, ready for the gossip.

"The delusional, media-obsessed lunatic you were just talking about." Sol could see Lola was enjoying telling her that story. But then again, Lola was a total gossip. "Simon Smith has been canceled."

Sol didn't follow. "Canceled?"

"You know he got a seven-figure deal to publish that tell-all book of his?"

"Yeah, of course!"

"He got some headlines because of that. So some people got interested. A couple of journalists started unearthing some of his not-so-old reviews . . ." started Lola. "And apparently back in the day, he'd said *Lady Bird* was a silly coming-of-age story for teenage girls and a bit limiting in its perspective."

"The fucking idiot! That movie is perfection."

"Oh, and he implied that *The Hurt Locker* could have been a better movie if it wasn't Kathryn Bigelow who directed it."

"Ugh! He meant if a dude had directed it," Sol said, and she could feel her blood boiling. "Why are you so peppy about the whole situation?"

"Because Simon Smith has been stalking my house, and I don't like that. My kid lives there. My husband lives there. I live there! I don't like him, and I'm glad some journalists found some of his old writing and showed the world he's an absolute idiot and a sexist. And that hardly makes for a commercial author these days," Lola reasoned, a smirk on her face.

"So he's been canceled for sure?"

"Yeah, the publishing company is backtracking, postponing the release. That book's not coming out anytime soon—if ever," Lola said.

"Is it bad to feel good about someone else's misfortunes?" Sol asked, and then she looked at her friend and recalled what Simon Smith had said about Greta Gerwig's perfect movie.

"Nah!" both Sol and Lola decided at the same time.

"I need to run something by you," Sol said, suddenly

remembering. "Emily told me something about not waiting for others to tell me what to do with my book. And it's really stayed with me. I think I'm going to self-publish it."

"So you're following the advice of a husband-killer?" Lola asked, her face not letting on what she was thinking.

"Sí," Sol said, reassured. "Let's not forget the husband was going to incapacitate her."

"Sounds good to me."

39

"Do we have everything?" Luke asked her when they got inside the car so Divya could drive them to the airport.

"We *finally* have everything," Sol said. Her suitcase had been delivered to their hotel twenty minutes before checking out and heading to LAX.

"You excited to go home?" Sol asked him.

"You have no idea," Luke said enthusiastically, and both Divya and Sol laughed.

"Believe me, mate, we *know*."

"I may have been getting used to everyone finding my accent irresistible here, though," Luke joked. "I'll miss that."

Sol rolled her eyes. "Please, as if people don't find you irresistible in London!"

"Exactly," Divya agreed. "Sol knows what she's talking about."

"And are you sure you'll be fine *here*?" Luke asked Divya for the umpteenth time, ignoring her jest.

"Moon gets here tonight. And for today, I have a full day of activities that Sol helped me plan," Divya dismissed him.

"She's going to Gold's Gym for a workout session, and she'll drive on Mulholland Drive," Sol said.

"Sweating and driving," Luke replied. "Very LA."

"That was the intention. And I'll be back in London in a couple of days, so you won't even have time to miss me," Divya continued, and it sounded like a promise.

"I'm sure I'll still miss you," Luke said. "But please be back. We've been getting calls nonstop for new cases, and it looks like we're going to be busy."

Divya dropped them off at the airport half an hour after that. She hugged Luke and Sol goodbye, then went on her way.

"She'll be fine," Sol told Luke, who was still eyeing Divya's car driving away from the departures level of LAX.

"That's what I'm worried about," he joked.

"Okay, London Guy, let's go home," Sol said, holding his hand while they walked inside the terminal.

"Now that you mention home, we never discussed what the living arrangements are going to be," Luke said as they lined up to check in Sol's newfound suitcase. "And you know this proposal of yours means you're stuck with me for the foreseeable future when it comes to Christmas."

"I'm perfectly aware and looking forward to it." She was.

"So, living arrangements?"

"I'm willing to look for a place together North of the Thames if you want," Sol said, turning to look at his chestnut eyes. "Or you can come to Roupell Street."

"Your place," Luke said, tentatively.

"Let's make it *our* place," Sol said.

"The idea of house hunting in London sounds as attractive as getting my teeth pulled," Luke admitted.

"Or getting a thousand paper cuts," Sol agreed. "So *our* place at Roupell Street?"

"I'm going to pay you rent," Luke said.

"The house is paid for. There's no rent. We can share the other expenses, but it's good to save a bit, no?"

"You know I've been a bit tight on money?"

"You told me! So yes. I know how to pay attention and listen too. I'll admit that half of the time, I'm completely and utterly clueless. But I care about you, Luca. No, I love you. So yes, I pay attention when it comes to you. Probably only when it comes to you, really."

"In the last couple of weeks, you've managed to make me enjoy being in Los Angeles, and now I'm agreeing to live South of the Thames." Luke sighed. "Sol Novo, I hope you realize I'm a changed man."

"Oh, I know that I got an upgrade," she said, teasing.

He grinned, arrogantly. "There wasn't much to be upgraded."

"I'm perfectly aware," she conceded. "Still got the upgrade."

"Next please. Miss," the airline employee called Sol as she and Luke were at the beginning of the check-in line.

"Miss, really?" Sol protested. "I'm forty-three!"

...

"You got us upgraded to first class?" Luke asked her suspiciously while they boarded their London Heathrow–bound plane.

"I have lots of miles," she explained. "It was easy, and we'll be more comfortable."

"You mean you'll be able to sleep even more?" he asked.

"With a little bit of luck . . ." Sol said. "You should try and get some rest too."

"It's barely afternoon!" he complained.

"Believe it or not, your body needs to get back to London time," Sol said. "Should we negotiate flight interactions now?"

"Meaning?" Luke said, not knowing what she was referring to.

"I packed a vampire novel by Ali Hazelwood that's going to keep me entertained. And I'm going to try to sleep as much as possible because, if not, flights get unbearably long, and I don't know what to do with myself."

Luke arched his eyebrows. "I thought you liked flying!"

"What? Of course I don't like flying! It's cramped. It's smelly. You get stranded in random cities you'd not be able to place on a map. Or worse, they lose your bag!" Sol scoffed. "I love traveling, normally, once the flying portion of it is *over*."

"And if you're not kicked out of the hotel," Luke continued.

"You get me." She smiled. "So, want me to not be completely isolated all the time that I'm awake this time? I'm sorry if I wasn't much company on our way here. It's been ages since I traveled with someone I like."

"I'd be up to watch *Anyone but You* simultaneously," Luke said.

"Rom-com, eh?" Sol said, raising an eyebrow.

"You know I like romance when we're traveling together."

Someone behind them let out a dramatic sigh. "Most tiresome awards season ever." When they turned, they saw filmmaker Greta Gerwig seated in the row behind them, deeply engaged in a phone conversation.

"I couldn't agree more," Sol said, giving Luke a sidelong glance as she shifted toward him. "But we managed to make the most of it, no?"

Thank you for reading *Scripted for Love and Poison.*

For a bonus scene featuring Sol and Luke discovering where their next adventure will take them, visit: https://BookHip.com/FNWXQBW

And if you enjoyed the book, please consider leaving a review on Amazon, Goodreads, BookBub, or wherever the cool kids are writing reviews these days. This indie author (and her books) could really use all the help and love you can spare.

Moltes gràcies!

ACKNOWLEDGMENTS

When I was editing this book and writing these lines, the house I'd called home for the last five years was in literal shambles as we prepared for a big move across the ocean. Surrounded by boxes and packing materials, I took stock of the 19 years we'd lived in the United States—most of them in California—and got ready to return to Barcelona. I'd be lying if I said it wasn't bittersweet.

Xavi, thank you for being the best partner in adventure—and in love—I could ever wish for. And for being mine and the dog's emotional support human.

To my family and friends: thank you for cheering me on these past few months and believing I could actually do what I've always dreamed of doing.

Thanks to Darinka Gadikota-Klumpers, Joan M. Griffin, Marta Franco, Marta Gené Camps, Sonia Fabre, and the team of ARC readers for your help in getting my novels into more readers' hands. Every review counts so much at this stage.

Thanks to Brenna Bailey-Davies at Bookmarten Editorial for her incredible editing skills—and for putting up with some of my more convoluted sentences.

Ashley Santoro, thank you for a beautiful cover. This one feels especially glitzy!

And once again, to every reader who's given this indie author a chance: *muchas gracias*, and please keep reading me :)

ABOUT THE AUTHOR

Patricia Puentes is a Barcelona native, expat, and recovering entertainment journalist who has been calling California home for almost 20 years. She can tell many funny (or just plain surreal) stories about the frequent times she has interviewed celebrities, but she mostly gets wowed by writers—and doggies.

She writes open-door romance mysteries with a Hollywood setting and where the leads have non-stop banter. You can check her previous rom-com mysteries *Cluelessly Unscripted (Sol and Luke Romance Mystery Romance #1)* and *Love, Lines, and Alibis.*

She lives in Oakland, California, with her romantic partner and their rambunctious Border Collie, Boira (aka Peluchín diabólico).

Find her online at www.patriciapuentes.com/books. To subscribe to Patricia's newsletter, visit this link: www.patriciapuentes.com/newsletter.

TikTok: @patriciapuentesbooks

Instagram: @patriciapuentesbooks

Goodreads: goodreads.com/patriciapuentes

BookBub: bookbub.com/profile/patricia-puentes